SANDY COVE

BY STEVEN RECHT

ISBN-13: 978-1-480-13405-8

ISBN-10: 1-480-13405-8

Cover design and formatting: www.damonza.com

The places, characters and events portrayed in this book are fictitious. Any similarity to real locations or businesses, or any persons, living or dead, is coincidental and not intended by the author.

For Geri:

Three Words

When one door of happiness closes, another opens;
but often we look so long at the closed door that we do
not see the one which has been opened for us.

Helen Keller

Conventional wisdom provides that a path exists for us to follow through life. For example, conventional wisdom teaches that to lead a good and proper life one is meant to go to school, learn a vocation, practice that vocation, retire, get old and die. Part of that conventional wisdom is obviously good. The other part . . . not so good. Grow up, get educated, get to work, stop working, enjoy the fruits of your labor. Get old. Die.

Along the way, conventional wisdom would have some good things happen to you. Maturity, relationships, accolades, success. Marriage, children, college for the children. Children's marriage, grandchildren. Maybe even great-grandchildren. In a perfect world.

In a perfect world, all goes according to "The Plan." Who or what originated, modified and finalized The Plan is a mystery. The Plan, by and large, is made up of good things, except for the death part. But what about when The Plan goes awry? What about the in-between-the-big-occasion events? Like puberty. Or illness. Or failure. Like dealing with adversity such as failing to make the team, or not getting into the school on which you had your heart set, or not getting the promotion you expected at work. Or getting laid off. Or the cruelty of other children to your child. Or the rejection of a lover. Or divorce. Or widowhood.

When The Plan goes awry, nothing anyone says to rationalize what has happened can soften the blow. You just have to live through the pain or the heartache, allow time to act as a salve, and have faith that the wound will eventually heal. Conventional wisdom dictates that it would be so. At least we have that to lean on. We hope.

Chapter 1

As the light of the emerging sunrise filtered through the curtains, his eyelids began to flicker, the knowledge of a new day dawning slowly seeping into his comprehension. He opened his eyes to the dim light, looked past the billowing curtains and through the opening between the windows, catching the purple-orange of the sky extending down to the deep blue of the Atlantic. This was going to be one of those days where the water was glass-smooth, with a timid curl of water lapping over as it hit the shoreline—a stark contrast to the normal roiling detonation of crashing waves. Before his eyes was displayed as beautiful and serene a sight as he could remember, but similar to his recent experience, he knew that the serenity could be gone in an instant. With something as innocuous as a puff of wind, everything would change.

The beach house was devoid of activity save for the fluttering of the curtains. He propped himself up, half lying and half sitting against the pillow pressed against the whitewashed headboard. He watched the curtains, caught by the wind and flapping here and there, ballooning and deflating with the ebb and flow of the air. They reminded him of a tragic movie he once saw, which depicted a plastic shopping bag flung abruptly by the wind, wildly changing directions along the ground, then getting caught by an updraft and floating away effortlessly. Gracefully. A thing of beauty. As he followed the flow of the curtains he thought of the gracefulness of the plastic bag in the wind, and looking beyond the windows and out at the ocean, he realized that he was surrounded by beauty. He had always been surrounded by beauty, as are we all. We just don't always see it through the fog of our everyday living.

The weathered clapboard house sat just off of the beach beyond the end of the paved road, partially hidden by a twisted pile of natural brush. The first time they came upon it was entirely by chance, a result of taking a wrong turn on their way to visit some friends. Lost and in need of a phone, they knocked on the door but no one had answered. They peered through the salt encrusted windows and saw that the house was empty. It was only then that they took in the view from the front porch: a sweeping panorama of the deserted beach in the fading sun, and realized that it was idyllic. It was love at first sight.

The house had been abandoned and was in disrepair, but to them it was perfect. After tracking down the absentee owner, they negotiated a fair price and bought it, then took pleasure in making it their own. The house became their respite from a life too full of work and travel and too many daily activities. It was their place of quiet nights with the windows open, listening to the waves and the chirping crickets, of lazy summer afternoons napping on the hammock they hung from the porch rafters, and of many nights of laughter spent with family and friends.

Ironically, the house that had provided so much joy and substance to their life together had become his own personal prison. He could no more leave and walk away from it as a parent could abandon a child. For embedded within its walls were the echoes of carefree days and nights, of discussions and debates, of the giddiness of playing board games together and the silliness that can only come from a family's intimate knowledge of its collective members.

Yet, a house is simply a structure absent the imminent

return of those souls that make it a home. Views and square footage and design are just sticks and mortar and placement. Where once there was laughter and touching and love, there now was sadness and solitude and loneliness. The building had become his torture chamber.

He avoided looking beside him on the bed—she wasn't there and he knew it. How many mornings had come and gone without her in this bed, the unnatural reality of his solo existence slamming into him as if for the first time. Some days, the weight of that reality was too great, preventing him from moving, depriving him of a day. One day excised from his life. If anyone knew the value of each and every day, lived to its fullest, it was he. Yet despite this understanding of the world and its machinations, he found himself paralyzed by sorrow, unable to function. Heartbreak is debilitating, and he was still trying to wrest control of his life back from that villain.

The light was gradually coming up, and he could see flocks of pelicans flying in formation over the shoreline. One or two were always peeling off to nose-dive into the water, disappearing for a moment beneath the surface, then coming straight out and into flight, like a missile shot from a submarine. Every morning he watched the pelicans. He was jealous of the simplicity of their existence. He wondered whether they thought, whether they hurt. Was their sense of such things so animalistic as to limit their ability to feel? Oh, to float on the air devoid of feeling, letting it take you where it would. A thing of beauty.

He willed himself out of the bed and walked into the kitchen to make coffee and to contemplate getting through the day. This is what his life had become: a monotonous routine devoid of any sense or meaning. Every day he told himself that this was to be the day, the day to resume his life. And yet he continued to find himself sleepwalking through it.

As the coffee began to brew and the house filled with its sweet aroma, he walked into the family room, opened the sliding glass door and walked through it, onto the deck overlooking the dunes and the ocean beyond. He took in the calm, waveless sheen of the water and noted the reflection of the sky on the smooth surface. Several puffy white clouds hovered in the sky, looking as if they were suspended by strings from the heavens.

Late Fall and early Spring were always his favorite seasons in Sandy Cove, to him the most beautiful time at the beach. In addition to the dearth of tourists that had of late discovered the isle, the days dawned crisp and clear, the beaches were pristine and deserted, and the bustle of the summer gave way to a slower and more casual solitude. He had always looked forward to the exit of the last of the visitors, leaving the small number of year-round residents alone to enjoy their piece of heaven on Earth, even as Spring brought with it the anticipation of a new season and the return of the tourists which were their lifeblood.

He leaned against the deck, staring out at the ocean. The water was smooth and calm to such an extreme that ripples could be seen from the movement of fish just below the surface near the shore. Farther out, he saw a school of porpoises crossing past the house, gracefully emerging from the water in groups of two, the sun reflecting off of their gray skin as they turned half circles and dove back into the depths. He stared out at them as they continued parallel to the shoreline, until he could no longer discern any movement above the water. His focus faded and he found himself daydreaming, staring out at the water without seeing anything, his memories taking over his consciousness.

He remembered the day he met her at college and the way she tilted her head when she asked if she could have the seat next to him. She was going to sit next to him! What great twist of fate had sent her to this seat, next to his? She was the most beautiful girl he had ever seen and he didn't know why God had bestowed such a gift upon him.

He remembered the time they were studying together and her hair fell across her cheek, when he reached out and pushed it back.

"Thank you," she said simply, looking up at him, a soft blush coming across her face. And then their eyes locked and they saw into each other's souls for the first time. The first of many.

He remembered their wedding night and the day their child was born and the day they moved into the beach house, the way she smiled and cried, the way she walked and the way that she looked when she was sleeping. He remembered how it felt to hold her in his arms while they danced, and what her hand felt like in his as they walked together along the beach.

He remembered the good times as well as the bad. But lately, he was trying to stay focused on the good times. And he was struck by the irony of our daily living, that when life is good and treats you well, time slips through your fingers like sand, the years passing by faster and faster. Yet when things go wrong and life gets tough, time slows down and each day seems endless, a sad, tortuous existence. He was buoyed by the thought that their life together had been good for a long time. Good and easy and happy.

The phone ringing from inside the house snapped him from his reverie, and taking one last glance at the ocean, he went back into the house. On most days he would hide behind the answering machine, not wanting to deal with the inevitable questions of "how are you holding up" and "why don't you come out with us tonight." But today the realtor was supposed to bring someone over to view the house and he'd said he would call in advance. The call turned out to be a wrong number.

He poured himself a cup of coffee, went back onto the deck and dropped into one of the wooden Adirondack chairs they had bought together at the local beach supply store shortly after they closed on the house. Soon, he thought, he would be away from here, away from this house and from Sandy Cove. Six months had passed and he was not getting better. In fact, he felt worse, and now he was selling out and running away. He knew it made no sense, because everything that mattered to him emanated from this place, from this house.

He hadn't arrived at the decision to sell easily, but he knew that staying in the house and in Sandy Cove was his roadblock from moving on with his life. He hadn't been able to figure out a way around it. Now, though, the angst over the decision to sell had replaced—he knew, temporarily—the sorrow that had taken over his heart. From one heartbreak to another.

Chapter 2

In the off-season the drive from the house into the village of Sandy Cove took all of five minutes, a stark contrast to the high season, when tourists clogged the roads with their overstuffed SUVs and minivans. During those times it could take upwards of thirty minutes on the winding two-lane road. Each year the traffic got worse as the area became more popular, providing the pretext for some of the local business leaders to again beat the drum for expanding the roads, adding bridges, building highways and otherwise easing access to the beachside hamlet. They seemed ignorant of the errors of so many other destinations whose planning failures had ruined both the ambiance and the character of the resorts. So far, their efforts had failed to attain enough momentum to gain a foothold with the voters, despite the maps and charts and traffic studies that they trotted out, annually.

He drove along the road deep in thought, oblivious to the landscape as he sped southward. The road meandered through newly-sprouted housing developments and passed by a century-old lifesaving station turned luxury Inn, as well as an old, abandoned military outpost, before curling along the soundfront and into the village. He pulled into the gravel lot in front of a small storefront adjacent to the Sound called the Cove Café, grabbed his backpack and trudged up the wooden steps toward the smell of fresh-brewed coffee and toasted bagels. He opened the door, making the small bell attached to the door jingle, and entered the store.

A burly fifty-ish man behind the counter was waiting on a couple with two unruly kids, looking perturbed and trying to be hospitable at the same time. He looked over them from behind the counter and rolled his eyes. But taking this opening as a way to break free, he shouted out at his good friend, "Hiya, Tommy Boy. How ya doin'?" And with that he moved away from the indecisive couple, came around the counter and proceeded to give his friend a bear hug.

Pushing the gregarious big man away in feigned annoyance, Tom quietly chided his friend. "How's it going, Sam? Still wooing the customers, I see."

"I kinda got used to being free of these guys over the winter," Sam half-whispered in Tom's ear.

"Now, how do you think you're going to pay for the mortgage on this place if you scare everyone away?"

"I have to put up with them all summer long. I can be mean until then," Sam replied with a wink as he moved back to behind the counter and returned to his position, patiently answering whether the smoked salmon cream cheese was better than the veggie. When the customers still couldn't decide, he looked back at Tom with another eye roll, then resumed explaining the attributes of the various bagel toppings.

Tom ambled toward his normal resting spot in the rear of the café, stopped to pour himself a cup of coffee and grabbed a section of the New York Times that had been abandoned by a previous customer. Slumping into a wicker lounge chair, he scanned the newspaper to find that it was filled with the typical hodgepodge of political conflict, international intrigue and pop culture nonsense. Nothing of real import managed to capture his attention and he quickly discarded the paper on the coffee table in front of him.

His attention returned to the two children in front of the

display case, their noses pressed against the glass, leering at the assorted pastries that were lined up inside. Their plaintive pleas for chocolate frosted cupcakes and doughnuts having been ignored by the parents, they returned to touching and pushing and pinching each other, their giggles rising in volume along with high-pitched screeches of feigned pain. The children, a boy and a girl, cavorted around their parents' legs, using them as shields, while the parents continued in their indecision, oblivious to the havoc reigning around them. Suddenly, the boy swung his arm to the side and inadvertently hit his sister on the cheek, which led her to shriek and begin to cry. Instinctively the mother picked her up and cradled her while the father reprimanded the boy, and they hurriedly exited the store without buying anything, the cheerful door chime conflicting with the state of the tearful little girl cuddled in her mother's embrace. Just before they pushed through the door he caught the girl's eyes, big and brown and brimming with tears.

Tom stared at the empty space in front of the counter, recalling summer in Nantucket from a lifetime ago. They had been on vacation and Emily was a little girl, about the same age as the little girl he had just seen. The art gallery near the pier had been their last stop before getting on the ferry to head back to the mainland. He and Sarah were wrapped up in a discussion about whether to buy the painting that they had seen early in the trip and which they had returned to view several times during their stay. Although they had negotiated a good price with the gallery owner, it was still a stretch, and they couldn't make up their minds. They were so preoccupied that they hadn't seen the door open, didn't hear the door chime jingle and didn't hear the door click shut. And then she was gone.

He recalled the utter fear that overtook him when they realized she was not in the gallery, when they frantically searched for her through the crowd awaiting the ferry on the dock, the look of desperation in Sarah's eyes and the dead, empty feeling in his stomach. And he remembered their relief when they found her safe, innocently kneeling on the pier, petting a dog.

"Hey, stranger. What brings you out so early in the morning?"

Tom looked up to see Jenny, Sam's sister, standing directly in front of him. She stood over him, smiling and wiping her flour-covered hands on her apron.

"How's the house coming along? Any bites yet?" she asked as she leaned over and kissed him on the forehead.

"Nothing solid yet, although someone's coming over to see it this morning." Tom smiled back meekly as he forced the memory back. He felt the cold sweat that had started to form on his forehead.

"You know, Sam and I are rooting against you on the sale. Why don't you just take your trip and give yourself some time to get back to normal? Do you really think you need to sell the house, too?

"Jen, I appreciate that you both need me around for entertainment's sake. But I'm wasting away over there. I just can't see any other way to move on."

She sat down next to him and put a comforting hand on his knee. "Tommy, it takes time. Give yourself some credit. You've been traumatized. You need to give yourself time to recover. It hasn't been long enough for you to make such a drastic change."

"I appreciate that," Tom said as he struggled to maintain his composure. "You've both been wonderful to me, having me over so much and looking in on me. But a clean break is for the best."

"Are you certain you need that? A clean break?"

"No, I . . . I have no idea what I need or what is going to work best. Nothing has worked so far. I just think that starting over without having to handle all of the memories lurking in that place—in this place—will give me a chance to move on with my life."

"Is that what you think? That you need to move on with your life?"

"I honestly don't know," Tom replied, looking absently at the papers scattered on the coffee table.

"Tom, I've been thinking that maybe that's the wrong approach." Jenny's tone was sympathetic but deliberate. Tom had been wallowing in despair since Sarah died. "Sarah's gone but she will always be a part of you. Of us. She was my friend, too, and you know what? I don't ever want to move on from her. I want her to be with me in spirit and in my consciousness, to be a part of all of the joys and sorrows that I experience in my life. I much prefer that than to move on from her."

Tom nodded, saying nothing in return, and they sat quietly, the random sounds of people coming and going providing soothing background noise and easing the need for additional conversation.

* * *

Tom Ralston actually met Jenny Powers long before Sarah came into his life. Tom had vacationed in Sandy Cove with his family since childhood, frequenting Powers' Mom and Pop, a small convenient mart that Jenny's parents ran, with Jenny behind the register most days. They had become friends the day that Tom's younger brother decided to find out if he could swallow an atomic hot ball, not realizing that the ball was too big to swallow whole, but big enough to go halfway down your throat and get stuck. Tom had panicked at the sight of his blue-faced brother motioning frantically, unable to breathe, and ran outside in search of—what, he could never figure out. When he came bursting back inside, he found his brother sitting on the ground, the atomic ball in his hand, and Jenny's arm around him. He never knew how she did it. He just remembered the look on her face and the smile she flashed him when she looked up to find him staring at her.

Although Jenny lived in Sandy Cove year 'round and Tom and his family only came for part of the summer, they were inseparable during those times. In the off-seasons in the age before the Internet, they wrote each other long letters about their lives, their hopes and aspirations and their love interests. They'd never dated, never went the route that most of the people around them thought to be inevitable. They simply became best friends, defying the age-old logic that such a friendship was impossible in the natural order of things.

When Tom and Sarah met in college and fell in love, the person he most wanted to meet her was Jenny. Her approval was essential. And Jenny loved Sarah from the moment they met, as Tom knew she would. Jenny and Sarah joked that Tom was their facilitator—the person whose efforts brought other people together who were a perfect match, while being incapable of making the same type of connections in his own life. That had always been Tom's problem, made even more pronounced after years of marriage had alleviated the need to seek companionship outside of his marriage.

Jenny's own marriage had lasted only a short time. It was the only time in all of the years that Tom had known her that Jenny had grown distant from him. For college she had decided that she needed to get as far away from coastal life as possible, partly out of fear that she'd never get to experience "real" life, which at the time she believed meant living somewhere that had a subway, a decent museum and enough people that she could live a blissfully anonymous existence. Her sojourn to city living was also based partly on her hope that such an experience would release her from what she perceived at that time was a pre-determined path which ended with her running her parent's store—and living the slow-paced life that coastal living afforded.

While all of her friends were planning to party for four years at State or at those other institutions along Tobacco Road, she had her sights set on Columbia and New York City. To say that her parents were surprised when she announced her intention to go to Columbia was an understatement, and was also prologue to their bewilderment at what came later, when she eschewed returning home and chose instead to stay in New York and work in a Soho boutique—a perfect avocation for someone with a degree in philosophy, she often joked. It was there that she met Robert Dixon, III (just call me "Trip"), who came in to her store one day with a friend and wouldn't leave until she gave him her number.

Tom could never quite put his finger on it but he just didn't like Trip. Tom always thought it was because he was one of those guy's guys. The kind who always has a sporting event to attend with other guys. The kind who always has a round of shots coming at the bar. The kind who seems to notice every good-looking woman who walks by and has a comment ready—even if his wife is standing right next to him at the time.

Trip was charming and always the life of the party, which is what drew Jenny to him. Everyone told Jenny how lucky she was to have him because he was such a great guy, and for a long time those comments are what kept Jenny from leaving him. After all, if everyone thought Trip was so great, how could she walk away from Prince Charming?

In hindsight, the telltale signs were there for all to see: the gradual separation from friends and family, the cryptic excuses for being unable to make plans to socialize, the hurried and infrequent telephone calls. Sarah voiced her concerns, but the prospect that her intuition was on the mark in this instance was too frightening to truly accept, and they never wanted to interpose in Jenny's marriage. They didn't find out about the physical abuse until after Jenny left him, in bittersweet validation of Sarah's perception. The experience left Jenny skeptical of the merit of relationships with men in general, and of the institution of marriage in particular. She also couldn't keep the failed marriage separate in her mind from her experience of living in the city, and shortly after the marriage ended she moved back home, back to the destiny she had fought so desperately to avoid.

While Jenny had sought to break away from Sandy Cove and establish a new life in the city, Tom had yearned for the welcoming embrace of the seaside retreat. He'd done his share of city-hopping and traveling, yet he never felt as good or as comfortable as when he was in Sandy Cove. Over the years he'd spent an increasing amount of time there, from college summers working as a beach guard, to the summer after graduate school which dragged into a year-long timeout from reality, to summer vacations and weekend getaways with Sarah and then family vacations. Each time he arrived he felt overwhelmingly relaxed, and each time he left he felt that he was leaving a part of himself behind.

When he and Sarah discovered the house at the end of Prickly Point Road, something inside of him sprang to life, an excited anticipation for what he always yearned. This wouldn't be a short-lived respite from their real lives; rather, the house would become the focal point of their future.

Initially, the idea was that they would repair it and rent it for part of the year. But once they undertook that task it became obvious to both Tom and Sarah that the house was a labor of love that they couldn't share with others. It was meant to be their own.

The first summer was a whirlwind of travel, meetings with contractors and making repairs on their own in an attempt to get the house habitable again. To start it needed a new roof, painting both inside and out and sanding and refinishing the porch and deck. Sarah took on the landscaping as her special project, personally removing and thinning out the overgrown foliage while adding native plantings which were geographically appropriate. She always cringed when she saw landscapers planting mini-palm trees in an attempt to give new homes a tropical appearance. Her repeated rant was "palm trees don't grow naturally 1,500 miles north of Miami! Don't they know that?" Her obsession became their inside joke, with Tom always nudging her on her obsession. "Why don't they make that house look more beachy and plant some palm trees?" he would say, chidingly. Sarah would bite her tongue as the blood filled her cheeks, such was her ire over the attempts to create a Margaritaville appearance.

They scoured the area for furniture to fill the house, seeking vintage pieces such as naturally-worn armoires, tables, lamps and headboards. The cottage industry of replica worn furniture seemed cheesy to them, and they marveled at the high prices stores charged tourists who were in search of so-called "beach" furniture, for which the customers would readily pay. It seemed that people would go to great lengths to add authenticity to their lives, even if the source of the authenticity was a fiction.

One day it occurred to Sarah that the local supply of vintage furniture was great enough to provide an alternative to the stores selling imitations, at a competitive price advantage. In the process of searching for their own purchases they had discovered the existence of a treasure trove of discarded "junk." Why not open a shop selling the real thing at reasonable prices as opposed to selling fabrications? Tom was easily sold on the idea, as demand for the furniture was obvious. As for the thought of relocating, Emily was on the verge of leaving for college and Tom had been looking for an alternative to the corporate world, as well as a valid excuse to make their move to Sandy Cove permanent. So began the next stage of their lives.

Their transition to coastal living proved to be easy. They had spent much of their vacation time over the years in Sandy Cove, and they had established friendships with several year-round residents. Jenny and Sam were thrilled to have them for more than the few short weeks that had been the norm. While Jenny and Sarah had grown fond of each other during the relatively brief periods in the summers, their friendship flourished and grew as they spent more time together. They became the best of friends, to the point where each of them thought of the other as the sister she never had.

Sandy Cove wasn't really a retirement destination. The population of year-round residents was small, and Sandy Cove was really just a village of less than a thousand people from September to May. Most of the restaurants and shops gradually cut back on their hours of operation in the Fall and Spring, and close entirely during January and February. This was the time that the locals used to relax and rejuvenate, and many who didn't have children still in school left to vacation in warmer climates.

The tourists still came in the Fall and Spring, but they were primarily couples seeking a quick weekend getaway from Washington or Philadelphia to stay at the famous Inn and Spa just north of Sandy Cove. They ventured out to the village mostly in the mornings before their massages and pedicures, seeking out bagels and croissants and scones, and browsing the shops along the main thoroughfare or in the quaint shopping plazas that lined the road and soundfront. Although far fewer in number than the hordes of summer vacationers, they were more likely to buy substantial items, as well as to spend more money. They ignored the t-shirt shops and surf stores, giving their attention to the specialty shops like Tom and Sarah's, the art galleries, and the stores offering literature on local history, shipwrecks and lighthouses.

Most days business was slow by late afternoon, and the store and sandwich shop owners, bored with the lack of traffic, closed early to seek out the company of the other late season hold-outs. Tom would often leave the shop and head over to the Cove Café with a bottle of wine or a six pack of beer to share with Sam while sitting on a bench that overlooked the sound. Sarah would eventually join them, then Jenny, after closing out the register.

They sipped on their drinks as they shared their stories of the day and watched the sun set on the sound, the light glistening on the water. Their talk would slow as the sun slowly tracked lower in the sky, first coming to rest on the tree tops of the mainland, then creeping behind the trees and disappearing beneath the horizon, leaving behind a collage of orange and pink and purple mixing in the sky and clouds. They'd sit watching the sky and listening to the frogs chirping beneath them in the bog underneath the deck, mixing with the sound of water softly lapping against the wood supports until the light finally disappeared from the sky.

Over time their impromptu get-togethers grew in frequency and size as other friends joined in to relax at the end of the day and to take in the sunset. Sam coined them "SLOBS," for "Sunset Lovers Out of Business Soon," but they all joked about how they couldn't live without their SLOB sessions. These were good times full of laughter and camaraderie that added to the special allure of Sandy Cove.

Tom and Sarah used the off-season to catch their breath from the hectic life of the summer months when they were busy running the shop, and to visit with Emily at college and family in the Northeast. Yet each time they returned, turning off the main highway onto Prickly Point Road and seeing the house emerge as they drove around the last bend brought a sense of relief and elation. Here they had found their respite, their escape from the fast pace of their former lives and from the form of life that grabs all of us, despite our best intentions. Materialism faded away from them in Sandy Cove, and the need to run the business was more a means to pay the bills than to accumulate things and to establish wealth. It was not an altruistic existence, but it was a far cry from the race to see who ends up first in the money ledger.

The house that was worn and faded and showing its years had been given new life. It was nothing like the ostentatious monstrosities that were being built on the isle as mini-hotels for rental. The locals called these new mansions monopoly houses, resembling the plastic game pieces being placed on tiny oceanfront plots and lined up for miles on end. Many wondered what would happen to these fragile homes in the event of direct hit of a summer storm or a strong nor'easter.

The house on Prickly Point Road was small in comparison, and had survived the weather over the years by being strategically placed farther back and at an angle to the shoreline, protected by a substantial dune covered with thick sea oats and native grasses. The angled placement allowed for views of the beach from both the front porch and the deck on the rear. Inside it was warm and comfortable, and the way that Tom and Sarah had refurbished it was a reflection of their easygoing approach to life. Overstuffed whicker chairs and couches inside, a hammock hung from the front porch rafters and Adirondack chairs and loungers on the deck. Framed family photos lined the walls and music could often be heard escaping through the open windows.

They became known for their get-togethers and hospitality, and in summertime they often had a house full of visitors. The house and the lifestyle they found in Sandy Cove suited Tom and Sarah, and they both adjusted seamlessly to their permanent move. It was a perfect fit for them, both individually and as a couple. And until their world was turned upside down, they were happy there.

Chapter 3

S omeone must have left the lights on. He woke up in the middle of the night and saw the light shining under the door from the hallway, casting a bright line across the bed. He looked over to the other side of the bed and saw that she wasn't there. A pang of anxiety attacked him and he quickly rose to investigate.

Life had become a series of fits and starts, good news—as good as such news could be—and bad. Their lives had become a roller coaster ride. Yes, he thought, a roller coaster aptly defined their lives now: the long, interminable climb up the big hill, the car teetering at the apex, then hurtling down the first descent and racing, seemingly uncontrolled, around the track until the car was abruptly brought to a halt so that the riders could exit, having dodged the contrived danger. In fact it was perfectly controlled, the physics of the ride purposefully calibrated to give the sense that the car was about to leave the track at any moment.

Theirs was a controlled ride, too. Controlled by the doctors and the specialists and the technicians who charted the course of treatment and who administered the drugs with clinical expertise. Whether all of that expertise would result in the happy ending, as if they had dodged the danger, was the only undetermined variable of their real-life roller coaster ride. Cancer was not something that could be calibrated with the certainty of physics.

Tom found her sitting at the kitchen table, writing. Sarah loved to hand-write letters and notes and thank you's, and she had different papers for each task. Her handwriting was unique and exquisite and she took great pride in her penmanship and in the praise she received from those to whom she wrote.

He pulled a chair out and sat down across from her, waiting for the proper moment to break the silence. He watched the pen float over the paper with ease and grace. She'd been having trouble sleeping through the night of late, and the lack of sleep combined with the medication was taking its toll on her. She'd started to get circles under her eyes and her temper had gotten short, the by-products of the poison that the doctors were feeding her.

"You don't need to keep getting up in the middle of the night to check on me," she said. Her words broke the silence so abruptly that Tom was startled by the sound of her voice. She kept writing.

"I know I don't have to get up. I just don't want you to be alone."

"I wasn't alone. You were just upstairs sleeping."

"Well, now I'm here with you. What are you writing?" Tom felt as if Sarah had been pushing him away of late and didn't want to give in to the temptation of sleep at the expense of spending time with her while she was awake.

"Just a letter to Emily. I know I could email her but this way it's more personal."

Tom watched as Sarah continued to write. She was still so beautiful to him, despite the ravaging effect of her disease on her body. She was one of the lucky ones who didn't lose her hair from the radiation, but she'd lost weight and looked somewhat gaunt now, and the tone of her skin color was not quite right. None of it mattered to Tom.

With some trepidation he spoke again. "Listen, Sarah. I

was thinking that once this round of treatment is over that we should take some time, maybe take a trip somewhere to decompress and allow us to get back to normal."

Sarah continued to write the letter, the slight rise of her eyebrow the only visible acknowledgment of his suggestion.

Tom sat staring at a spot on the table, waiting for her response. Although it was natural to try to do so, it wasn't easy to suggest something to Sarah that took her out of the mode of thinking exclusively about her condition. Lately, their lives consisted solely of going from treatment to treatment and from doctor visit to doctor visit. It was all-encompassing and didn't leave much room for planning for the future, especially given the fact that their future was so uncertain. Still, they had hope for a successful outcome, and if so, for their old life to resume anew.

Sarah finished her writing, put the pen down and folded the letter, then focused her attention on Tom. "Where were you thinking we should go?"

Tom was relieved that she asked the question with sincerity. Still, he replied tentatively, unsure of how Sarah would respond to his suggestion. "I don't know. It doesn't matter where. Just so we're moving from place to place and not worrying about meeting any kind of schedule."

Sarah, ever the pragmatist, responded not to the suggestion but with the obvious. "What about the store? Who's going to be there to run it while we're off having fun?"

Good question. Tom had been flying solo running the shop while Sarah was undergoing her treatments, and despite his efforts to find someone to manage things in his absence, he'd failed to find anyone reliable enough to do so. Certainly none of their current employees would fit the bill. There just weren't many people available to whom they could entrust their business, and the college-aged kids who swarmed in for the summer season could barely manage to pay close enough attention to learn how to run the cash register. Still, he knew Sarah—knew that she would hone in on the key point, and he'd thought of all of the potential responses.

"Why let the store dictate our lives to us? Maybe we wait until the Fall, close the store early this year and just stay away until Spring," Tom said this while avoiding Sarah's gaze, that knowing, accusatory look that said that he was being irresponsible and short-sighted. Instead, she surprised him.

She came around the table and sat on his lap, folding her arm around his shoulder and nuzzling against him. "I think you're on to something, Mister," Sarah said as she gave him a kiss on the cheek. "I think it's a fantastic idea."

"You do?"

"Yes, I do. If I've learned anything from this nightmare it's that if I make it through I'm going to do all of the things I never had time to do. Well, all of the things I thought I never had time to do. The only thing is, can we afford to close the store early?"

Tom paused before replying, if only to gather his thoughts due to Sarah's unexpected response. He'd done his best to hide from her how emotional he'd become since the diagnosis. His job was to be strong for her. He pulled her to him and hugged her. "At this point money is the last thing on my mind. We'll be fine," he said, then stood and led her by the hand back to bed.

Chapter 4

He'd been gone for a year, yet as he drove along the rural road—one that he'd driven a thousand times—it occurred to Tom that nothing had changed. A year in time is nothing. It doesn't even register, except when every day, every minute, every alive moment matters. The way it did when Sarah was sick. But time stopped mattering for Tom the day that his wife died.

When he left he'd felt irresponsible, childish. He *was* running away. Running away from Sandy Cove, from his store, his daughter and his friends.

He had no set itinerary or agenda. He didn't care about how much money he spent. The credit card was his best friend. His primary focus was his immediate next stop, as if at the next destination he would find salvation. Yet as soon as he arrived, in whatever town or state or country, he was already planning his getaway, knowing that the answer he sought wasn't where he presently stood. He was in search of the holy grail at the end of the rainbow, and although he knew that he was never going to find it, he was intent on continuing the quest.

He hadn't thought much about when he would return. But he had loose ends to tie up, and when the realtor got ahold of him and told him that they had a buyer for the house, Tom came back. Reality beckoned, and Tom knew he needed to take care of the things from which he had run: a house to sell, a business to close, friends to whom he needed to bid farewell. He was back to finally end his former life, and he had no idea where he would go afterward.

As he drove down the peninsula toward Sandy Cove he passed through Alikay, a little town that failed to register any significance to Tom other than a single house by the side of the road. He glanced over at the house as he sped by and continued driving, then abruptly slowed the car and turned back. If he was going to wrap things up, the old house he had just passed was the place to get started.

* * *

There wasn't much to the town of Alikay. It couldn't even be said that it was past its prime. It never had a prime. In fact, no one who was born and raised there could figure out a reason for the town's existence. As towns go, it didn't really qualify. No factories were located there. No jobs of any kind existed to provide any of the residents with a way to make a living. It only consisted of a smattering of single room homes, trailers on blocks, crumbling antebellum farmhouses and two fifties-era service stations that still stood but hadn't doled out any service since the new BP up the road opened and put them both out of business inside of a year. Alikay was actually just a pass-through that vacationers sped by on their way to and from the coast.

So it was quite odd to the locals when Miss Rayleigh Williams moved into the old Crawford house on State Route 158 and turned it into a living antique store. Miss Ray, as she told everyone to call her, had lived her entire life in a not-so pleasant neighborhood on the South side of Norfolk. Moving to Alikay and opening an antique store was her idea of the perfect retirement, something she had dreamed of while raising four kids on her own. The locals couldn't figure out what to make of Miss Ray, or her decision to move *to* Alikay, as opposed to the universal exodus that had taken place over the previous thirty years to . . . anywhere else. They'd joked about her and wagered on the amount of time it would take for the store to close, the consensus being eight months. As it turned out, Miss Ray had done her homework, or at least had followed her intuition, which led her to believe that Alikay was, in fact, the perfect place to open a store.

The Crawford House was most recently occupied by Beau Crawford, a farm hand of ill repute who died as a result of a bullet to the head fired by a jilted lover. There was no reason for the house to have been named The Crawford House save for the fact that someone named Crawford had lived in the house for as long as anyone could remember. It had sat empty and for sale for over two years since poor Beau was caught in bed with another woman. It was located on the main highway and was large enough to incorporate a store as well as to double as her home. No other antique stores were located on the entire stretch from Norfolk to the coast, and it was exactly the right distance from the beaches for tourists to take a break from their driving. And it was a bargain.

Miss Ray moved into the house and quickly stocked it with items which the locals called junk and the tourists called antiques. She picked up old fixtures and lamps, curios and art glass from estate sales and abandoned farmhouses. She had a knack for seeing value and sensing demand, and the cars, minivans and SUVs that piled in the front yard of the house validated her insight.

Although she made good money on her sales, she ran the store without assistance, and the local customers who occasioned the store often wondered how Miss Ray managed to maneuver the bigger items into the store and around the abundant antiques that made for cramped quarters. On this early Spring day she was at the rear of the home in the kitchen sipping her breakfast coffee when she heard the front door open and close and the hardwood boards of the flooring creaking under someone's foot. She emerged from the kitchen and her shoulders slumped visibly upon catching sight of her patron. She made her way through the labyrinth of chairs and floor lamps and vases, reaching out her arms as she drew near. Tom allowed her to capture him in her abundant embrace, and they stood in the middle of the floor as she attempted to comfort him, patting him on the back.

Eventually she released him, but grasped his hand in hers and said, "I've been waiting so long for you to come see me."

"I'm sorry it's taken me so long to get here," Tom replied, suddenly a bit unsettled. A year ago he had grown accustomed to such greetings, but it had been some time since he'd been away. Miss Ray's embrace had the effect of transporting him back to where he had been when he left, and he felt the emotion start to well up inside of him.

"You know, Tom, I was very fond of Miss Sarah." She reserved passing on her title to the few people with whom she felt a special bond. She continued to hold his hand in hers, caressing it as she spoke. "She was a special, special woman who loved you dearly. How can one account for such a tragedy?"

Tom simply nodded in return.

"Come—come with me and sit." She turned and pulled Tom behind her to the kitchen where she directed him to a chair at a small table. She retrieved a cup and saucer and poured him coffee, then sat down next to him. They sat in comfortable silence, and then Miss Ray began humming softly.

After several moments she stopped humming and said, "When someone so full of life passes from us we're tempted to question ourselves about our existence. Some fall back to prayer for comfort and reassurance in the goodness of life.

Others fall into a remorse so deep it seems impossible that life goes on. But, Tom, life does go on. Life has to go on."

Tom, who had been the recipient of this advice many times over, sat listening respectfully. He'd come to see Miss Ray out of respect for Sarah more than anything else. Sarah had formed a special relationship with Miss Ray, first as a result of their mutual admiration for antiques and vintage furniture, then, as they spent more time together, as a result of the unique bond that they felt for each other. They had a fondness for each other that defied their difference in age as well as their divergent social backgrounds. They'd become close friends, and Sarah got into the routine of driving out to see Miss Ray once every week or two, even during her treatment which left her weak and tired and deflated, to sit at the kitchen table drinking coffee and ruminating about life. Tom daydreamed about those times, imagining Sarah sitting in the same chair, drinking the same coffee from the same cups and saucers, and thought that Sarah was as happy in that setting as in any other.

"Tom?" Miss Ray had noted the glassed over look in Tom's eyes and looked at him with concern.

"Sorry about that," he replied. "I was just thinking that Sarah really loved this place, loved coming here and spending time with you. It was one of the joys in her life."

"For me, too. For me, too." She pulled a tissue from inside her sleeve cuff and dabbed at her eyes and nose, then placed the tissue back in her cuff. "Sit still for a minute, I have something I want to show you."

She rose and shuffled out of the room, disappearing up the stairs. Tom sat at the table looking out the window to the backyard. Nothing was in bloom this early in the year, but he could see she had planted a rose garden in a semi-circle around a small pergola. Vines grew up the posts and over the top of the pergola, which hovered over a cast stone bench. It was a beautiful, restive area. Tom had accompanied Sarah to visit Miss Ray on several occasions, but he had never before noticed the quaint setting. He wondered how Miss Ray managed to maintain the garden in summer, given the coastal climate that was so hot and arid.

"Here we are," Miss Ray said as she re-entered the kitchen. She was carrying a cardboard box, which she placed on the table in front of Tom. He sat looking at the box, unmoving. "Go ahead, take a look at it," she said, as she nudged the box toward him.

Tom reached out tentatively, opened the lid and pushed aside the tissue paper, revealing a small lacquer box. He lifted it out of the cardboard box and placed it on the table. The lid had a floral design and was hinged. He opened the lid and the box began playing music. Inside were pop-up figurines–a couple in an embrace, dancing in slow circles to the music.

"She loved these things," Tom remarked, as he watched the figures turn round and round.

"I know she did," replied Miss Ray. "My mother gave me a music box just like this one when I was a little girl. I keep it upstairs. Miss Sarah fell in love with that box from the first time I showed it to her. She couldn't help herself but to open it and watch the couple dancing every time she came to visit me. This one was meant to be a surprise—a gift from me to her." She was looking at Tom now, watching him stare at the figurines.

The music started to slow, then stopped. Tom slowly closed the lid, watching as the dancers folded inside. After a moment he asked, "Did Sarah talk to you about me?"

"Yes, she did," Miss Ray replied. "We talked about a whole lot of things, including you and Emily. We discussed the cancer and how the treatment made her feel. She spoke very lovingly of you and of how appreciative she was having you to take care of her."

"And she told you that she loved dancing?"

"Slow dancing and taking long walks on the beach. She said those were her favorite things to do with you. That those were the times that she felt closest to you."

Tom was unconsciously nodding his head as he listened. He wanted to inquire more into what Sarah discussed with Miss Ray, but thought better of it. Some things were better left undiscovered.

He managed a feeble smile and rose to leave. Miss Ray stood as well and embraced Tom again. As he turned to walk out Miss Ray said, "Aren't you forgetting something? She picked up the box and pushed it into his hands. "I want you to have it,"

Tom stood looking down at the box in his hands, then placed it back on the table. Miss Ray looked at him, quizzically. "Not yet," Tom said. "Not yet."

Miss Ray nodded, knowing that in due time he would come back to retrieve the dancers.

"She was lucky to have had you as a friend," he said.

"Miss Sarah was a special soul. We were all lucky to have had her in our lives, even if it wasn't for as long as we had hoped. Remember that, Tom."

He nodded at her and walked out to his car, Miss Ray following behind him. As he started the car and put it into gear, Miss Ray stood at the front door watching him. He waived goodbye, then steered the car onto the highway and headed toward Sandy Cove.

* * *

Tom spent the trip back to the coast contemplating his conversation with Miss Ray. Sarah had always returned rejuvenated after her visits with Miss Ray, even during the times when her treatment was most debilitating. They had joked that Miss Ray was her spiritual advisor. Tom thought he now understood the therapeutic effect of those visits. Visiting with Miss Ray was soothing, like sitting with a grandmother who dispenses wisdom borne of years of life's experiences.

He approached a traffic light and slowed to a stop behind a row of cars. The car in front of him had large white acrylic letters pasted to the rear window, which said, "In Loving Memory of Jessie Lynn, 1989-2006." He had seen such memorials in the past and thought them a bit much. Why would people torture themselves with a constant reminder of what was obviously a young life taken too soon? Even in his current state, he could not imagine having to endure the stark reminder every time he drove his car.

Maybe it was the sage advice that Miss Ray had imparted on him, or maybe it was just time for him to break out of his melancholy, but as he watched the car pull away from him, he had his epiphany: *You have to just let it go at some point*, he thought, and for the first time since Sarah died he didn't feel that aching sadness that had been his relentless companion. Instead, he felt a sense of relief wash over him—relief from the grief and the sorrow he felt as a result of Sarah's death, and relief from the guilt he felt for failing to protect her from her fate. For the first time in a very long time, he felt . . . alive.

The remainder of the drive went quickly as traffic was light, and Tom drove with a renewed energy. As he approached the last curve in the road before entering Sandy Cove, Tom slowed the car. He had been gone for a year and was unsure how he would feel when he finally drove down Prickly Point Road and caught sight of the house for the first time. He was terrified but also eager.

His soul-searching trip had lasted for a year and had taken him all over the world, but until this morning he had never had an epiphanic moment, had never felt a release from the dread and despair of his mourning. Suddenly, he felt like he could breathe again.

He drove through Sandy Cove, looking left and right as he passed by the storefronts and cafes. The village felt oddly deserted to Tom, and it reminded him of the Twilight Zone, where on the surface everything looks normal but where something evil lurks. He chuckled to himself at the absurdity of the notion and continued along, catching sight of his store, closed and looking forlorn. He had an urge to pull into the parking lot and go inside, but thought better of it. That was a task better left for another day.

Ahead of him he caught sight of two friends jogging alongside the road. He considered stopping to say hello, but instead he pressed on the accelerator and turned his head away from their view as he passed, hopeful that they hadn't recognized him. He felt odd being back, having extricated himself from Sandy Cove and failing to maintain contact with anyone while he was away.

He drove on, through the rest of the village and then along the Sound, which was frothy with waves from the wind. When he finally made the turn onto his street he felt a surge of adrenaline run through his body. The feeling of being back was exhilarating, and it made him wonder why he had been so concerned about returning. He felt his heart pounding in his chest as he covered the last hundred yards to the last curve before the house, and then, there it was, right in front of him.

He pulled into the carport and parked, then practically leapt from the car and up the front stairs. The house looked the same as he had left it, save for the windows, which were dirty and in need of a good cleaning. He walked briskly to the end of the porch and looked out over the dunes at the ocean, which seemed to be calling out to him, welcoming him back. He took in the sweeping vista: the deserted beach and the tumultuous waves, the sea oats swaying in the wind and the specks of blue trying to break through the dark, brooding clouds. The wind whipped around him and he breathed in deeply, taking in the air thick with the smells of the sea.

He walked back to the front door and stood in front of it, unmoving for a moment, before he unlocked the door, turned the handle and began to enter. He paused, as his one last reticent feeling overtook him, before he pushed it aside and pressed onward. He was home.

* * *

In the morning Tom jumped in his car and headed North to Crystal Cove, the next village up the road from Sandy Cove. He turned into a parking lot, parked, and briskly climbed the stairs to the B & R Realty office. As he entered, Charlie Reynolds rose from his desk. Charlie was a good old boy who spoke with a slow Southern drawl.

"Tom, good to see you," Charlie said with his hand outstretched. "I've got the papers all ready to sign. Are you ready to get this thing done?"

"Good to see you, too, Charlie," Tom replied, while shaking his hand. "Umm. Can we talk for a minute?"

"Surely can. No rush, no rush. What've you got on your mind?"

Tom paused, not sure how Charlie was going to take what Tom had to tell him. "Uh, Charlie, I've decided not to sell the house."

The smile quickly faded from Charlie's face.

Tom continued quickly. "It's just that . . . I think I acted a bit hastily in deciding to sell. It was more of a knee-jerk reaction—an attempt to solve what's been going on in my life—than a real desire to sell the house. I don't know what I was thinking, to be honest with you."

A smile crept back onto Charlie's face as he listened to Tom explain his decision. "Tom," he replied, "I could be a selfish SOB and try to talk you back into selling, but then I'd have all of Sandy Cove breaking down my door to get at me. And I personally would rather see you stay than go. Don't worry yourself about the listing. I've got more than my share, and I'd rather sell one of those new-fangled rental homes than a year-rounder's."

"No hard feelings, then?"

"No, sir. No hard feelings," Charlie responded. "But you can buy me a beer at the next SLOB session."

"Deal," Tom replied, giving Charlie a hearty handshake.

As Tom headed to the door, Charlie said, "I guess this is gonna work out the way it was supposed to, after all."

Tom stopped and thought about the comment for a moment, then turned, and said, "How so?"

Charlie hesitated, now thinking that maybe he shouldn't have opened his mouth. But Tom was waiting for him to answer, and he didn't really have a choice any longer.

With a shrug of his shoulders, he said, "Well, Jenny told me a year ago that if anyone was ever really interested in the house that I should let her know, because she would bid higher and buy it."

"Jenny was going to buy my house?" Tom said, incredulously.

"Now, Tom, don't go getting yourself in a tizzy," Charlie said, certain now that he should have kept quiet. "She said she was doing it for you."

Chapter 5

S pring is symbolic of renewal. Nature's re-set button. The beginning of Spring in a coastal tourist town is more than a figurative notion. In Sandy Cove, the onset of Spring evidenced the emergence of its residents from their cocoon-like winter existence, both personally and business-wise. Whether they left the area for the winter months or simply holed-up in their homes for the duration, Springtime was the time for them to end their hibernation and to begin preparations for the coming onslaught of tourists.

For Tom the Spring was going to be more anxiety-filled than in past years. He wasn't just returning from his year-long interlude--he was also emerging from the loss of his wife and the depression that had controlled him since. And now he had the store to get up and running.

He and Sarah had decided to close their store, The Cottage Shop, in the Fall and he hadn't stepped foot inside since. The store had remained closed for a year in his absence. He wasn't sure how much of their revenue was based upon repeat business, but if it was a lot, then he was in for a rough time upon re-opening. He also hadn't obtained any new pieces to stock the store, and he had no employees.

Tom was hopeful that the store would do well upon re-opening, as long as the tourists decided to show up. As for the other store issues, finding employees would be the easiest to rectify. By the end of Spring semester, colleges would provide an ample supply of potential hires, all looking for an easy way to make some money over the summer while partying every night. The only limitation was that they weren't available until May. Tom was on his own until then. He did need to pick up some items to re-stock the store, but Miss Ray had graciously offered her help in that regard.

Since his return Tom felt that he had been doing relatively well, although he knew that he would never fully excise the pain that he felt over the loss of Sarah. Still, he couldn't shake the feeling that something felt "off." Other than the obvious fact that he was now a widower, the general aura of the store (and that of Sandy Cove) was different to him now. Although he knew that his reality changed when Sarah died, he didn't anticipate the changes to his perception of his surroundings and of people with whom he came in contact. In fact, with Sarah's death the environment in which he had been accustomed to living for his entire adult life had been irrevocably altered. The saying that life will never be the same was apt. He simply hadn't adjusted completely to his new life without Sarah in it.

Getting the store ready for the season was therapeutic and kept Tom busy. He dove into the logistics and spent days cleaning up the months worth of dust and dirt that had accumulated in his absence. He and Sarah always had an unspoken division of labor. Sarah was in charge of purchasing and selling. He was in charge of the books and financial matters. Together, they made it work.

He knew that he would be fine in the actual running of the store. The one thing that concerned him was how he would handle all of the other tasks--those which had made The Cottage Shop attractive to its customers. Sarah had always been the front person, while he had operated behind the scenes. Couples typically came into the store together, with Sarah engaging the women while the men moped around looking bored. Tom wasn't sure he could step into Sarah's shoes and bridge the gender gap. Time would tell if he could.

In the meantime he was doing the work of two and it was consuming all of his time, so much so that he'd dropped out of sight and out of touch. He hadn't spoken to any of his friends since he'd returned, least of all Jenny. To say that he'd been caught by surprise when Charlie told him that Jenny was buying his house was an understatement. It was more like a blind side, and the questions it raised in his mind were many. A long discussion was definitely in their future. But it would have to wait.

First, he had business to take care of, both in regard to the store and in regard to his personal life. One of the things on his agenda before opening the store, and which was compelling him to accelerate his schedule, was to visit his daughter and explain some things to her. He spoke with Emily often by phone and they emailed each other daily, but Tom felt that he had failed her after Sarah died. Although he attempted to shield the difficulty he experienced in resuming his life, he'd done a poor job of it, and Emily had noticed his descent into depression. Rather than providing a strong shoulder for her to lean on, they had reversed roles, with Emily supporting him for those many months that he struggled. The opposite of Tom, she'd been stoic in handling the loss of her mother, but he knew that she'd been hurting as badly as he. She simply hadn't let it overwhelm her life like he had.

Emily was living in D.C., having settled there after spending several summers during college interning on Capital Hill. Tom and Sarah had worried about their idealistic daughter's choice to enter the cynical and insular world of politics inside the Beltway. She was their only child, and like most parents of only children, they were overly protective of her. They wanted the best for her but mentally they were unprepared for her transition from student to young working adult. They gradually accepted that their little girl wasn't little any more, and that she had to find her own way, had to experience her own successes and failures. Over time they became pleasantly surprised at their daughter's self-confidence and single-minded assuredness maneuvering in the working world.

Emily found work at a lobbying firm engaged in environmental causes, which meshed well with her idealism and work ethic. The job provided enough income to pay for a small one bedroom on Dupont Circle and spending money, with a little left over for savings. Her plan was to work for a couple of years before returning to graduate school, of which there were several exceptional options in the District. Washington was full of bright young people starting out in the world with similar aspirations, and provided good work opportunities both in and tangential to the government, as well as a vibrant social scene. Emily made friends easily, and she quickly developed a nice core group of friends with whom she spent time in the city as well as in the summers as the D.C. population migrated to the Delaware shore. She was happy and thriving and was enjoying her life. And then her mother died.

Although she had always been somewhat of a daddy's girl, Emily was an only child, which enabled her to spend significant time alone with her mother and her father—more-so than most children—and she was very close to both of them. The difference in the relationships she shared with each of her parents could be measured in qualitative terms, rather than quantitatively. They each fulfilled a unique and complimentary role in her life and her psyche, and now the role that Sarah had played was gone forever.

After the funeral Emily stayed in Sandy Cove with Tom for a week. They were both numb, operating on autopilot. They spent each day as if sleepwalking, neither able to communicate their feelings of loss to each other or to come to grips with it themselves. For the better part of the time they simply sat on the deck staring blankly at the ocean, both alone with their thoughts and not able to share with the other.

Toward the end of the week Tom was able to think clearly enough to be able to see that his sorrow was so great that he was incapable of being a father to Emily, and that if he didn't force her to go back to Washington she would be drawn into his depression. Emily felt it, too. When he told her that she should leave, she initially protested, then acquiesced relatively quickly. It was time, already.

It was not that Emily was any less devastated by Sarah's death than was Tom. The distinction between what the two were feeling was more about the *type* of loss each felt as a result of Sarah's death. Where Tom lost a best friend, a lover, a life-partner, Emily lost a confidante, an advisor, a female role model. While Tom questioned his *raison d'être*, Emily pondered the end of her *joie de vivre*. Where Tom knew he needed to move forward and put Sarah in his past, he held on to her as if with an iron grip, while Emily, by virtue of her age and the newness of the life she had found, imperceptibly pushed away, the genesis of her new life already taking root.

Outwardly, she left her father alone in Sandy Cove reluctantly, while inwardly she was relieved. She needed time to herself to grieve and to make some sense of life without her mother. Month by passing month Emily gradually found a new equilibrium. She realized that her life would never return to normal. That life was lost, forever. Over time the feeling of loss hollowed-out and grew more distant. Laughter returned. Yet as her sorrow dissipated, the guilt over leaving her father grew. In her mind, as much as Sandy Cove was the best thing to have happened to her parents, day by day it was sucking the life out of her father as he remained there alone. In those first months after Sarah died, despite her calls and the many attempts she made to get Tom away from Sandy Cove, even for a short trip, he refused, and she could sense his continuing malaise.

Still, she'd had mixed feelings when he told her that he was leaving Sandy Cove and was putting the house up for sale. She was happy that her father was going to travel, although his lack of any set plan or course, as well as the open-endedness of his journey, concerned her. The sale of the house was another matter. So many memories had been made there, and she loved the house as much as her parents had. She had a feeling that selling the house was a sign that her father was still struggling, and while she believed that the trip would be beneficial to him, despite the fact that he was, to an extent, running away, he needed a place to which he could return and resume his life.

Thanks to the Internet he never seemed to be far away from her during his time abroad, even when he was half-way around the world. They emailed each other regularly, and she knew that they could speak daily, but she did her best to let him have the space away from her that he seemed to need. She was elated when he told her that he was returning, but her elation was tempered when he told her that the purpose of his return was to finalize the sale of the house.

When he called from Sandy Cove and told her that he had changed his mind about selling the house and that he wanted to travel to visit her in Washington, Emily was both surprised and overjoyed. When she picked up the phone she heard the salutation that never failed to put a smile on her face and make her feel secure. "Hiya, babydoll. How's my favorite daughter today?" For the first time since her mother died, the voice she heard on the other end of the phone sounded like her father, rather than the feeble, dejected soul that had replaced him for so long. She would never tell him for fear of adding guilt to his despair, but he had disappeared from her life, and now she felt that she needed him. She had weathered the loss of her mother essentially on her own. She may have become an independent young woman, but she had lost one-third of her family, and she was still her Daddy's little girl. She wondered what had turned him around, what was the source of his rediscovery of enthusiasm for living. Ultimately, whatever caused the change in him was irrelevant to her. She had her Daddy back.

Chapter 6

T om decided early on after Sarah's diagnosis that he would never allow Sarah to see him waiver from his certainty that she would beat the cancer. No moments of doubt could be revealed, no pangs of despair could seep out. His job was to keep her positive and to maintain as normal an existence as was possible under the circumstances. He felt helpless, and in fact he was helpless in the face of her formidable foe. But Sarah would never know of his feelings. Ever.

Sarah was by nature an upbeat and optimistic person, but the fear that overtook her when the doctor pronounced her illness was palpable. She put on a brave face, but Tom knew her too well, and it broke his heart. She changed forever with three words: "You have cancer."

The range of emotions she went through ran the gamut. First was fear, then angst, then hope and then despair. It all happened so quickly. Diagnosis, prognosis, preparation for surgery and on to chemotherapy and radiation. And yet, Sarah tried to remain upbeat. Although it ebbed and flowed, she still had hope.

* * *

In hindsight, Tom and Sarah seemed destined for each other, from the first day of classes at Penn to summers at the Jersey shore, and then into marriage and parenthood.

Despite coming from vastly different backgrounds: he from a blue collar family on full academic scholarship; she from the Main Line, of money and polished pedigree, they shared the same politics and ideals. They joked easily together and complimented each other's traits. And their friends chided them as being a perfect couple.

They were engaged while he was still in graduate school and married shortly after. Their singular life began in a one bedroom walk up, living off of his meager salary while she studied for her teaching degree. Life as a young couple in the city was exciting and vibrant, filled with good food and good music, Sunday morning jogs along the Schuylkill River and shared beachhouses at the shore. It was there that their love blossomed and matured, the complexity of the relationship growing and strengthening with each shared experience, each setback and each achievement.

They wanted children but agreed to put it off until their careers took hold. The time came, sooner than he expected, when Sarah told Tom that she was ready, and to appease her, he acted as if he were. He thought it was too soon. They were too young. They had more to do, more to see, more to experience before going down that road.

They soon learned that deciding that you want to become pregnant and achieving that desire were two different propositions. The initial excitement of making the decision to have children was followed by several months of hopeful expectation, which was replaced with several more of cautious optimism, and then concerned frustration. As time went on Sarah became more determined to become pregnant, and exceedingly disconcerted by her failure to conceive.

In contrast to Sarah, Tom was initially secretly relieved by their inability to conceive. He just didn't feel sure that the timing was right. He was comfortable with the life they had established together and the lifestyle they were leading. But as time passed he, too, became disappointed by the monthly revelation of the negative results. Gradually, he had started to warm to the idea of being a father. He also worried that Sarah's frustration was turning into obsession. She had become weepy and disconsolate. He would come home from work to find her sitting on the couch in the darkened apartment, Kleenex scattered around her, and his attempts to console her proved to be futile. She was putting undue pressure on herself to get pregnant, and with each passing month that pressure grew.

Although Tom had grown frustrated as well, he felt that eventually they would be successful, and that the timing and physiology would take care of themselves if they just relaxed and let nature take its course. Sarah was not easily assuaged.

Finally, Tom showed her a medical journal article that identified stress as a contributing factor to a woman's inability to become pregnant. The premise was that stress compromised a woman's fertility by adversely effecting ovulation as well as the quality and quantity of the eggs produced. Sarah was offended. "So, you're blaming me. It's my fault, all my fault." She spat out the words at Tom and burst into tears.

"I'm not blaming you," he replied as he reached for her. "No one's to blame. But if it's meant to be, it will happen. And if it's not . . . ."

Sarah sat weeping in his arms. "Do you hate me?" She managed to ask through her muffled sobs.

"Of course not," he said as he raised her head off of his shoulder and brushed her hair away from her face. "I just want you to be happy."

She nodded, then buried her head back into his arm like child.

"Hold on, I have something for you," he said and rose

to retrieve a small package from his coat pocket. "I thought this might cheer you up."

She sat up on the couch and took it from him, sheepishly. Her nose was wet and her makeup was running down her cheeks. He reached out with his hand and turned her face toward him, wiping away her tears with his thumb and trying to clean up the lines of mascara that ran southward from her eyes. Even this way, looking like a mess, she was as beautiful to him as ever.

She opened the bag and the small box within, and sniffed back her tears. She looked coyly at him and picked up the necklace that lay in the box, letting it dangle from her fingers. A small silver pendant hung from the necklace——a couple in an embrace.

"Oh, Tom. It's lovely," she said as she examined the pendant.

"Stand up," he said, abruptly, as he stood, pulling her up with him. He took the necklace from her and snapped it into place around her neck, then wrapped his arms around her and they stood, embracing. Slowly, they started to move together. She grasped his hand and put her head on his shoulder, and as they stood in the middle of the room they began to sway, rocking back and forth, slowly dancing in the quiet room.

Eventually, all of the angst and anxiety gave way to happiness and jubilation when Sarah became pregnant and later, when Emily was born. They didn't know at the time that Emily was truly a blessing, as they would not be able to conceive another child. But Tom and Sarah never forgot the night they danced in silence, and despite accumulating jewelry over the years, Sarah's most cherished item was the simple pendant Tom gave her that night——she and Tom in each other's arms.

Chapter 7

Tom had always had an affinity for diners, and the one downside to Sandy Cove was that it had none. If you wanted a good greasy spoon you had to head south a couple of miles to find one. Before Sarah got sick, several times a week Tom would schedule his morning around the trip to feed his habit. His favorite was Bob and Shirley's, which was neither owned nor run by either namesake.

At every stage of his life, in whatever location, Tom had always found his diner, and he was picky in that regard. He tested them to see if they met his standards: could they make the simple staples the way they were supposed to be made? Eggs over with sausage and home fries. Was the sausage fresh and crisp, or overcooked and dry? When he asked for his home fries well done, did they come blackened around the edges or just heated up a little more? Was the coffee refilled when needed, not every time a waitress picked up the coffee carafe?

Once a diner passed the staples test, it became a part of his normal routine. Bob and Shirley's had passed with flying colors. In addition to the food and service, he liked it because it wasn't one of the faux, replica diners placed in a trucked-in railcar, and because it wasn't a dump. It was neither old nor new, neither shiny nor dull. It defied definition, but it fit the bill.

Tom was such a regular at Bob and Shirley's that he

never had to bother placing an order. His coffee was poured and ready for him at the counter—second seat in from the left—as soon as he pulled into the parking lot. The food followed in short order, after a ten minute delay to allow him to scan the morning newspaper before he was ready to eat. On most days few words were exchanged until the food was gone. Then it was time to talk and catch up on the local scuttlebutt. On a good day they might sit and talk the morning away, a slow, leisurely and thoroughly enjoyable pastime that rural beach life afforded those lucky enough to experience it year-round.

After Sarah's death, Tom's diner sessions had waned along with other staples in his life. Tom was cognizant of the mental condition to which he had descended, and of the fact that he was now resuming his life, or an adaptation of the life he led before Sarah died, and each item that he restored to his daily routine was another step in the direction of recovery.

To those who experience the loss of a parent or spouse, a child or a close friend, the "finality of death" is an oxymoron. Whether after a long and agonizing illness or with the suddenness of a horrific accident, death isn't final. For survivors, death provides a new beginning without the deceased. The collective lifetime experiences and human interaction which molded us and sustained us are still present, but without a major component. The loss leaves indelible scars and enduring heartache, and the mind and heart struggle to adapt in the absence of that essential, missing element. The only finality that death affords to the survivors is the inability to engage in human interaction with the deceased, the inability to see and hear and touch and *feel*. *That* is final.

By Tom's calculation he was doing well, all things considered. He still suffered his fits and starts, his moments of despair and feelings of hopelessness. He was not out of the woods, but he was on the right path to getting there. He also was ahead of schedule in preparing the store for its re-opening, so he decided to treat himself to a morning off and headed south to Bob and Shirley's.

When Tom entered the diner Dexter Limas was sitting in his designated seat at the far end of the counter, next to the TV hanging from the wall and within steps of the grill, where a hodgepodge of meat and eggs and potatoes were sizzling and spewing smoke into the air. Dexter turned, and looking over his reading glasses gave a simple nod to Tom and a subtle wave of his upraised coffee cup. Tom climbed onto the stool next to Dexter and breathed in the diner smell that he loved so well. It was the commonness of a diner, the down home and welcoming feel of it, the unpretentiousness, that appealed to Tom.

"How goes it, Tom?" Dexter didn't look up from the newspaper spread on the counter in front of him as he made his inquiry.

"Good, Dex. Good," Tom replied as he scanned the restaurant and nodded at the other regulars. The restaurant and its patrons were the same as the last time he ventured there, over a year prior. Nothing had changed, which is what drew him there in the first place. It existed as if suspended in time. Coffee appeared before him without comment from Wendy, the normally irascible proprietor, who winked at Tom as she moved quickly behind the counter preparing plates for the other diners. They all knew Tom, knew about Sarah, and silently felt for his loss. "Pass over the cream, would you, Dex?"

"Sure thing, Tom," Dexter said, as he slid the container to Tom, his eyes never leaving the paper. "You see that game last night? Carolina wupped on Duke. That Calvert is a monster. Thirty points, fifteen rebounds. He's a first rounder, for sure." Dexter was a college basketball junkie and March was his nirvana.

"Didn't catch it. Been kind of busy getting the store ready."

"Carolina's definitely gonna win the tourney this year. Just a matter of putting in the time."

"If you say so, Dex." Tom was settling in to the flow and feel of the place, and it fit like a glove. "But I think Duke's going to have their number at crunch time in the tournament." Tom didn't know this to be true and wasn't even following the season. He was just stirring up trouble.

Dexter simply grunted his disagreement, finally looking up from his paper to cast a disapproving scowl at Tom.

This is what Tom loved about the diner. He *knew* these people. With every reprise of interaction Tom was coming to the realization that he had taken for granted all of the people around him who normally provided a cocoon of comfort and safety. The irony was that when he needed them the most, when he was suffering, he had pushed all of them away. He wondered whether he would have been better able to deal with his tragedy if he hadn't isolated himself from them. In hindsight it seemed so, but at the time he was so raw with emotion that he couldn't think rationally, couldn't function beyond going from point A to point B, and the comfort of others was not in his frame of reference.

When he finished his meal he sat and talked and caught up on everything he had missed over the preceding year. Life had gone on for these people, while his had remained in neutral. Wendy, who usually limited her discussions to exhortations to the patrons to eat and get out so that others could take their seats, actually poured herself a cup of coffee and stood at the counter talking to Tom. He was one of them, and even though they only knew each other within the four walls of the diner, they were like family.

Chapter 8

People make the locale. As was the case elsewhere, Sandy Cove had its share of local characters who seemed to have been there forever and who provided a unique flavor to the area. LenDale Avery added that spice in abundance to Sandy Cove.

LenDale was one of the few residents who could trace his roots to the area back more than a generation or two. Sandy Cove had existed as a seasonal hunting destination until relatively recently, and its permanent population in the early part of the 1900's was nil. When exactly LenDale Avery's grandfather, Woodrow Walker Avery, came to the area or why was the subject of local lore and much speculation. Everyone had their own theories and stories to tell on the matter, and no one was knowledgeable enough to separate fact from fiction. The most popular theory was that he was a gin runner who purposely sought out the area during Prohibition to lay low from the authorities. At the time the area was desolate, densely filled with scrub and brush and barely habitable. Access from the mainland was by a once-daily ferry or local watercraft. Once on the peninsula the only access to present-day Sandy Cove and the surrounding area was provided by narrow dirt paths which bird hunters had worn into the landscape. The area was not for the faint of heart or those lacking in fortitude. The land was raw and unforgiving, the insects intense.

According to the most accepted bit of folklore, Woodrow was a moonshine man out of Buffalo City, an old timber town that had become a hub for moonshiners who supplied the entire Eastern seaboard with hooch during prohibition. Allegedly, Woodrow commandeered a boat from a mainland dock under cover of night with G-men in hot pursuit, making land on the isle and disappearing in the brush as if an aberration. Once across the Sound and on the narrow strip of land he was virtually invisible, and as a practical matter, the G-men figured that if he had been stupid enough to seek refuge in such an unforgiving landscape, his fate was probably sealed. The land would take care of him. On the other hand, if somehow he survived, he'd eventually emerge from the wilderness and resume his activities. They could always pick up their pursuit at that point, rather than chase him amidst the thistles and having to endure the deprivations that would entail. So they waited at the end of the trail, enjoying some of the hooch that they had confiscated along the trip. After several days, hot, tired and in need of proper facilities, of which the area had none, they gave up the hunt, packed up and left, confident that old Woodrow would soon follow.

What happened to the elusive Mr. Avery after the authorities gave up the chase and how Woodrow's descendants ended up owning the lion's share of the land was the part of the lore where opinion diverged. Some believed that he continued to live in hiding on the land and eventually claimed squatter's rights to much of the property in the area. Others believed that he set up a clandestine operation hidden somewhere on the Northern end of the beach and ran liquor up and down the coast by boat. Still others believed that Woodrow left shortly after the feds, but making note of the land and the isolation (and safety) it provided, he proceeded to use his ill-gotten gains to buy a safe haven to use if ever the need arose. No one ever claimed to have laid eyes upon the man, either at the time or thereafter, thus adding mystery to the lore.

Over time Woodrow Avery became a vibrant figment of everyone's imagination, a folklore hero of sorts, much like Blackbeard, the notorious pirate who plied the waters off the coast seeking bounty and who met his fate not far to the south. Woodrow was such a part of the history of the area that locals invoked his name when someone went missing, stating that he or she "pulled an Avery." A local historian once attempted to put fact to the fiction on how the Averys came to own such a large amount of the local real estate, even going so far as to hire attorneys to conduct title examinations to trace the origins of the purchases. What the lawyers found was such a hodgepodge of names and entities and transfers and reverse transactions that they were unable to sort through the mess. The historian's attempts to trace Woodrow's fate also proved fruitless, which added further still to the intrigue.

What people *did* know was that his son, Woodrow Walker Avery, Jr., whom everyone came to know as "Woody," settled in the area in his twenties and established a lucrative cement and contracting business. There was nary a public works project within a 75 mile radius that Woody didn't manage to secure, and he quickly locked-up the cement supply to such an extent as to create a virtual monopoly, enabling him to freeze out potential competitors and to set prices as he saw fit. Shortly after Woody showed up, he sent for his young bride to join him, and that was when Margaret Lipscombe Avery, of the Newport, Rhode Island, Lipscombes, came to the area toting little LenDale. But Margaret was not much for coastal living, having been born of great wealth and social status, and in short order she left the area to return to Rhode Island, leaving a good portion of her money, as well as LenDale, behind.

LenDale was an insecure, precocious child who needed to be heard—and often. His insecurity was a mystery to those who knew only of his father's massive land holdings and wealth, which translated into a "if LenDale wants something, LenDale gets it" upbringing. But having lost the company of his mother to her selfish needs, and some said, alcoholism, the child developed an inferiority complex that no amount of money in the bank or toys in the house or garage or boathouse could ameliorate.

He bounced from one New England prep school to the next, getting kicked out for committing a variety of insubordinate acts. He learned from his father that he should use money to try to buy happiness, and he spent most of his early years attempting to do just that. He had no true friends, just hangers-on who knew that LenDale would pick up the tab and bail them out if anything got too out of hand. Yet those leeches eventually grew up, grew out of their youthful dalliances with alcohol and drugs and moved on, leaving LenDale alone and with a serious substance abuse problem. His story was the stereotypical rich boy's, and coupled with a father who was either incapable of or disinterested in providing guidance, he floundered into adulthood.

When Woody Avery dropped dead of an aortic aneurism at the ripe old age of 52, he left LenDale as his sole heir and as sole proprietor of the multimillion dollar Avery business empire. LenDale, who was ill-equipped to run the business, was astute enough to realize his limitations and made what would turn out to be the smartest business decision of his life: he sold. LenDale would spend the rest of his life doing his best to spend the millions that he made selling his father's business.

To those who had known him since he was a child, LenDale was annoying, but harmless. To the tourists and those who only visited Sandy Cove briefly, LenDale was a curiosity. He was a fixture at the local watering holes and was Sandy Cove's comedic muse, usually at his own expense. He dressed like a surfer, yet he drove exotic cars. He was quick to buy rounds for the house, but was always waiting for a friend who never appeared.

Some of the locals in Sandy Cove did their best to avoid him and treated him poorly when he showed up uninvited and unwanted. Others felt sorry for him: here was a middle-aged man who was rich beyond imagination monetarily, and yet who was poorer than poor socially. He was desperate for attention and pined for friendship, and he roamed the local stores seeking personal interaction, striking up conversations with customers and shop owners alike. He seemed to always appear at the most inopportune times, always sticking his nose into others' business and always ready with a contrary opinion or inappropriate comment.

One person who was never dismissive of LenDale was Sarah. She welcomed him when he appeared in the store and made a point of inviting him to their SLOB sessions. She was not his friend, per se, but her inclusion of him was neither patronizing nor self aggrandizing. She was just a kind person, and she was appalled at how others were disdainful of, and many times, cruel to LenDale. She included him because it was the right thing to do, and in a strange way it made LenDale a part of their crowd, even if he was odd and inappropriate and annoying.

Sarah was a beloved member of Sandy Cove, in large part because of the kindness that she afforded everyone. When she died most of the community came to the funeral, as is often the case when a prominent and relatively young person dies. Hundreds of people had crammed into the small cemetery to pay their respects and to provide support for Tom and Emily.

After the funeral, after everyone had left, as Tom was getting into the limousine, he turned to look back at the gravesite. He was surprised to see LenDale, dressed in a suit, standing over Sarah's grave. He was holding a single rose. Tom watched as LenDale leaned over the grave and tossed the rose inside. As he began to walk away from the grave, he turned in Tom's direction. What Tom saw next warmed his heart, as few things could do on such a day.

LenDale was crying.

Chapter 9

They had been sitting in the hospital for over an hour, waiting. The thing about hospitals that Tom hated the most was the waiting. They were always waiting for the treatment to be started or for the treatment to be finished; for the doctor to finally appear to explain the situation or for a nurse or aide to carry out the doctor's directive. Time melted away while you waited in the hospital.

The only time Tom was happy in a hospital was when Emily was born. All of the other occasions were filled with angst and anxiety, the worst of which occurred when Tom was a child, when his father took him to the hospital to see his grandfather, who was dying. He remembered walking into the room and seeing all of the machines and all of the tubes which ran out from under the sheets. His remembered seeing his beloved grandfather, who had always been so happy and who always made Tom feel like the most important boy in the world, lying on the bed, unshaven and in pain. Tom remembered when a nurse came into the room and rushed out to get the doctor, and then the room filled up and someone pushed him outside and slammed the door shut. Tom stood outside of the room, shifting from one foot to the other, crying. Finally the door opened and his father walked out and hugged him tight—tighter than he ever had before.

Tom was on edge whenever he had reason to go to a hospital, and Sarah's treatment saddled him with a heightened level of anxiety with each additional foray they made into the hospital. To Tom, treatment for cancer was counter-intuitive. Treatment is supposed to provide relief. Instead, Sarah went into the hospital appearing and feeling well, received her treatment, went home and got sick—sicker than one could imagine. All the while, in the hospital Tom sat and waited as Sarah received the poison that posed as her medicine.

It was a depersonalizing atmosphere. The staff moved about with purpose, and Tom receded to invisibility before them. It wasn't their fault. They went to the hospital five days a week to do a job. Inevitably, the idealism that led them into the medical field gave way to the reality of work being work. Some still tried to be sympathetic to the patients and their family members, but in Tom's experience most of them had become numb to the suffering and the indignation that they witnessed day in and day out. That their work happened to take place in a hospital, where the fate of your loved one hung in the balance, eventually became secondary to the paycheck they were there to earn.

But this day was to be the end game. Sarah had finished her course of treatment. They were waiting to meet with her doctor to go over the results of the test that would determine whether the treatment had been successful or not. If all went according to plan, this would be the first day of a new beginning for them, a fresh start on a life together that had taken a horrific turn for the worse. Everything else in their lives had been pushed aside in anticipation of this day, a day which they previously wouldn't even allow themselves to imagine, for fear of it never coming. They were cautiously optimistic but not quite ready to assume the best.

Tom reached over and took Sarah's hand in his and nudged her with his shoulder. "Where are we going to go tonight to celebrate?" Tom asked, as he squeezed her hand.

Sarah nudged him back. "Don't jinx us." They sat holding hands, both of their minds racing with thoughts of what-ifs. "I just want this nightmare to be over with," Sarah sighed.

"That goes double for me."

"We'll have to remember to call Emily after we leave here. I promised her that we'd call."

Tom nodded. Emily had come home at every opportunity to be with Sarah during the ordeal. "Maybe that's the first place we should go on our trip. To see Emily."

"That would be wonderful," Sarah said, then fell silent once again while unconsciously toying with the pink plastic wristband that Emily had given her. It had the word "Hope" stamped into it.

Tom stood and was about to bother the nurse again when the doctor walked into the room and sat down next to Sarah. They both stared at him, trying to discern whether the news was positive or negative. It seemed to take an eternity for him to open her file and find the test results. When he finally looked up they each had a knot in the stomach and feared the worst. But then he broke into a broad smile. "Good news. Very good news. You're clean. Totally clean."

Chapter 10

Jenny was ill at ease about what was going on with Tom, especially after Charlie Reynolds called and told her that he'd spilled the beans on her plan to buy the house. She'd called Tom several times but never succeeded in getting through to him. It became obvious that he was avoiding her, so she decided to give him his space. Tom had become aloof and distant after Sarah died, going out only sporadically and declining most dinner and social offers. Then he left town and it was as if he had disappeared from the face of the earth. He had been gone for a year and no one had heard from him or knew where he had traveled. This was different, though. She knew he was back, but she hadn't seen or talked to him since he returned to town, and that had never happened before.

Sandy Cove was a small place and it was almost impossible that they hadn't run into each other. She'd heard from some of their mutual friends that they'd seen him outside his store and that he'd been busy getting The Cottage Shop ready for the season. Jenny decided that it was time to break the ice and headed over to the store to talk to him.

When she arrived she found a sign taped to the door. It read "Be back in 15 min. Have a seat and make yourself at home." A small Parisian table was set up outside the door on which sat a pitcher of sweetened tea and a stack of paper cups, as well as some dipping pretzels and an open jar of dip. Several chairs with hammock cord seats and backs were spread on the porch, hand-made by a local merchant who gave other store owners free use of the chairs as a marketing ploy. This is what made Sandy Cove special. It felt relaxed and homey, and the feeling was genuine rather than manufactured. Not that it was perfect, as all places had their peccadilloes and flaws. But the merchants were mostly good and kind people, and their personalities were reflected in the communal feel of the place.

Jenny poured herself some tea and sat down to wait for Tom. The weather was starting to warm up and she leaned back to take in the sun. A gentle breeze was blowing to offset the hot sunlight. It felt good to be outside and have the heat spread over her skin. Her mind drifted and she thought about the numerous items on her to do list. She loved the Spring and getting ready for the onslaught of tourists. It was rejuvenating, and it forced her to resuscitate herself from the dormancy of winter.

She felt a shadow over her and opened her eyes, squinting into the bright sunlight at the silhouetted form in front of her. They just looked at each other for a moment, then Tom moved toward the door and fumbled for his keys as he juggled an overloaded bankers box. "Grab the pitcher and the dip, would you?" Tom said over his shoulder as he headed inside.

Jenny followed Tom into the store and waited for him at the checkout counter. She looked around, checking out the store and the new items Tom had picked up. She had always liked the feel of The Cottage Shop, which was upscale in an understated way. Tom emerged from the stock room and stopped, hands on hips. "Let me guess," he said. "You're here because you want to take over my store."

"What? Don't be ridiculous, Tom." They stood staring at each other. "Are you at least going to let me explain?" Jenny said to break the uncomfortable silence.

"What's to explain? You don't owe me any explanations."

"I think I do. I . . . ." Jenny looked around the store as she tried to find the right words. "It's just that you weren't thinking rationally, and I wanted to save you from making a mistake."

"You wanted to save me from myself?"

"Listen, I just want you to know that I only did what I did because we're friends, and you'd been struggling so badly. I just didn't think you were making a rational choice."

Tom thought a moment before responding. "So, what were you going to do if you bought it?"

"I was going to hold it for you. I knew that no matter what happened, no matter where you went, you'd come back. And I was going to hold the house for you." When Tom didn't respond, Jenny continued. "What did you think, Tom? "That I wanted your house?" Tom just shrugged his shoulders and continued avoiding her eyes. "Well? Did you really think I had some ulterior motive?"

"I don't know what I thought. I wasn't thinking, actually." Tom took a step toward her and stopped, grappling to explain himself. "When Charlie told me that you were the buyer, I didn't sort through it. I just reacted. I know it's a lame excuse, but I didn't want to deal with it. I just stayed away."

"But you know me. You know that I wouldn't do anything to hurt you."

"I know that." Tom dug his hands into his jean pockets and looked at the floor. They'd known each other almost their entire lives. Here was this person who didn't have a lot of money, who was willing to go out on a limb and deep into debt for him. They were best friends and this was an indicator of the strength of their friendship. Tom had just been too blinded by his remorse to see it at the time, and too busy since. He looked up, gave an embarrassed half-grin and threw his hands up.

Jenny wasn't about to let him off so easily. "So, what was it Tom? Really."

Another uncomfortable silence enveloped them as Jenny waited for Tom's explanation. Tom moved across the room and began rearranging a table full of knickknacks. Over his shoulder he asked, "How come you never talked to me about Trip?"

"Trip? What does he have to do with anything?"

Tom continued to work with his back to Jenny. "You never told me what was going on with him. I didn't find out about it until after you left him."

Jenny was dumbfounded. Her failed marriage was the last thing she expected to be discussing with Tom. In all the time that Jenny was married to Trip she never complained about him to Tom or Sarah. She just withdrew from them. When she finally got up the courage to leave him, she was so embarrassed by the fact that she had pushed them away that she couldn't bring herself to re-insert herself into their lives. The chasm was too wide.

Initially, Tom and Sarah kept a respectful distance, affording Jenny space, which is what she appeared to want, but neither of them were happy with the situation. Ultimately it was Sarah who showed up on Jenny's doorstep brandishing a bottle of wine who succeeded in getting through to Jenny, convincing her that she had no reason to feel shame or embarrassment. Jenny had poured her heart out to Sarah, had sought out her companionship and her shoulder to cry on. But she and Tom had never really discussed the gory details of the abuse. Sarah had been her confidant, not Tom. And not until after the fact.

"I wasn't comfortable sharing the details with you," Jenny tried to explain. If only it was so simple, she thought.

"That's not what I'm talking about. Why didn't you tell

me while it was happening?"

Jenny thought about why she didn't tell Tom. It was such a traumatic time. She had become a different person, a shell of the person she had been before getting married. When the abuse started she blamed herself. She thought she must have been doing something wrong to cause her husband to become abusive toward her. The abuse sapped all of her energy and warped her sense of right and wrong. It was embarrassing and it was part of her marriage. She didn't think it was something to share with anyone.

"I didn't tell anybody," she said as she fought back tears. The tears caught her by surprise. She thought she had conquered the hurt. She was amazed that she was still emotional after such a long time.

"I'm not just anybody. I'm . . . I thought I was your closest friend."

"You were. And you are. But that was ages ago. It's over and done."

Tom stopped and turned to face her. "You shut me out, Jen. You didn't give me a chance to be there for you."

"He was my husband, Tom. It was awkward for me. Don't you see that?"

"Not really. I could have protected you. That's the part I don't understand. I was the one person who could have protected you from that jerk."

"How? How would you have done that?"

Tom thought for a moment. It was a good question. He never quite thought through what he would have done had he known. "I would have gone there and beaten the crap out of him. Or at least I would have threatened it." Tom wasn't talking out of a false sense of bravado. It was more of a figurative than a literal idea. He knew that there wasn't much he could have done for Jenny in that situation. She just never gave him a chance to do anything.

"And then what, Tom? You'd leave and he'd take it out on me."

Tom moved toward Jenny, who was now dabbing at her eyes with a tissue. "I just wasn't able to be there for you."

Jenny nodded her head. They stood facing each other, each contemplating what to say next.

"Wait. Hold on a second," Jenny said as she took a step back. "Maybe I'm missing something. What does my relationship with Trip have to do with anything now?"

"You didn't let me in to your life, and yet you inserted yourself into mine. You were going to buy my house, for God's sake."

"It's a little different situation, Tom. I was trying to protect you from making a bad decision."

"Exactly. You wanted to protect me, yet you didn't allow me to protect you. You didn't even let me know that you needed protecting."

Jenny considered Tom's logic. Nothing she could say would get him to understand her mindset during her marriage. It was an abusive relationship, with all of the manifestations of anger and guilt and embarrassment that normally attach to the abused. She also had never told Tom that Trip's overwhelming jealousy toward him was the initial cause of the abuse. At least that's what appeared to be the case. Her arguments with Trip always migrated from the original topic to his jealousy over her relationship with Tom. Outwardly, Trip acted as if he liked Tom. Whenever they got together Trip was his normal gregarious self, the guy's guy. But when he got home, behind closed doors, Trip erupted with jealousy, and nothing Jenny could say would appease Trip.

Jenny never revealed the situation to Tom, or even to Sarah after the fact. She could never place the burden of the abuse on his shoulders. In hindsight she regretted that she had pulled away from them. She had believed that the abuse would stop if she could eliminate the source of Trip's anger. It was her way of trying to appease her husband and to save her marriage. But the abuse continued even after she distanced herself from Tom. In time she came to doubt that her relationship with Tom was in fact the trigger of the abuse, rather than a convenient excuse for Trip. She became convinced that Trip was predisposed to being abusive, irrespective of what she did or didn't do in their marriage, or what relationships she had with others, including Tom. With this realization, she knew that the marriage was doomed, and she eventually worked up the nerve to leave.

It would prove to be harder to do than she anticipated. The first time she tried to leave she made the mistake of thinking that she could sit down with her husband and tell him that she was leaving. Trip broke down and begged her to stay, promising that he would change his ways. He even agreed to go to counseling. And for a short while he was on his best behavior. But one night he came home drunk and reverted back to what was his true nature. Jenny bore the brunt of a night of abuse, waited until Trip passed out on the bed, and quietly slipped out, leaving all of her belongings behind. She never spoke with him again, despite his many attempts to contact her.

Leaving Trip was a quick fix to quell the abuse. Her physical injuries eventually dissipated, leaving no visible evidence of the damage she had suffered. The effect on her mental state would take longer to heal, as would the relationships she had neglected, including with Tom. Yet, she had never let on to the alleged cause and effect that her close relationship with Tom instigated.

As she stood before him, it occurred to Jenny that Tom was right. In all of the time that had passed since she left Trip, she never fully mended fences with Tom. She had confided in Sarah in a way that she couldn't with Tom, and they were closer for it. Her family had welcomed her back with unconditional love, no explanations or descriptions being required to be exchanged between them. And so forth with other friends, all of them eventually reaching out to each other and reconciling over what had occurred. Yet the same could not be said about Tom. Once she confided in Sarah, Tom was there for her. He consoled her and they had discussions about her relationship with Trip. But there was never a time when they sat down and discussed—really discussed—what she had experienced in her marriage. Now, for the first time, she became aware of the wedge that had developed between them. They had never resolved the impact that her marriage had on their friendship, although Tom was apparently aware of it, if only subconsciously.

Tom put his hand on her shoulder. "Listen, I didn't mean to upset you like this."

"It's ok, I'm fine." she said as she quickly dabbed her eyes and pivoted away from him. She didn't like him seeing her be so emotional. Suddenly, the normal coziness and warmth she usually felt being in the shop began to make her claustrophobic. She felt a strong desire to escape the confinement of the store to be outside in the open space with the breeze and sunlight.

Tom watched as she started to move away from him, speaking to him with her back turned. "Not to make a bad situation worse, but this is exactly what I'm talking about," he said as he reached out and turned her around.

Jenny was surprised and confused by his firm grip on her arm. "I don't know what you mean."

"I mean you're not opening up to me. You have a tell, like in poker. Your actions betray thoughts. Every time we discuss a topic that's too close for comfort you turn away from me."

"Tom, I'm not avoiding the topic. We're talking."

Tom shook his head. The wall that had developed between them had dissipated but hadn't disappeared entirely. He saw it so clearly, but Jenny seemed oblivious to the subtle yet persistent change in their relationship.

He knew that in the natural order of things it was inevitable that their friendship would be diminished over time. It was natural for his wife and her husband to question the relationship, although Sarah had seemed to do a good job of understanding the bond that existed between him and Jenny. Cultural mores do not accede to such strong opposite-sex relationships of those who are married. Ironically, their friendship was just that—a friendship. It had never been anything more. And yet the immutable societal forces put the imprimatur of scandal on it, a scarlet letter, to which reality took a back seat.

Once Jenny left Trip he thought that they would become close yet again, but the opposite occurred. They grew even more distant from each other. He had thought that it was due to Jenny's attempt to get back to normal mentally before resuming her old life. He felt that the barrier would erode in due course. Yet the chasm persisted well beyond the time that Tom had anticipated it would take for it to wane.

Sarah had succeeded in getting Jenny to open up about her troubles with Trip, and they became closer for it, but that created yet another curious, subtle strain to their relationship. It was almost as if Jenny was suddenly more attuned to her friendship with Sarah than to him, and as that relationship grew, theirs became secondary.

Timing is everything. It bothered him to not be able to speak with Jenny as he had in the past. For so long she had been his friend and his confidante. He felt the loss of that friendship, felt the void of her presence in his life. Originally, it was his doing. He had pushed her away due to the exclusive devotion that he felt he properly needed to exhibit toward his wife. Then it was Jenny's turn, beginning with

Trip and after she left Trip. Then once again, his, after Sarah died. Until Jenny was going to buy the house. That was the fork in the road, the path back to where they had started. And it caught him by surprise. What was Jenny saying by taking that step? That the wall between them was coming down? It had been so long he almost didn't know what to make of it. It made him happy and it made him angry at the same time. Why had it taken so long? Did it matter?

He looked at Jenny, who was trying and failing to keep her emotions under control. Women were such different creatures than men, Tom thought. He knew it was acceptable for him to cry. Any man who lost his wife is given a pass to cry. But his father was old school, and he'd been hard-wired to keep his emotions under wraps. It was all he could do at times to keep a firm upper lip in the face of losing his wife. For the most part he succeeded on that front, at least in public. Women on the other hand were the polar opposite. Their emotional wellbeing seemed to be tied to the necessity of revealing their emotions, as if it was therapeutic.

Tom took Jenny's hands in his. "Jen, I'm sorry for letting this get so out of hand. I don't want you to cry over it. I know you had good intentions and meant well." Jenny was looking at the ground and nodded her head in agreement. Tom continued, gently reaching out and lifting her chin up until she was looking at him. "But if you think this is 'talking,' you're wrong. Dead wrong. On both our parts."

"I don't know what more you want from me," Jenny said and looked plaintively at Tom.

"I want you to . . . . *We* should work on our friendship."

Again Jenny nodded. They had allowed too much to build up between them, and regardless of why or how, they both knew now that their friendship required repairing. And they both knew that it was a long time coming.

They looked at each other, then both broke out laughing. "How's this for a start. How about you come over for dinner tomorrow night? I'll cook some of my famous pan seared Snapper and open up a good bottle of wine," Tom said. "We'll eat good food and drink good wine and get smashed, just like the good old days." Tom looked expectantly at Jenny.

Jenny was relieved that the gravity of the conversation was dissipating. She had started to feel as if she was reliving the whole Trip experience over again. "Alright. I'll come over and let you cook for me on one condition," Jenny teased while wiping her face. "I get to pick the wine. None of that Two Buck Chuck that you like to pawn off as the good stuff."

Tom feigned pondering the proposition, then stuck out his hand. "Deal."

"Deal," Jenny replied. And they shook on it.

Chapter 11

"Hey Reggie, what's with these Blue Points? Are they fresh, today?" Tom asked kiddingly as he reached out to grab a handful of oysters from the bin. He knew they were. That's why he was there.

Reggie Gordon, the proprietor of the roadside seafood stand, guffawed at the suggestion that his product was anything less than stellar, mumbled some unintelligible derogatory comment and waived Tom off in feigned disgust.

Tom smiled. One of the benefits of living on the coast was the abundance of fresh seafood, but more importantly, the benefit of knowing where you could locate the best of it. When they lived in Philadelphia Tom had frequented the South Philly produce shops or Reading Terminal Market, each of which provided him with the same feeling as places like Reggie Gordon's: a sense of freshness and purity that Tom could feel in his soul, like it blended in to his own body–a feeling which Tom imagined was part of the farmer's experience. A oneness with nature that can't be substituted or bought—just felt. Like standing in the rain looking up at the sky and having the raindrops splatter on your face and stream down your cheeks.

Tom was feeling better and better every day, and he had a purpose to his life. He knew that idleness was the enemy and he was doing his best to hold it at bay. Not that every day the reality of his life didn't seep into his consciousness.

He knew it was always going to be there, lurking in the background. But he was in charge now, and he was plowing forward. And he was starting to feel good again.

The conversation with Jenny had to happen and he was happy with the course it took. As time goes by we realize that true friendship is fleeting, that our intimate circle of companions grows ever smaller with the passage of time, whether by virtue of death or by the fact that things and people change or because we simply start to follow different paths through life's journey. Certainly, he and Jenny had started off on the same path, from which they had both been diverted.

The one positive change that Tom could identify in himself after Sarah's death was a rejuvenation for the activities which he had previously enjoyed. Foraging through the roadside markets for the best produce and fish and cooking up the fresh catch, making the shop ready for the season, and now, getting his social life back in order.

One of the truths of marriage is that, in most cases, the collective entity that is the married couple develops relationships that supersede the individuals'. Not that any of Tom's singular friends, nor Sarah's, were bad people or necessarily unpalatable to one or the other. Rather, once married, the socialization that occurs is that of the couple, at the expense of and to the exclusion of those that came before the marriage. Even in the case of Sarah and Jenny, a social divide had persisted.

After Sarah died that theorem had turned back around on Tom. The entity of "Tom and Sarah" had ceased to exist, as had Tom's social life within the circle of couples with whom he and Sarah had socialized. He knew he was a third or fifth or seventh wheel, as did they, and though on occasion he would accept their entreaties and join them, to Tom it now felt forced. Those couples with whom he and Sarah had spent so much time did not immediately distance themselves from him, but over time they gradually asked him to join them less, they eventually stopped having him over for their little get-togethers, and finally Tom and Sarah were replaced in their group by another couple.

Tom was not entirely put off by this change in his social life. Although he enjoyed the company that he and Sarah had kept, he found the group dynamics more tedious than the simplicity of one-to-one friendships, which seemed more true to him, more real, and more about true friendship than having to please or appease one or the other member of the couple. This was one of the reasons that Tom was looking forward to Jenny coming over for dinner. He wanted to be able to relax and talk to her, without any barriers or inhibitions. Just the two of them. It had been so long since they both were unencumbered by their significant others. He and Sarah had been together since college, and he had spent his entire adult life with her. For the first time since he was a teenager he did not have Sarah as part of his life or of his identity. He felt odd even thinking it, but the fact that he was now single and free to lead a single-man's life was somewhat exhilarating. Of course that type of life came at the expense of companionship as well as with indescribable loss. But he was on the path to recovery, and despite his feelings of loss and loneliness, he had started to feel the desire to start his new life, with the world of opportunities that it afforded him.

Tom grabbed a couple of handfuls of the oysters, paid for them and jumped in his car to head toward home. He had a lot of work to do to prepare for the night and he had several stops to make on the way. He turned onto Beach Road, the two lane road that paralleled the shoreline, and reached down to tune the radio to an Oldies station he liked. It was one of those days that was a precursor to the upcoming season—a pristine, cloudless, cobalt blue sky, a wayward puff of wind here and there, and the warmth of the latitude starting to kick in. It was easy to be happy here, and it took tragedy to be sad here, Tom thought. He felt no shame for the time he had spent in mourning, no matter how long he allowed it to drag out. He now knew that whatever time it took was the appropriate amount of time. No one could tell him otherwise. Like most other life events that one experiences, it is personal, it is individualized, and it is whatever suits you that matters. It is the human element, which doesn't fit uniformly into a one-size-fits-all box. Rather, it takes on a myriad of sizes, shapes and forms. And Tom had found his. Now, he had placed that box aside and was beginning to develop the next shape and form into which his life was to evolve.

Up ahead of him on the right he started to make out the form of a man walking alongside the road. As he came nearer he recognized that the man was LenDale Avery. He thought for a moment whether he should pull over and offer LenDale a ride, chose otherwise, and continued driving past without slowing the car. He watched in his rearview mirror as the form grew smaller and smaller. Tom knew he should have picked him up, but he wasn't ready yet to cross that path. He was still taking baby steps. This was a good day and he didn't want to sully it with the conversation that was sure to take place with LenDale. That conversation would occur, sure enough. But at another time and another place. And at a time that Tom would be able to handle the horror that would accompany it.

Chapter 12

"Do you think we need to pack anything warm?" Tom called out to Sarah from inside his closet. They were set to leave in the morning and he'd been so busy he hadn't even thought about what the weather was likely to be and what he should pack. They were headed to California wine country. If they were just going to San Francisco he'd pack all warm, but once they got away from the city and into the valleys to the east the weather would be much more temperate.

They had decided on the wine country not because they were connoisseurs, but rather because they both loved the rustic feel of the area. They had traveled there to vacation several times and had fallen in love with the land and the scenery and the people who made their homes there. Wine country was really just a bunch of farms whose sole crop happened to be grape vines. They preferred the Sonoma Valley, which tended to be less commercialized than Napa and more like the way they envisioned the entire area to have been 25 years earlier.

Tom and Sarah had been giddy since her doctor gave them the good news. Of course Sarah would have to continue to get check-ups and would never been totally free of the specter of cancer, but she had been given a reprieve. It was a blessing, and she agreed with Tom that it was her second chance at life—at living it the way that she wanted to live it, free from the clutter of daily living. In other words, she wasn't going to sweat the small stuff ever again.

The trip was a break from reality as well as a reality check. They were running away in order to get back to where they had been before the diagnosis. The relaxed and leisurely lifestyle that they loved was awaiting them in California and they were both in dire need of the break. It would be the perfect atmosphere to allow them to reconnect to each other, enabling the dams that had been holding back their emotions to open. They had been in tune with each other from the time they first met, yet now they were worlds apart, living two solitary lives in the same house, talking to each other but not really hearing, reaching out for comfort without really touching.

Tom was holding two light sweaters in his hands, weighing whether to bring both or one or the other, when Sarah came into the bedroom and sat on the end of the bed. She was holding the phone in one of her hands and a tissue in the other.

Tom heard the mattress squeak as she sat, and he came into the room to see Sarah sitting quietly, staring blankly at the floor. "What's wrong? Who were you talking to?" Tom asked, as he felt his stomach tighten.

"Emily. I wanted to talk to her before we left."

"And that's why you need the tissue?" Tom asked, motioning to her hand.

Sarah shrugged and crumpled to tissue into a ball in her hand. "Do you really think we should go?"

Tom dropped his hands and looked at her. She was still beautiful to him, and when he looked at her he still saw the 18 year old co-ed with whom he fell in love. He sat on the bed next to her and nudged her with his shoulder. "Come on now, what's the problem?"

"I just don't know if it's the right thing to do right now. It feels like we're running away."

Tom put his arm around Sarah's shoulders and pulled her toward him. He had been anticipating this conversation. Sarah had always been a reluctant traveler. To her it was a form of change, and she was averse to any type of change. He knew that once they stepped foot on the plane that her demeanor and outlook would change. He just had to get her to that point. "We're not running away. We're getting away. I think it will be good for you. For us," Tom replied. "I think we should go."

"But what about the store? We've neglected it for so long. We've neglected everything," she said as she wiggled out of Tom's embrace and sat facing him. What she really meant was that the upheaval in their lives was her fault. Tom had been hearing Sarah make such comments more frequently as the trip got closer.

"Sarah, we can do whatever we want to do. It's our decision. And if I can take anything positive away from this whole experience, it's that it doesn't matter. The store just doesn't matter. Nothing really matters, except for the fact that we're both here and we have a second lease on life, and I intend to take advantage of every minute of it."

Sarah, usually so self-assured, had lost her ability to judge right from wrong, appropriate versus inappropriate. Weren't they being irresponsible? Or did the responsible part of her life disappear with the words "you've got cancer?" She and Tom had always acted responsibly and conservatively—personally, in their work and in their finances. They had put their money into all of the right stock funds, had bought all of the right investment vehicles. They had raised their daughter without giving her too many of the material benefits which would make her expectations in life too unrealistic and too unobtainable. So wasn't this being hypocritical? Throughout their life they had avoided the mistakes that so many of their friends had made: overextending themselves financially, indulging in a must-have, live for today and don't worry about the future mentality.

This was not their way, and it was virtually impossible for Sarah, despite her recent life-altering experience, to actually change her way of doing things.

Sarah looked questioningly at Tom, surveying his face. She wondered: Could she trust him? Could she place her blind faith in him, and put the weight of her uncertainty on his shoulders? Was that even fair to him? She was always amazed that her love for him continued to grow, day by day, year by year, and that when she looked back in time to when she had thought their love was as great as it would ever be, she was always wrong, as it had grown even more. When she looked at Tom these days she felt such overwhelming guilt, even though she knew that the changes in their lives were not due to any purposeful act on her part.

"I see that look in your eyes," Tom said as he moved closer to reassure her. "This is going to be a great trip, a great time for us to get back to being 'us.' Trust me."

And she did, as she always had, and always would.

Chapter 13

"*So this is what my life has come to.*" It was a statement, not a question, that rifled through LenDale's brain as he walked along the side of the two lane asphalt road that served as the local rendition of a State highway. He had recognized Tom's car as it sped by him headed north toward Sandy Cove. He thought he caught Tom's eyes peering at him in the right side view mirror, but he wasn't certain of it. The car was moving too fast for him to hone in on them.

He had watched the car continue up the road, the image first becoming blurred by the heat plumes rising off of the asphalt, then getting smaller and smaller as it continued on its course away from him. But now he knew that Tom knew what was what, and he also knew that a sit down with Tom was due in his future. *That* was a discussion that LenDale was going to do everything in his power to avoid.

"*Perfect,*" he thought. "*Once again I'm in the shit.*" Things like this always happened to him. If things could go wrong for a person . . . . No, he thought, if someone could chart how wrong things could go for a person, in theory, their attempt to quantify how badly things had gone in his life would fall grossly short. Call it jinxed or cursed or just call it karma. LenDale had considered all of the possible names, sayings and definitions for his affliction, and the one that seemed most apropos was "bad luck," as in "I have the worst luck of any human being, *ever.*"

He was aware that others might offer up argument against his self-evaluation. After all, LenDale was one of the wealthiest individuals in the area and had never had to work a day in his life for all of that money. And therein, he knew, lay the rub: Oh, but if money was the only scale against which success, failure, happiness or sadness was measured. The cliché was reality: money doesn't buy happiness. This was a fact of life of which LenDale became aware early on in life, despite many attempts to prove the principle wrong.

He could never understand why people were so enamored of the money. His family had all of the money in the world, but it didn't keep his mother from abandoning him. In fact, he had become certain over the years that the money was the reason that his mother had left. The money hadn't made his father spend more time with him or listen to him. It hadn't kept his father's heart beating until a ripe old age, nor given him a "heart" in the sense of showing his son any sense of sentimentality.

It always came back to the money. How many friends over the years had turned out to be anything but, all hangers-on because of the money. And the women. He knew he wasn't tall enough, thin enough or good looking enough to attract the women. It was the money. For a while, after he had been hurt and abandoned time and time again, he had turned the tables on them, unabashedly using money as bait to gain companionship. Eventually, though, those conquests left LenDale feeling as hollow as when the women walked out on him.

Everyone thought that money defined him, but over time LenDale had decided that he would never let that happen. It was why he had a garage full of exotic cars but often found himself walking, why he had the means to travel but never left Sandy Cove, why he had the ability to accumulate jewelry or art, but often had to borrow money to pay for a meal. He knew people talked about him, knew that they thought he was eccentric, and knew that they had coined him Sandy Cove's Howard Hughes. He could live with it, and sometimes even embellished it when it was to his benefit. But he never let it become reality.

Unfortunately, LenDale *had* suffered some bad luck over the years, starting with the fact that his mother seemed to lack that most inherent of all female traits: love for her child. It was LenDale's bad luck to have been borne of a woman without a heart for her son. His existence was a product of his father's desire for offspring, and despite his mother's desire to avoid pregnancy. From his birth she had been burdened by his presence in her life. She didn't want to raise a child, didn't want to be nurturing, didn't want to be a mother. In fact, LenDale was one of those most unfortunate children to have actually caused his parents to break up. His mother was selfish to the core, an immature and coddled child who had been raised in such a cocoon of indulgence by her parents that the prospect of having to be giving to another being was a literal impossibility. Raising a child was not on her life's agenda, and from the outset she struggled with parenting. Out of necessity they hired a full-time nanny, who as luck would have it provided a special allure to LenDale's father. Bad luck. If LenDale hadn't been born the nanny wouldn't have been in the house, the affair would never had happened, and his mother would never have been provided with a moral pretext to leave. But leave she did, leaving son and husband behind and never looking back.

Other instances of misfortune, some minor, some major, were sprinkled throughout LenDale's life. He had gotten used to living his life with the expectation of the next bad thing being around the next corner. Bad luck was his unwelcome companion through life. And of course the Sarah situation was the latest rendition of that. He hadn't planned on that. It was just what always happened to him. Plain, old, bad luck.

Chapter 14

Tom was putting the finishing touches on the meal preparations when Jenny arrived toting a bottle of wine and a box from the local bakery. Tom didn't even have to ask what was in the box, and when he glanced at it and caught Jenny's eye, they both said in unison, "Leave the gun, take the cannoli," quoting from The Godfather. It was an old inside joke they had, the origins of which were long forgotten. Jenny stuck her cheek out and Tom gave her a kiss.

"So what's cookin'?" Jenny asked as she sauntered into the kitchen in search of a corkscrew. "It smells fabulous in here."

"You'll find out soon enough." Tom replied as he gathered two place settings. "Is the counter okay with you?"

"Sure, as long as you don't spray the food all over me with your fancy pan flipping." Another inside joke. At one of Tom and Sarah's dinner parties Jenny had been sitting at the counter while Tom was using the adjacent cooktop, and when Tom attempted a culinary school move with the fry pan Jenny ended up with a lap full of diced vegetables. Tom ended up with a tongue lashing from Sarah.

Jenny rifled through a drawer, found the corkscrew and opened the wine. She grabbed two bulbous wine glasses from the cabinet and filled them half way, handing one to Tom. "Cheers," she said as she proffered her glass and clinked with Tom's. It was a good Chardonnay and it felt good and cool going down her throat, which was a bit parched. For some reason she was nervous. In fact, she had felt nervous since she left Tom's store. It was a tingly anxiousness that she hadn't been able to shrug off.

While Tom moved about the kitchen continuing to get the food ready, Jenny roamed around the living room. She hadn't been in the house since immediately after Sarah died. Despite the fact that Tom hadn't changed anything and everything seemed to be in the same location, it felt odd. Off. In some way the house was different without Sarah's presence. The pictures on the coffee table and shelves were the same—the same scenes from vacations at the beach and in the mountains, the same smiling faces. The same artwork adorned the walls. Yet there was a palpable difference. For some reason it made the level of her nervousness rise and she felt her stomach clench. She felt like an intruder. She took a gulp of the wine and simultaneously thought that she could use something stronger right now. A big glass of vodka would be much more satisfying.

"Hey, could you come in here and give me a hand?" Tom called out to her from the kitchen. "Bring that over to the table, if you don't mind." He was working on a sauce at the cooktop and he gestured toward a platter on the far counter next to the oven adorned with two pristine filets of Red Snapper.

Jenny obliged him and then sat down on one of the bar stools. She grabbed the wine bottle and re-filled her glass, which was almost empty. Tom hadn't touched his. She was starting to feel the effect of the wine. The nervousness was melting away and she felt a looseness start to overtake her shoulders and neck. "Better be careful not to go overboard tonight," she thought to herself as she instinctively raised the glass back to her lips.

"Voila! Specialties of the house: oysters to start, then Tom's famous Snapper," Tom said as he reached over from the stove and spooned out a silky sauce over the fish. "Let's eat!"

* * *

After gorging on the oysters, Snapper, roasted potatoes and sautéed greens they both sat back and rested. Neither had spoken much during the meal.

"That was fantastic, Tom," Jenny said as she pushed her plate away. "I'd forgotten what an accomplished chef you are."

"I do my best to please, ma'am," Tom joked. "It's been a while since I had someone to cook for." The words were out of his mouth before he realized what he was saying. An uncomfortable silence followed.

"So, did you know that I told Sam that he should take the summer off?" Jenny said to break the mood.

"You did what? What's he going to do?"

"I think he's going to go abroad."

"Abroad?" Tom asked as he poured himself another glass of Chardonnay. "It's a little odd in the timing, don't you think? Why not wait until after the season is over?"

"It has to be summer. He always wanted to go to Greece in the summer and bum around the islands. He's afraid his window of opportunity is closing."

"Yeah, but it leaves you all alone at the shop. Are you going to be able to handle it?"

"We'll see," she said with a shrug as she used her hands to gather the crumbs that had accumulated on the counter and dropped them onto her plate. "I might have to hire someone to help me, but if that's what it takes, I'll do it. He deserves to take a summer off. He never got that chance like I did." She stood and began to clear the dishes.

"Don't," Tom said. "Just leave them. Let's go sit on the deck. It's beautiful out tonight."

Tom grabbed the wine and they went outside. The sky was clear and the moon was full. The landscape was lit with moonlight. They could see the waves curling over and crashing into the surf. The air was chilly and Tom went back inside to retrieve a throw blanket as Jenny sat and listened to the sound of the waves. She had spent virtually her whole life here, watching the waves and looking out at the sea, wondering what mysteries lay hidden underneath the surface. When she was a little girl she used to sit on the sand and imagine the Pirate ships that had sailed these waters, and more so those that sank right off of the shoreline. What terror the shoals had caused those outlaws, fearless men brought to justice by the shallow waters that reached up and grabbed sturdy ships overladen with bounty, pulling them underneath for eternity to a watery grave. From the days before the Pirates to her days as a little girl to the present, how quickly the years passed, yet as the rest of the world had seen monumental changes in technology and medicine and mechanics, the waves and the sea had remained constant. That was why the ocean had always been her respite. It was her re-set button, and it was why, when her life had spiraled out of control, she had sought refuge here, why she returned to Sandy Cove despite vowing to herself when she left that she would never return.

All things considered, when she looked back on her life, she felt blessed. Blessed with good health, blessed with family and blessed with friends. Few people live life impervious to some manner of hardship or heartache, and she was no exception, as her foray into marriage had proven. Her recovery from that experiment took time, but she had gotten over her failed marriage and the psychological damage caused by it long ago.

Initially, she vowed that not only would she not marry again, but she swore off men altogether. Over time her view

on men softened and occasionally she found someone interesting enough to date, but she never allowed herself to be
drawn into a long-term relationship. Her relationships with
men had never ended up well. She found that ending things
before they got serious was a more logical and reasonable
method of controlling her life. She needed companionship,
to an extent, but she did not—would not—allow herself to
be swallowed up with love. Love was an unnecessary evil,
as she had found in her relationship with Trip. Love had
made her a victim.

Tom emerged from the house, placed the throw over her
and sat down in the chair next to her. The wine had worked
its magic on her and she was feeling relaxed. She was content sitting and watching the waves, and the constant roar
of the ocean washing over her was soothing. They sat in
silence listening to the sound of the ocean. After several
minutes Tom leaned forward and looked at Jenny to see if
she was awake. She looked over at him and smiled, both because she was feeling good and because she found it funny
that he was checking on her.

"I'm so glad you decided to keep this house. I love it
here," Jenny said as she clutched her wine glass in both
hands, as if to warm herself. "But I really wanted to buy it
for myself," she deadpanned.

"Ah, sarcasm," Tom laughed and lifted his glass to her
in salute. "I almost made a colossal mistake, didn't I?"

Yes, you did."

"I think . . . that Sarah would have wanted me to stay
here."

"I don't doubt that for a second. But I'm also glad because that means you're here. It would have been difficult
for me if you had left."

"For me, too. I was trying to run away, yet everything
that mattered to me was located here, with the exception of

Emily. The only thing that made sense other than staying put was to go to D.C. to be nearer to her, but I didn't think that would be fair to her. She deserves to find her own way without having me hovering nearby. And speaking of Emily, she's doing so well. She just got a promotion at work and she seems to have a good group of friends around her. I was worried about her but she seems to have everything under control."

"I'm so happy to hear that, Tom. She's grown into such a lovely young woman," Jenny said, stopping short of what they both knew was on the tip of her tongue: that Emily looked and acted just like Sarah at that age.

Tom rose from his chair and walked over to the railing. "You know what's funny?" Tom said as he stood looking out toward the ocean. "I haven't been able to step foot onto the beach since Sarah died."

Jenny sat up as if at attention in her chair. "Oh, Tom."

"Yeah, I know it sounds quirky. But I really can't do it. Sarah used to drag me out of bed at dawn and we'd go on these endless walks on the beach. It was one of her favorite things. I'd grouse and complain, but over time my complaining became part of the routine. I grew to love those walks with her." He turned around and leaned back against the rail, as if to block out the view from his consciousness. "The day she died she wanted to go for one of those walks, but when she tried to wake me I guess I wouldn't get up."

"But you couldn't have known, Tom."

"No, I couldn't have known. Early on, though, I beat myself up about it. I wondered if things would have turned out differently if I had woken up, if we had gone for that walk together on the beach. Was what happened to Sarah fate, or could it have been altered by what I did or didn't do? I'll never know, but what I wouldn't have given for one more of those walks."

Jenny sat still trying to decide how to respond. She was surprised by how matter-of-fact Tom was in discussing Sarah's death. He had made more progress than she had thought.

"Some times I think that we *can* alter the outcome of events," Jenny said, choosing her words carefully. "But it's more subtle than waking up and taking a walk versus what ended up happening. It's in the details of things: how much time and effort you put into something or how much you pay attention to detail. Like the saying goes, you make your own luck, and usually it's due to hard work." Tom was looking off into the distance and he seemed to not hear her. He wasn't responding, so she continued. "You're thinking that just by getting out of bed you could have altered the outcome, and that maybe Sarah would still be here. What you aren't considering is that you had already altered the course of events, through the support and love and compassion you showed her. You helped make things better for her in the face of chemotherapy and radiation and depression. If you hadn't been there for her she may not have made it through all of that."

Tom still didn't reply, but now he was clearly listening and contemplating Jenny's philosophy. The wind picked up and it seemed as though the temperature dropped ten degrees in less than a minute. They both felt the chill of the air. "Why don't we go back inside?" Tom said, and Jenny nodded enthusiastically.

Once inside Jenny rubbed her hands up and down her arms to warm up. Tom went for the scotch. He didn't need to ask if Jenny wanted to join him. He grabbed two highball glasses from the kitchen cabinet, added two ice cubes and poured two fingers in each. He came back into the living room, handed Jenny a glass and without exchanging a word each took a swig. It was warm and smooth going down. The scotch made the back of Jenny's throat feel scorched and she could feel the warmth spread through her body. Tom might be cheap with wine but he never scrimped on the scotch. Single malt, and good ones at that.

Tom settled into a wingback chair and Jenny sat on the sofa. She was starting to lose steam and the couch didn't offer any assistance in keeping her awake. Her eyes had started to feel heavy from a combination of the scotch and the exhaustion she was starting to feel take her over. The thought ran through her head that if she could just close her eyes for a minute she'd be fine, but just as her eyelids started to flutter she was snapped back to the moment by Tom's voice.

"Speaking of one's actions having an effect on the course of events, what about you trying to buy this place?" Tom said as he swept his hand to indicate that they now were discussing the house.

Jenny had to shake off the sleepiness before responding. She took another sip of the scotch, which this time had the effect of snapping her awake. "Different story," she said. "If anything, my decision to buy the house was to buy you time—to give you an opportunity, later, to recoup what you had lost, if you chose to do so. And if not, then I'd have a really wonderful place to hang out," she said with a flip of the wrist. She was tired and the scotch was going straight to her head. She had hoped that Tom wouldn't broach the subject again. The night had gone well and she was in no shape to have a serious discussion. But his mood was lighthearted, a stark contrast to their earlier conversation.

"I would have given you this house if I knew you wanted it that badly." Tom said with a smirk. "Or you could have just moved in with me." He was goading her.

Jenny rolled her eyes and readjusted on the couch, slipping her sandals off and pulling her legs up onto the couch. She was up to the challenge. "Like that's what I need in my life—to take care of your daily needs," she said, her eyes gleaming as she moved in for the kill. "The house I'd take.

You, not so sure."

"Touché," Tom said and half-bowed toward her in submission.

Jenny nodded her affirmation and smiled smugly. They both sat quietly and listened to the soft jazz that Tom had playing. After several minutes Tom noticed that Jenny's eyes had closed and he sat watching her as she moved toward sleep. He rose and carefully plied the glass out of her hand. He stood over her wondering whether he should wake her, but concluded that there was no use. She was in no shape to drive, nor was he. After contemplating the options for a moment, he retrieved the throw and put it on top of her, carefully tucking it under her.

Tom stood looking at Jenny who was sleeping soundly on the couch. How many times had he stood watching Sarah sleep, listening to her breathing and thinking that each breath was precious, a lasting gift that all too often we take for granted, as if an infinite supply existed, never to be exhausted. Tom resisted the urge to fall back into his old sorrow-filled thinking. It would be easier just to give in to it and become morose once again, easier to feel sorry for himself. He wasn't going to allow that to happen again. He'd come too far. Sarah wouldn't have wanted that, either.

Lately, he'd thought a lot about what Sarah would have wanted. She was the eternal optimist, even through all of the hard times. Certainly she'd had her moments of doubt, but by and large she'd maintained her usual sunny countenance, and it had helped pull Tom along the way, keeping him from falling into despair. And it continued to carry Tom through his recovery.

He grabbed the scotch glasses and went back into the kitchen to clean up from dinner, thinking about the irony of the moment. Sarah had always fallen asleep after their parties, while he stayed up late to clean up. He had never complained about clean up as he found it to be brainless and therapeutic. He would usually put on some good music and pour himself another drink. It was his time to unwind and think about the night's events and conversations.

It was strange for him to think that he'd have to plan for a future without Sarah. What was his life going to become, he wondered, as he moved instinctively through the kitchen, hand – cleaning the pots and pans and leaving them on the counter to drip dry. When he was finished he switched off the kitchen lights and went back into the living room, sitting down heavily in the easy chair with his now-watered down scotch. Jenny hadn't moved much and she slept quietly on couch.

It was not late—only a little before midnight—but Jenny was never a night owl. He remembered the time when, as children, they had decided that it would be fun to stay up all night and watch the sunrise over the ocean. They had spent a whole day planning out their adventure, taking care to cover all of the details, from the food to the flashlights to the sleeping bags. Their parents had agreed to let them sleep on the beach, splitting the chore of checking up on them periodically throughout the night. The era allowed for such an adventure. It would be unheard of today.

At sunset the children loaded up a wagon and pulled it behind them to the beach access, then made several trips to the beach carrying their supplies. They laid down a large beach blanket then a sheet over top, taking care to not splash sand onto it, then rolled out their sleeping bags and carefully placed their pillows inside them. Their parents came shortly after carrying a picnic basket full of goodies to last the children through the night, then left at the kids' insistence. The parents wagered as to how late the kids would make it before getting spooked and trudging home. No one gave them a chance of going past midnight.

Jenny and Tom made themselves busy with chores to get their sleeping area ready and organizing all of their supplies until everything was just right. Then they sat on the blanket and tore into the picnic basket, balancing their flashlights in the nook of their arms as they explored the contents to find their favorite treats. They gobbled the cupcakes and candies that their parents had packed for them as if they hadn't eaten in days.

When they finished eating they lay on their backs and pointed their flashlights straight up at the sky, two light beams that seemed to shine all the way into space, and battled in the dark sky like two light sabers. They identified the constellations and argued with each other about which star was the North Star, then told each other made up stories about space travel. They looked at the full moon and wondered out loud about what the astronauts felt like blasting off into space and jumping down into the moon dust.

When they switched off their flashlights the moonlight lit up the beach eerily, as if in subdued daylight. They decided to walk down to the surf and there they watched the crabs scuttling in and out of their sand holes, scurrying little creatures going about their business without paying the two children any heed. Tom chided Jenny and told her that he was going to drag her into the water, while Jenny shrieked playfully as he stepped toward her, knowing that he was too kind and would never do such a thing to her. They parried back and forth in the sand and Tom chased Jenny back to the blanket where they both collapsed out of breath.

They lay down again on their backs looking up at the stars and silently contemplated the heavens. Eventually Tom spoke, asking Jenny a question, but she didn't respond. He rolled onto his side and looked at her face and saw that she had fallen asleep. The wind was blowing off of the ocean and her hair covered her face. He stared at her and reached out to push the hair away from her face, watching her as she drifted deeper into sleep, and at that moment he knew, as much as a twelve year old could know, that she was the love of his life. He leaned over, and as gently as he could, kissed her on the cheek.

Tom found himself smiling at the memory of that night. He remembered when their parents gently shook them and woke them from their sleep. They hadn't made it to midnight, and they put up little resistance to their parents' prodding to return to the warmth and comfort of their own beds. Life had seemed so simple and pure then. You liked who you liked, you did what you wanted to do, and the world seemed to hold endless possibilities and prospects.

The memory was good and pure and reminded him of the sweetness of their youthful friendship. What Tom didn't, and couldn't, remember about that night was what happened between the time that he fell asleep and when their parents roused them. He didn't know that after he fell asleep Jenny had awakened to find him asleep with his arm over her. She had wiggled out from under him and sat up to survey the scenery. Clouds had moved in and the temperature had dropped. The clouds concealed the moon and the beach was much darker. Her eyes were adjusted to the dark and she could see the wind-whipped whitecaps of the waves. The tide had come in and was marching steadily toward their perch. She lay down facing Tom, their faces inches apart, reaching over and placing her hand on his face, cradling it. He was fast asleep. Then she did something that Tom didn't, and couldn't, know that she had done: She leaned over and kissed him, and whispered, "I love you Tommy Ralston, and I always will."

Chapter 15

The morning arrived quickly and abruptly for Jenny. The sounds and smells and feel of the room struck her senses and she instantly realized that she was in a foreign place. She snapped fully awake as soon as she became conscious that she wasn't lying in her own bed. Consciousness, then the moment of dread that accompanies waking in someone else's bed. The thoughts cascaded through her brain as she tried to shake the cobwebs of deep sleep mixed with the remnants of the alcohol she had consumed the night before.

After her initial disorientation dissipated (and a quick peek under the sheets to make sure) she realized that nothing untoward had occurred. She rolled off of the bed and glanced at herself in the mirror to make sure she didn't look too horrid, then made her way to the kitchen. The coffee was made and she poured herself a cup. She looked out the window and saw Tom sitting on the deck with his coffee, reading the paper. With an almost imperceptible exhale of breath, she willed herself to go sit with him and have him fill in the gaps of the previous night.

As she pushed through the patio door Tom looked up from his paper and smiled at her, waving her into the chair adjacent to his. Without saying a word Jenny took the chair and then sat silently, cradling the cup between her hands.

"You were a barrel of fun last night," Tom said, chiding her.

"You got me drunk to take advantage of me?

"A lot of good that did me. You fell asleep mid-sentence."

"As usual?" Jenny said, coyly.

"As usual."

"I can't hold my alcohol like I used to. It puts me right to sleep." Jenny wasn't being facetious. She had always been able to drink the boys under the table.

"I noticed," Tom said, then playfully reached over and squeezed her knee. "That's ok, though. Your secret is safe with me."

Jenny let out a half grunt. "Well, that makes me feel better about things," she said, sarcastically. "How late were we . . . did you wake me . . .?" She wanted to know but she didn't want to know. Finally, she blurted out, "How did I get in your bed?"

Tom laughed at her squirming. "Wouldn't you like to know," Tom joked, reveling in her unease. He looked over at her and raised his eyebrows two or three times.

"You're a jerk."

"Oh, hold your horses," he said. "Nothing happened."

Jenny just sat, looking expectantly at Tom for further explanation.

"You fell asleep during our conversation, I finished cleaning up, then I picked you up and put you on the bed," Tom explained. "I slept on the couch."

Tom chuckled to himself as he watched Jenny squirm. He could really milk this moment and make her uncomfortable if he wanted. Instead, he decided to take the heat off of her. "What are your plans for today?" Tom asked. "Want to do something?"

Jenny's face betrayed her relief at the change in subject.

"Other than the million things I need to do on a daily basis for the shop, nothing," she said. "Why, what did you have in mind?"

"I was thinking of heading down to Ocracoke for the day. It's been forever since I've been there and I need to pick up some things for the store. How about joining me?"

Jenny hesitated. It wasn't that she didn't want go. She loved Ocracoke and she and Tom always had a great time there. When they were younger they'd hitchhike down the coast and spend the day on the beach with not a soul in sight, then eat enormous amounts of food at one of the roadside seafood shacks. Right now, suffering from a hangover, she wasn't too interested in the food part, but once there, a bucket of cold beers and a plate full of fresh seafood would be heaven. But despite that allure, she hesitated. A strange feeling had settled over her since their confrontation and kept gnawing at her. Something had changed between them. It wasn't necessarily good or bad. Just . . . different. Their equilibrium was off, and that was the strange part. Their equilibrium had never been off. Not since the day they first met.

"Look, if you don't want to go . . . ," Tom said, his disappointment obvious.

Jenny thought about all of the things that she had to do, all of the reasons to not go. They just kept getting bumped back by the fact that something inside her did want to go. "It's not that I don't want to go, Tom," Jenny said as she struggled within her mind to make a decision. "I do want to go. It's just . . . well . . . oh, what the hell. Yeah, sure. I'll go."

"Great!" Tom replied as he clapped his hands together. "How about you go home and get yourself ready and I'll pick you up at around 11:00. Will that give you enough time?"

"It should," Jenny replied as she moved inside in search of her purse and keys. Her movements seemed disjointed and stunted, like she was trying to move through molasses. *"Way too much to drink last night,"* she thought to herself, again making a mental note to put the brakes on earlier the next time. She found her things inside on the kitchen counter, swigged the last of her coffee and headed toward the front door, all the while trying to push the strange feeling out of her head while simultaneously trying to convince herself that she wasn't making a mistake. *"It's gonna be ok, it's gonna be ok,"* she kept thinking over and over again. She was almost through the door headed toward her car, when she heard Tom yell, "And don't forget to bring your bathing suit and a towel."

* * *

Tom was at her door at 11:00 on the nose and they were soon cruising along the shoreline. The trip to Ocracoke would take them about two hours—two hours of driving along some of the prettiest scenery to be found. Once they were south of Nags Head they entered the Cape Hatteras National Seashore, the first of its kind established in the U.S., which had succeeded in keeping the shoreline almost as pristine as before man ever laid eyes on it. The two lane road hugged the beach as the land mass narrowed and expanded, never really becoming wide enough in any place so that they couldn't see both the Pamlico Sound and the Atlantic with a swivel of the head. The land narrowed to the point in places where it was barely wide enough to support the road, and it seemed that all it would take was a big wave to wash it out. In fact, that's what happened in some of the bigger storms, Mother Nature's way of sending a reminder as to who was really in charge.

Tom and Jenny made their way south, driving through fishing villages named Rodanthe, Waves, Salvo and Buxton. The beach along this portion of the Outer Banks was wide and deserted, and couldn't have offered more of a contrast to the development that had occurred farther north. Once the land ended they would have to take a ferry over to Ocracoke, which was less an island and more a lowland whose north and south attachment to the rest of the barrier seemed to have simply washed away.

Neither said much to the other as they drove. The windows and sunroof were open and the wind whipped through the car as they sped along. Pickup trucks and Jeeps laden with fishing poles sticking up in front from grille carriers roared past them, rushing to get to their lines in the water, as if the fish might not wait for them. The sunshine and scenery lended to one getting lost in the beauty of the ocean and the wildlife and the notion that not much had changed here over time. When they reached the ferry to Ocracoke Tom pulled the car onto the back of the boat and they got out and stretched their legs and allowed the sun to wash over them. They were the only passengers on the ferry and as the boat prepared to cast off Tom asked the boat captain to hold off for a second as he jumped back onto the dock. Tom ran over to the little provision store next to the dock, the kind that was valued as much for supplying bait and tackle supplies as it was for food. After a few minutes, and a few testy comments to Jenny from the captain about keeping on schedule, Tom came trotting back toting a bag in his hand and a smirk on his face. He winked at the captain as he jumped onto the back of the boat. The captain threw a sneer Tom's way and sounded the ship's horn, and within a minute they were underway for the forty minute trip to Ocracoke.

They sat on the side rail on the stern as the boat pulled away from the dock, holding onto the rail as the boat rolled with the movement of the waves. The smell of the diesel exhaust mixed with the water, filling their nostrils with the odor and spurring memories of a youth spent on fishing boats and at the shore.

Jenny was lost in nostalgia and looking out blankly at the water when Tom's words brought her back to the present. "Aren't you going to see what's inside?" Tom asked mischievously as he nudged her with his shoulder and held the bag he was holding out to her. Jenny looked at the bag for a moment as if it were a foreign object that she couldn't quite place, then snatched it from Tom's grip. She looked at Tom as if to say "I know what this is," then slowly opened the paper bag, peered inside and let out a chuckle.

* * *

When they were kids, but old enough to take care of themselves, Tom and Jenny, bored of the same old routines and hangouts, convinced their parents to let them head out on their own to destinations unknown. It was a hard-fought battle that started well before their parents could give them such latitude. In fact, Tom and Jenny were caught so off guard the first time their parents agreed to allow them to go that they hadn't even figured out where it was they were headed. The battle had been fought to gain their freedom, not to travel to a specific destination. When they got down to the task of figuring out where they might like to go they were underwhelmed by their choices. Sand and beach and beach and sand pretty much summed up their options. So, in an effort to make their first day trip into something of the exotic tilt, they decided to pick the farthest point south that they could reasonably go—and where they would have to ride a boat. A boat ride seemed exotic at their age.

If, in the minds of its present day admirers, the area provided a natural landscape, then the Outer Banks of Tom and Jenny's youth could have been looked upon as downright pristine. There wasn't much in the way of commercial development or amenities. Most of the homes were low-risers that appeared to be half-buried in the sand, the better to withstand the storms and constant battering of the ocean winds and salt, or beach shacks propped up on stilts right on the beach. Tourists were few and far between. The majority of the summer population consisted of summer locals—those people who lived a couple of hours away for eight or nine months out of the year and who migrated to the shore in the spring or early summer. Traffic didn't exist, and rides by hitchhiking were hit-or-miss, but odds were that if you were lucky enough to actually catch a ride, you'd know the driver. More importantly, in Tom and Jenny's case, the driver would know you, and your family, and be able to report back that the kids were fine when dropped off at the ferry.

That first trip, the getaway that Tom and Jenny forever referred to as their "Grand Excursion," turned out to be thrilling and scary and worth the fight. They'd set out early in the morning wearing flip flops and bathing suits, carrying rolled up towels and a bag full of fruit and sodas, trudging together toward the main road with the concerned faces of their mothers staring after them from their front porches.

It took a while, but just as the rising temperature was starting to get to them, they hooked a ride. Ed Stanley was the one who stopped to pick them up. They knew him as Mr. Stanley, the post office man. Turned out that Mr. Stanley was on his day off and was headed to Hatteras to try to nab some bluefish. This time of year they were hopping and easy picking. "Where you kids headed?" he called out as his old International pickup sputtered and came to a stop beside them.

"South," Tom responded simply and pointed down the road as Jenny nodded in agreement.

"South, huh?" Stanley chuckled. "Well seein' as I'm headed that way y'all can hop in back and catch some wind. I'll take you 'far as Hatteras Village, then you're on your own to go farther . . . *South*."

"Thanks, Mr. Stanley," they said in unison as they lumbered over the side of the truck. They adjusted their towels underneath them to act as cushions against the steel bed as Mr.Stanley put the truck in gear and it lurched forward. They looked at each other and smiled in an attempt to show the other that they were happy to be doing what they were doing. But as hard as she tried to cover it up, Jenny's fear and anxiety got the better of her, and her lower lip started to quiver and shake. Tom had feared that this would happen. He wasn't one hundred percent sure about this excursion thing, but once they had started scheming to get permission and then pleading their case, the whole idea had gained momentum and the plan had taken on a life of its own. Their trepidation gave way to blind enthusiasm as they began to believe what they were working so hard to convince their parents that they could do.

"So, what do you want to do first when we get there?" Tom said in an effort to calm Jenny down. "Wanna go swimming? Or maybe we hang around the docks and see if anyone needs a couple of extra hands for a deep sea fishing trip."

Jenny just shrugged her shoulders and turned her head away as she wiped a tear away in as unobtrusively as possible.

They sat in silence as the truck chugged along the roadway. They each quickly came to the conclusion that riding in the back of a pickup under the broiling sun was no picnic, nor was their excursion turning out to be what they had conjured up in their heads. The worst part of it was that their rear-ends were getting more and more sore with each bounce and jolt of the truck. They were hot and sore and having a hard time remembering what was supposed to be so good about this day, and a tinge of regret began to seep into their consciousness, as well as a secret yearning for an end to the excursion.

When the truck pulled off of the road and into a service station they were silently thankful for the reprieve. Tom jumped down over the side of the truck and reached up to help Jenny, who playfully swatted his hand away, climbed over the back gate and hopped from the bumper to the ground. They stood by the side of the truck and tried to stretch and twist their bodies back to normal.

They were at the last bit of road before the seashore portion of the trip. Mr. Stanley was leaning against the side of the truck with his hand in a tobacco pouch talking with the attendant who was busying himself pumping the gas, cleaning the windshield and checking the oil. Tom walked over to Mr. Stanley and stood silently before him, unnoticed, so deep was Mr. Stanley's concentration in packing tobacco into his corncob pipe. When his presence was finally noted, Mr. Stanley appraised Tom with a skewed look, as if to say, "Well, out with it, boy."

"Do you mind if I run to the store over there?" Tom asked as he pointed in the general direction of a store that was two lots away.

"Go on ahead, but get a move on. I've got a schedule to keep," Stanley said with mock sternness as he carefully folded up the tobacco pouch and stuffed it into his back pocket.

Tom turned on his heel and started to jog toward the shack of a general store. "Wanna come?" he asked over his shoulder to Jenny as he ran by her, but Jenny, not feeling up for anything except seeing an end to their daytrip just shook her head "no" and acted busy examining the contents of the bag her mom had packed for her.

Tom got to the store and entered through the screen door. The heat was stifling outside, but inside was noticeably cooler, as somehow the wind found its way through the screened windows. An old lady sat at the counter on a barstool concentrating on a crossword puzzle, and seemed to barely notice that he had come in. Tom looked around the store at shelves stuffed with tin cans and fishing gear, hardware items and household goods. A Coke machine sat whirring in the back corner—five cents for a bottle. Next to it was a rack full of sweets: lollipops and candy cigarettes, redhots, lemonheads and sourballs. Tom's eyes roamed up and down the rack, finally landing on the item he was seeking, and he grabbed it with satisfaction. He paid the woman, who took the coins in her hand and deposited them into a drawer without so much as looking up at him, and he hurried out of the store, breaking into a run back to the service station.

The truck was running and Jenny was already back in the bed. The smoke from Mr. Stanley's pipe was floating out of the open driver's window in a steady stream as if from a smokestack, and as Tom approached Stanley stuck his head out to let Tom know he had better hurry. Tom jumped up onto the bumper and into the truck without breaking stride and settled next to Jenny as Mr. Stanley pulled back onto the road. Tom, out of breath, leaned back and closed his eyes. His heart was beating fast in his chest and sweat was beading on his forehead. As the truck picked up speed the wind began to swirl around them and the air cooled him off. He opened his eyes and looked over at Jenny, whose head was turned toward the ocean and was gazing at nothing in particular. He nudged her and held out the little brown paper bag that he had been clutching in his hand, urging her to take it from him. She looked at the bag for a moment before reaching out and taking it in her hand, then opened it and peered inside.

She tried to hold back the smile, but her lips betrayed her. She reached into the bag and pulled out a handful of Atomic Hot Balls and looked gleefully at Tom. Ever since Jenny had popped the Atomic Hot Ball out of Tom's brother's throat, it was their inside joke. It meant nothing, but it meant everything. It was symbolic—it was their connection to each other, the first thing that had brought them together, and the thing that reminded them of their friendship. It had become their constant, and it instantly cheered her up.

Without a word, Jenny handed one to Tom, opened one up herself and popped it into her mouth, and Tom did the same. As the truck continued its solitary journey on the desolate seaside road, the precious baggage in the back bounced and bucked in silence, all the while contentedly sucking on Atomic hot balls, ready again to take on the world.

Chapter 16

Few locations along the Eastern coast of the United States are as isolated as the far barrier islands of the Outer Banks, nor are many as full of rich folklore. Isolation, killer storms, shallow shoals and prowling pirates were the spicy ingredients that mixed together to fuel vivid imaginations and to form thrilling stories about conquests and tragedies, murderous clans and broken-hearted settlers. Hundreds of years have passed since Edward Teach, better known as Blackbeard the Pirate, was killed at Ocracoke Inlet, yet his legend is still fresh, and tales of pirates stalking merchant ships along the coast give the island a mysterious feeling.

The present day incarnation of the island is comprised of the small Village of Ocracoke and miles of unspoiled beaches and sweeping dunes. The village is home to galleries and shops, home-grown seafood restaurants, and a bevy of bed and breakfasts and quaint inns. Tom was headed to Chaunessey's, a shop known for its collection of maritime artifacts and alleged pirate plunder. The owner of the shop, Ronnie Willis, had called Tom to tell him that he'd come across some items that he thought would sell well at Tom's store and suggested that Tom come take a look. This was normal practice in the area. Local businesses looked out for each other, the thought being that they all needed help to survive, so if the opportunity presented itself, why not lend a hand and expect that one would be outstretched in reciprocation at some later date.

Tom had always liked Ronnie as a person and admired his staying power as a businessman. It wasn't easy making a business successful in Ocracoke, which was a much quieter destination and attracted far fewer tourists than the more accessible areas to the north. Ronnie was a transplanted New Englander who appeared one day and seemingly opened up his shop the next. He started his business from scratch without the benefit of having local connections or anyone on which to rely to send customers his way. He'd been in business for over twenty years, and he either had a knack for knowing what people wanted to buy, or a bank account filled with an inheritance.

The shop was a half a block off of the harbor, on British Cemetery Road. Tom parked his car in front, no small feat given the limited spots available around the village, and he and Jenny made their way into the store. Ronnie greeted both of them with a warm hug and appraising look. The look he gave Tom was the unspoken *"how are you doing"* that Tom had become accustomed to hearing since Sarah's death. Coming from Ronnie, with whom Tom had always had a collegial bond, the look was appreciated. Tom returned the look with his own tilt of the head, as if to say, *"It's all okay. I'm okay."*

Ronnie took Tom into the back of the store while Jenny perused the new season's collection. Jenny was always amazed at the endless supply of stuff that showed up for sale at shops carrying "authentic" local items. Hadn't the pirates disappeared hundreds of years ago? Still, wherever she went on vacation she found herself drawn to local shops such as Chaunessey's.

Tom and Ronnie emerged from the back room with Tom carrying a banker's box. "Told you it would just take a minute," Tom said as he walked toward Jenny.

"That's why we drove all of the way down here?" Jenny said as she sized up the box. "Didn't you ever hear of Fe-

dex?"

"Jen, why can't you and Tom ever get along?" Ronnie said, sarcastically.

"We get along just fine. See?" Jenny replied, as she playfully dug her elbow into Tom's ribs. Tom, feigning pain, bent over at the waist and grimaced.

Ronnie rolled his eyes as he walked backward toward a wayward customer. "Sorry I can't hang out with you guys—business calls."

"Priorities, priorities," Tom said as he and Jenny pushed through the door, Jenny blowing a kiss in Ronnie's direction.

Tom loaded the box in the back of the car, slammed the door shut and rubbed his hands together as if to say "done." "So, what do you want to do now? A little swimming? Or are you hungry?"

It was already past two o'clock and Jenny, who was still feeling a bit hung-over, had been running on empty all morning, save for the cup of coffee at Tom's. Food was the call. "Food," she replied, bluntly.

"Then, food it shall be," Tom said, and they headed toward the harbor.

* * *

After ingesting a monstrous serving of mussels, french fries and cold beer in such a frenzy as if to imply that they hadn't eaten in days, Tom and Jenny, fortified with sustenance, both leaned back in their chairs and allowed the food to start to digest. They sat in silence, neither capable of overcoming their engorged stomachs to engage in any sort of conversation. Theirs was one of only several tables occupied on the outdoor terrace of the restaurant adjacent to the harbor, and they both sat silently watching the boats bobbing up and down and from side to side with the movement of the water. The sounds and smells of the harbor and the movement of the boats were calming on their senses, and melodious bits of music drifted over from one of the adjacent cafés and set upon them. Jenny couldn't place the exact songs but pieces of the tunes and the sound of steel drums struck a chord, and she felt as if she might be sitting in at a harbor bar in Key West rather than a thousand miles north.

They sat and sipped their beers as they watched the harbor at work. The ketches and sloops, trawlers and motorboats tied down in the harbor were being tended to in a futile attempt to counter the inexorable effect of the sea. Decks were scrubbed and cleaned, sails were unfolded, checked and refolded, and engines were examined and retooled in a never-ending cycle. The term "pleasure craft" was certainly a misnomer, as the ratio of pleasure compared to the hard, backbreaking work involved in getting a boat ready to sail, or securing it after a trip, was very much skewed to the work side of the equation.

Tom and Jenny could relate to the tasks being carried out in front of them, as they had each put in their share of time working on or around boats——Tom especially, as he had spent one grueling month-long period when he was seventeen working on a shrimper. After about one week everyone involved knew that Tom was better suited to work on land than at sea, but he managed to stick it out for three more weeks. The only lasting effect of his failed attempt at being a deckhand was that it became fodder for his friends' ribbing later in life.

The two of them continued to sit as though hypnotized, caught up in their memories. Finally, Tom suggested that they walk off their lunch and they paid the bill and then strolled around the harbor.

"Boy, it really is nice to be back," Tom said as he playfully bumped Jenny with his hip toward the water's edge.

"Hey, watch it, cowboy," Jenny said, and bumped him back forcefully, causing him to half-stumble. Jenny had always been more coordinated than Tom, and they laughed together at his lack of dexterity.

"I'm serious," Tom said. "I'm so glad that this place makes me happy again. I don't know how to describe it, but for the first time in my life, I was feeling uncomfortable here. That's why I decided to leave."

"I felt the same way when I went to college. Suddenly, I felt claustrophobic and I had to get away."

"But you came back."

"Yes, I did. But I had to come back. I had no where else to turn." Jenny paused, contemplating how she should ask Tom what she wanted to ask. "So, why did you come back, Tom?"

"Well, we both know why I came back. To sell my house to you," he said in mock consternation. He continued after Jenny shot him a look back. "Alright, I know why you did it. To be honest, I had no intention of staying after the closing on the house. I fully intended on turning around and leaving again. In fact, I thought I would never come back again."

"I'm confused then. What happened?"

"I know it's cliché, but something just clicked in my head. A switch was turned back on, and this became my sanctuary again. "And I realized that I missed . . . this," he said as he waved his hands back and forth between them to emphasize their interaction.

Jenny nodded. "Me too," she said as she stopped and looked at Tom. The years had passed and they had gotten older, but at their core they were still the same two kids who used to kick around together. She reached out her arms for him and they hugged, an affectionate, reassuring hug.

They resumed walking up and down the piers, casually looking into the boats and speaking with the people working on them. Maybe it was the moment or maybe it was the two days spent together, or maybe it was just the two days-worth of drinking, but they each had begun to feel an ease with the other that seemed old and new at the same time.

"This was a nice day," Tom said as they began to walk back toward the car. "I hate to have to head back."

"I know. But reality beckons."

"You want to hitchhike back, for old time's sake?"

"No, thank you," Jenny said with a chuckle. "I think I'm a bit too old to sit in the back of a pick-up truck."

As Tom began to reply his cell phone rang, and he gave Jenny a "sorry" look as he reached into his pocket for the phone. He looked at the screen before answering. "It's Emily," he said, and answered the call. "Hiya, babydoll."

There was a muffled response on the other end. "Emily, are you there?" he asked. Still, she did not respond. Like any parent his anxiety immediately spiked.

"Daddy? Daddy!"

Reflexively he grabbed Jenny's arm and pulled her along as he began to run to the car. Emily couldn't say anything more. She was crying.

Chapter 17

The trip back was endless and a blur at the same time. The desire to get somewhere fast, when distance (and method) precludes doing so, is torturous. Tom's natural inclination to jump in his car and get to Emily caused more anxiety than if he had stayed in Ocracoke. Cell phone reception in the area is spotty, at best, and was nonexistent on the ferry and along the seashore. So, for more than two hours Tom was unable to find out what was happening with Emily.

What he had ascertained once Emily had stopped sobbing into the phone was that she was in the emergency room at George Washington University hospital, that she had been in an accident while she was riding her bicycle, that a car was involved, that she was in pain and she needed to have surgery. Additional details were not provided as Emily broke down again and then the phone went dead.

All of this hit Tom hard, as he was immediately transformed back to that place he thought he had escaped when he lost Sarah. The trauma of that event was still close to the surface, and Tom's wounds were flayed open upon hearing the pain in his daughter's voice.

Jenny did all she could to allay Tom's fears. She told him that Emily was safe and would be fine. She told him that he would be with her soon enough, that it wasn't worth driving like a maniac and getting hurt himself by being reckless. The level of his anxiety shocked her, as he was close to hysteria and was almost incoherent.

"I shouldn't have left her alone," he said at one point as he pressed the accelerator even closer to the floor and the speedometer shot over 100.

"She'll be fine, Tom," Jenny said. "If they felt she was well enough to call you then she's going to be okay."

"She didn't sound fine to me. She got hit by a car, Jen. People aren't fine when they get hit by a car."

"Don't jump to conclusions. Your mind will play tricks on you and drive you crazy with what-ifs. Don't let yourself do that."

"You didn't hear her voice. She's . . . she's still my little girl," he said as his words caught in his throat. He was starting to lose control. "I don't think I'll survive if I lose her, Jen. There's only so much I can handle."

"You're not going to lose her. Don't even think that way."

"I can't help myself," Tom said as he pushed the accelerator closer still to the floor. "I've just got to get to her and see that she's okay with my own eyes."

No discussion took place about whether or not Jenny was going to come along with Tom or if he should drop her off. Tom had only said, "Do you need to be anywhere?" His failure to suggest an alternative to her, not ruling her out of this equation, was as clear a signal as he could give off, short of directly asking her to accompany him. Nor had Jenny had to reply. All she did was shake her head "no," and she was in for the duration.

They sped along in a wild dash up the coast. Tom was gripping the steering wheel so hard that his hands cramped up, but he refused Jenny's entreaties to allow her to drive. The scenery that had captivated them earlier in the day flashed by, unseen by eyes that were blinded by anxiousness and worry. They made it through the seashore portion of the trip, past Nags Head, Kill Devil Hills and Kitty Hawk, then over the bridge to the mainland and began the long trek toward Norfolk, Richmond and finally to Washington. The route was dictated by the randomness of old hunting roads and jutting estuaries, which made for no quick way of getting to where they needed to go, until they reached the interstates around Norfolk and made it through the harbor tunnel.

Both Tom and Jenny had settled into their own thoughts, the events of the day a surreal mix in their minds. Tom was consumed with a parent's guilt—guilt for living away from his daughter and guilt for being so weak during the aftermath of Sarah's death. Even the fact that he had been relaxed and enjoying his day made Tom feel guilty.

Jenny also felt guilty, but her guilt was different from Tom's. Hers involved anger, at herself, in that she had failed Sarah. She should have stepped into a mothering role with Emily once Sarah had died, but she hadn't done so. She hadn't visited Emily or reached out to her, other than to call to check in on her once in a while. And to add to her guilt, some of those calls were made more to find out about where Tom was and how he was doing than for Emily's sake. Now, she could almost feel Sarah's presence over her, urging Jenny to be her surrogate with Emily.

The clarion ringing of Tom's cell phone startled both of them. He had tried Emily's phone several times earlier to no avail, and calls to the hospital only revealed that she was in surgery. They wouldn't give out any other information over the phone, despite Tom's entreaties. The picture of Emily that appeared on his cell phone when she called stared smilingly at him as he answered.

"Hello? Emily?" Tom said, expectantly.

A male voice answered. "Mr. Ralston?"

Tom was instantly on edge. "Who is this?" Tom replied, warily. "Where's my daughter?"

"Mr. Ralston, this is Bobby. I'm Emily's . . . friend."

The hesitation in the young man's voice was not lost on Tom, but now was not the time that Tom cared to address it, and he wasn't in the mood for niceties. "Where's my daughter?" he repeated, more emphatically.

"She's fine, sir. She's out of surgery and in recovery, but she hasn't come around yet."

Tom was immediately overcome with such a feeling of relief that he almost cried. He kept repeating, "Thank God," over and over again, as Jenny patted him on the arm. Then, remembering that "Bobby" was still on the phone, he said, "Thank you for calling me. I'm sorry if I was curt with you, but under the circumstances. . . ."

"Don't give it another thought." Bobby said, cutting him off. "I've been sitting here for what seems like forever and I'm just happy to be able to relay the good news. It's been quite a day."

"Yes it has. Were you with her when it happened?"

"Yes. We were near the Jefferson, at the tidal basin, when this idiot came across the road and hit us."

"Us?" Tom said. "You got hit, too? Are you okay?"

"Relatively speaking, I'm fine. A few scrapes and bruises, and I'm sure I'll be black and blue and sore all over when I wake up tomorrow. But I was lucky. We *both* were lucky."

Scores of questions raced through Tom's mind, not the least of which was who was this young man to whom he was speaking and what was his relationship with Emily. Those questions would have to wait for their answers. More pressing was where Emily was and where they were going to put her for the night. After discussing the logistics of her stay, Tom said, "Can you promise me something, Bobby?"

"Sure thing. What is it?"

"Hang up the phone and go to Emily. And promise me

that you'll be by her side when she comes to," Tom said. "Would you do that for me?"

"I'm on my way," Bobby said, and the phone went dead.

* * *

By the time they reached the Northern Virginia suburbs on the outskirts of Washington, their trip to Okracoke was long-forgotten, and the anxiety level rose again. This time it had more to do with maneuvering the car through the maze of the D.C. highway system. Bobby had given them directions, and they exited I-395 at Crystal City and got onto the George Washington Parkway. They passed the Pentagon and Arlington Cemetery, then over the Roslyn Bridge to M Street in Georgetown. From there it was a short ride to Foggy Bottom and finally, after the eternity of the ride, they rushed into the hospital where their momentum finally ground to a halt.

Bobby had called several more times to provide updates, but Emily hadn't been able to talk to them. She was out of recovery and in a private room, sleeping. After working their way through the hospital's winding corridors, Tom and Jenny managed to find Emily's room. Just as he was about to push through the closed door, he paused, and steeled himself to what he might find on the other side of the door. Jenny put a reassuring hand on Tom's shoulder and nudged him forward.

The door swung open and inside Emily lie sleeping, the crisp white hospital sheets wrapped around her. Her casted foot protruded from under the sheets at the end of the bed, and a semi-sock was covering her toes. The room was lit by a fluorescent light on the wall above the head of the bead, and cast a sterile pallor over the room. An IV and electronic monitor were positioned to one side of the bed, an easy chair on the other. The only sound was the sporadic beeping of the heart monitor. Otherwise, the room was still. Still and quiet and calm. After their frantic chase to reach her, after all of the introspection and mental self-flagellation, here she was, safe, and sleeping soundly. Tom sat in down in the chair, reached over to the bed and cradled Emily's hand in his. She was safe. His baby was safe.

Chapter 18

When Jenny showed up the next morning at the hospital she found Tom fast asleep in the easy chair next to Emily's bed. After first convincing Bobby to go home to get some sleep, Tom had succeeded in persuading Jenny to stay in a hotel while he would stay with Emily. Jenny really had no alternative and trudged off to a Foggy Bottom inn frequented as a place for Congressional liaisons. She had brought coffees and pastries and a newspaper, and she pulled another chair into the room and sat at the foot of the bed.

Emily stirred with the sound of the chair scraping upon the linoleum. She looked at Jenny with sleepy, pain killer-addled eyes, no quite comprehending what she was seeing. "Jenny, what? . . . .," she said as she tried to clear the cobwebs from her head.

Jenny rose and came to the side of the bed opposite Tom and stroked Emily's face. "Hey there, kiddo," she said as she brushed Emily's hair behind her ear. "You gave us quite a scare yesterday."

Emily sat up and scanned the room, her eyes coming to a stop on the figure of her father curled up on a chair that was too small to hold his frame. Then, as if on cue, the pain from her leg started to creep into her consciousness and she started to feel nauseous.

"Take it easy, Em," Jenny said as she watched the color

draining away from Emily's cheeks. "You're going to have more than enough time on your hands, so no need to jump right up out of bed."

Emily nodded slightly and lay back, closing her eyes. She was having trouble piecing together the timetable since she found herself lying on the ground under the grill of the car. It had all happened so quickly—in fact, she still wasn't quite sure what had happened to her. She and Bobby had taken the day off and decided to ride their bikes over to Virginia and along the G.W. Parkway bike path to Alexandria for lunch. They never made it to Virginia. It happened along the tidal basin as they neared the Jefferson Memorial. In one instant she was laughing at something he said when she saw a strange look come over Bobby's face, then she was on the ground. She didn't remember the impact or what had happened to Bobby. She just remembered looking up at the sky and wondering how long she had been dreaming.

The police came, then the EMTs, and they all merged together around her in one indistinguishable blur of movement and commotion as they immobilized her and placed an air splint on her leg. Somebody must have given her a shot of painkiller because she didn't recall feeling any pain. Bobby was kneeling next to her holding onto her hand and looking worried every time he glanced at her leg. She couldn't see anything other than that which appeared directly above her—the immobilizer kept her head and neck from moving—and people moved in and out of her visual range as they hovered around above her.

The ride to the hospital was full of fits and starts, the siren wailing sporadically to clear a path. Then she recalled the ambulance pulling up to the hospital, being pulled through the back of the ambulance and being wheeled into the emergency room, past the other patients she could feel gawking at her as she was wheeled by, and then into a room full of doctors and nurses and technicians who seemingly were awaiting her arrival.

She didn't remember much of what occurred from that point until she awoke the next morning. She had no recollection of calling her father or of telling Bobby to make sure that he keep Tom informed. She didn't remember waking in the middle of the night and having a conversation with Tom about how things were going in Sandy Cove, or telling him that she was famished and asking him to get her something to eat, and then falling back asleep before he was able to leave the room. Everything just felt like a dreamy blur of images and sounds and people.

Jenny stood by the side of the bed as Emily, awake, but with eyes closed, started to make sense of the last twenty-four hours. "You know, all you had to do is ask, and your father would have come to see you, rather than staging this whole scene," Jenny joked.

Emily opened her eyes and smiled. "I don't even know what you guys are doing here."

"We got bored on Ocrakoke, and we wanted to see how fast we could get here from the most remote location on the East coast."

"Ugh. I'm so sorry. I ruined your trip."

Jenny laughed and said, "Honey, we wouldn't have missed this for the world," as she gently rubbed her hand along Emily's arm. She caught herself looking down at Emily in wonderment. Gone were the girlish affects and lingering immaturity, both having been replaced with a new self-assuredness. She had really grown into a woman since the last time Jenny had seen her—at Sarah's funeral.

Tom stirred and stretched out his legs from the fetal position he had assumed on the chair. Emily and Jenny both looked expectantly at him as he awakened. Having warded off the queasiness, Emily managed to sit up and did her best to smile despite the pain pulsing through her body from her leg.

Tom's eyes opened and he jumped out of the bed as soon as he saw that Emily was awake. He looked over to Jenny on the other side of the bed who was holding Emily's hand in hers, then he looked down at Emily. He struggled to come up with the right words to say to his daughter, more-so because of the hours worth of worrying he went through while driving to see her than because of her actual injuries, although a child's injuries are never routine or insignificant to the parent.

When he continued to stand over her without saying anything Emily broke the ice. "God, Dad. Stop looking at me with such morbid fascination. I just have a broken leg," she said.

Tom laughed and leaned over the bed to give his daughter a kiss on the forehead. "You're right. I'm getting to be an old softie," he said. "I'm just happy that you're alright, broken leg or not."

Emily adjusted herself on the bed again and lifted the sheet to see what had happened to her leg, but she couldn't see much of the actual damage. Her leg was encased in a cast and wrapped with an Ace bandage, and it stretched from mid-thigh to her foot. This was not good, she thought, and not what she expected to see when she decided to take a peek. She dropped the sheet and looked upset.

"It's okay, sweetie," Tom said as he squeezed Emily's hand. "You're going to be just fine." Then, to change to a subject he thought would cheer her up he said, "So who's this Bobby, and why haven't I heard about him before?"

Emily's demeanor brightened. "Bobby? Oh, well, we're friends."

"Friends, huh?" Tom and Jenny shared a knowing look. "Well he was hell-bent on staying with you last night. I nearly had to drive him home myself."

Emily realized that she hadn't even asked about Bobby.

"He's at home? Is he okay?"

"Yes, he's fine. More shaken up than physically hurt."

"Thank God," Emily said, simply.

"So are you going to tell me? What's the deal with him?"

"He's just a friend. Well, more than a friend. I . . . we've been dating for a little while now."

"Is it serious?" Tom asked.

"It's . . . percolating," Emily responded, then noticed the blank look on Tom and Jenny's faces. "That means that we're getting to know each other," she said in explanation of her generation's lingo. "I met him at a congressional fundraiser in Bethesda. He was there trying to round up votes for some Bill. We got into a discussion about the environmental impact that passage of the Bill would have. Actually, it was more of an argument. But anyway, by the end of the night we ended up at a diner discussing it over fries and gravy."

"So how long have you been dating?"

Emily hesitated before answering. She had wanted to tell him but had never thought it was the right time. "It's been going on for a while."

"How long's a while?"

"Six months," Emily said under her breath.

"Six months? Why didn't you tell me about him?"

"I was afraid to tell you. I don't know. In some weird way I felt like it would upset you."

"Honey, of course it wouldn't have upset me. I want you to be happy."

"I am happy, Dad. Very happy."

Tom looked down at his daughter and despite the accident and the trauma and the surgery, as well as the fog of the painkillers she was taking, he saw her eyes sparkling. She had her mother's eyes, and in that moment of looking into them, a thousand memories, as well as a sharp pang of hurt, hit him, which by sheer will he pushed aside. His time of mourning had been put to rest. This was him being a father, and this was one of those moments that was to be remembered forever. All of the worrying and worst-case scenarios that he had gone over and over in his head during his race to reach Emily had been erased, and here she was, smiling at him through it all. She did have her mother's eyes, and Tom realized that those eyes had been Sarah's eternal gift to him. For the rest of his life Sarah would be with him and would be there to share with him, and he would be reminded of her, each and every time he looked at Emily and saw Sarah's eyes. Starting today, this moment, when one look into Emily's eyes spoke a thousand words. She was in love.

Chapter 19

O ver the next few days Tom divided his time between the hospital and Emily's apartment, shuttling back and forth on the metro and getting the apartment ready for Emily in her less-than-mobile condition. Jenny had driven Tom's car back to Sandy Cove to handle some business and to check in on Tom's store. She insisted that she would drive back on the weekend to be with them. Emily had been itching to get out of the hospital from the outset but the doctors insisted that she stay for a couple of days of observation. She had suffered a compound fracture, and in addition to allowing the new hardware the surgeons had attached to the bone to take, the doctors wanted to make sure that the leg didn't become infected.

Bobby had camped out at the hospital since the day after the accident and Tom observed their easy and loving interaction. Tom found it interesting to watch the two of them together. Fathers typically struggle to deal with their daughters' love interests, but Tom had never felt threatened by that malady. Emily had boyfriends in high school and college but had never fallen head-over-heals for anyone. Tom got the impression that Emily felt differently about Bobby, and he enjoyed being there to witness the blossoming of their relationship, even though his presence was brought about by such an unfortunate circumstance.

Bobby had understated his injuries from the collision and was sporting a massive bruise that had turned deep purple and covered the entire left side of his body. Tom had insisted that Bobby leave on the first night, and took on a parenting role over him, making him follow up with his doctor and ensuring that he got enough rest. He also insisted that Bobby call his parents and let them know what had happened after Bobby told him that they didn't need to know because it would only worry them. As a parent Tom cringed to think about what important events had been kept from him over the years so that he "wouldn't worry." He knew that Emily had shared things with Sarah that were private between the two of them, as daughters and mothers should do. He just hoped that Emily would allow him to take over that role in Sarah's absence.

Bobby and Tom took shifts staying with Emily and had time to sit and talk and get to know each other. Bobby was lanky with olive skin and unkempt black hair. He grew up on the North Shore of Chicago, where his parents still lived and where he expected to return in the future. He had graduated from Georgetown law school and decided to stay in D.C. for a while before getting serious about life, putting off a job that awaited him at a big firm in Chicago. He was working on the Hill as an aide to the senior Senator from Illinois, which is what placed him at the fundraiser where he and Emily met.

Although they hadn't spent much time together, Tom liked Bobby and was pleased that Emily had found him. He seemed kind and warm-hearted, intelligent and inquisitive. He was young and idealistic but seemed much more focused than Tom had been at that age, and he seemed to have charted out his future in a very strategic way. Tom knew, from age and experience, that Bobby and Emily were naïve and would have their idealism challenged many times in their lives. Perhaps the events of that past few days were the first of those that they would experience, and that would mold them and affect their future. Fortunately for all of them, Emily would recover and they would get to resume their lives, eventually. What impact all of it would have on them, only time would tell.

The guilt, on the other hand, was not so easily dispelled, as Tom was unfortunately well aware. Tom found it odd—a psychological anomaly—that one felt guilt for events over which one had no control and bore no responsibility. Tom hadn't caused Sarah's cancer and played no role in her death, yet he had felt an enormous amount of guilt over both. Similarly, Bobby felt guilty—guilty that he had been the one who insisted on taking that route over to Virginia, guilty that Emily was the one who was so badly injured, and guilty that he escaped the brunt of the collision with mere bruises. As they discovered, the collision wasn't anyone's fault. Apparently, the driver of the car was a diabetic and had passed out in the car from low blood sugar. The police told them that it was just a matter of Emily and Bobby being in the wrong place at the wrong time. One of life's tough lessons.

The doctors had good news for them at the end of the third full day. Emily would be discharged that evening, but under strict limitations. By the time the paperwork was finalized and Tom and Bobby managed to get Emily safely home, she was exhausted and immediately maneuvered her body onto the bed. Tom sat on the side of her bed and pulled the comforter up to her chin and straightened the sheets with his hand. Emily let out a contented sigh and smiled at him before closing her eyes and almost instantly falling asleep. Tom looked down at her and thought about how many times this same scene had played out when she was growing up, how many times he pulled the sheets up and tucked her in to the safe cocoon of her bed. When he looked at her sleeping he still saw his winsome young daughter, still innocent and unaware of the perils of the world around her.

He came out of the bedroom and carefully pulled the door shut behind him. The apartment was a one bedroom that was not much bigger than a studio, but was updated, comfortable and affordable by Dupont Circle standards. Bobby was sitting on the couch randomly flipping channels. Tom looked at the television and then at Bobby, who then decided that it was time to excuse himself, averting an uncomfortable situation of deciding who should stay with Emily. Tom wasn't foolish enough to believe that Bobby never slept over, and the second toothbrush and men's deodorant he had found in the bathroom cabinet confirmed it for him. But he felt that his role was still to tend to his daughter at this point in her recovery, given that he was here and available to do so, and irrespective of Emily's relationship with Bobby.

The next morning Tom was awakened from his exhaustion-aided sleep by a plaintive call from the bedroom. He jumped up and practically leapt through the door, only to find Emily sitting up in bed with a smile on her face.

"I knew that would get you here quickly," she said as she patted the bed next to her, instructing Tom to sit.

Tom, his head still foggy from his deep sleep, but also surging adrenaline, took a moment to get his wits together. "Em, you scared me to death," he finally managed to say. He sat on the edge of the bed and surveyed the scene. Everything looked normal, save for Emily's casted leg. "How'd you sleep?"

"As well as could be expected. My leg itches like crazy, but otherwise I know it could be worse. Sorry about calling out to you like that. I was just kind of stuck here."

"No apologies necessary," Tom said as his eyes began to focus on her nightstand. Somehow he hadn't noticed the pictures before now: one of Tom and Sarah, one of Sarah and Emily, one of the three of them together. Sitting next to the pictures were some earrings, rings and necklaces that were laying haphazardly in her open jewelry box. He recognized Sarah's engagement ring and felt a lump begin to grow in his throat.

Emily saw the look on his face and followed his stare to the stand. "Daddy, I'm sorry . . . I should have put those away."

Tom did his best to downplay it. "I'm fine, honey. Really. Sometimes I just get caught by surprise by a memory or a picture and I get stuck there. I'm getting better at dealing with it, though."

Emily looked at Tom, trying to determine whether he was truly okay or if he was just putting on a good face for her benefit. He seemed to be sincere.

He picked up the engagement ring, twirling it in his hand.

"You can take that back if you'd like," Emily said, sorrier now that she hadn't been able to put things out of sight.

"No, I'd rather you have it." Tom said as he placed the ring down. He ran his fingers over the picture frames and the jewelry, then pulled his hand back. "Where's the necklace?" he asked as he looked down quizzically, pushing pieces of jewelry about, then looked at Emily, noting that she wasn't wearing it. He didn't need to say which necklace. It was the one that he had given to Sarah in Philadelphia. The one that she always wore.

"I don't have it," Emily said as she tried to move closer to him. "I couldn't find it the last time I was home."

"Well, when I get back I'll find it and get it to you."

"Dad, you really don't have to do that."

"Emily, I want you to have it. You *should* have it."

He continued looking absently at the nightstand, then shook it off. "Hey, how 'bout I make you some chocolate chip pancakes," Tom said, clapping his hands together. "Bet you haven't had those in a while."

"Not since I realized that they go straight to my thighs.

Give me a hand?" Emily asked as she began to swing her legs around to the side of the bed.

Tom stood, looked around the room and found the crutches perched against the closet door. He grabbed them and reached over to help Emily get to her feet as she pushed off of the bed. She wobbled a bit from the sudden change from horizontal to vertical, then righted herself and reached for the crutches. "Take it slow, honey," he said as he helped keep her steady. "Rome wasn't built in a day."

Emily struggled a bit with the crutches, realizing that having to use them was one of many limitations to her life with which she would become acquainted in the coming days. She also felt her leg begin to throb as she stood, yet she put on a brave smile for Tom. "I don't know about those pancakes, but I sure could use a cup of coffee. And some ibuprofen."

Emily sat at the round Parisian table just outside of the kitchen as Tom made breakfast. He found the galley kitchen almost claustrophobic, and not dissimilar to the apartment where he and Sarah had lived in Philadelphia. He sat with her as she ate and they talked about Emily's work and about her relationship with Bobby. Tom was amazed with her and he chastised himself for missing her transition from book-toting student to adulthood. She had become so self-sufficient and self-assured. Even the setback of the past few days did not seem to dampen her spirit or her drive to push forward with her life.

As she gobbled up the last of the pancakes, which she claimed to have eaten only under protest, Emily let out a contented sigh. "Those were so good," she said as she used her finger to scrape up the last of the chocolate on the plate. "You can come and cook for me anytime."

"My pleasure, Madame," Tom said with an exaggerated bow as he poured each of them more coffee. He retreated to the kitchen with the coffee and returned to his chair. He stared at her cast and then tapped it two times with his knuckle for effect. "This thing is going to be a pain," he said. "I may just have to stay up here for a while."

"No way, Dad," Emily said a little too quickly and with a little too much force for Tom's liking. Emily noticed the effect of her comment on his demeanor and attempted to soften the blow. "I mean, well, I appreciate everything you've done for me, but you have to get things going back at home and I have to learn to manage for myself."

"My situation at home is fine and I can afford to spend whatever amount of time is necessary to help when you're in this condition."

"If you say so," Emily said absently as she shifted her weight in the chair, attempting to find a comfortable position for her leg. It was painful for Tom to watch.

"So what's up with you and Jenny?"

"Jenny?" Tom said with a confused look. "What does she have to do with how long I stay here with you?"

Emily rolled her eyes at him. "You're totally clueless, aren't you?" she said, but Tom continued looking at her for an explanation.

"It just seems to me that you have been spending a lot of time together lately," Emily said, trying to sound matter-of-fact, then looking away from him in embarrassment, concentrating on the fork she was using to swirl the left-over syrup on her plate. Tom wasn't sure if she was making a rhetorical remark or an indictment. His cheeks flushed and he felt his temperature begin to rise.

"Maybe you don't know what you're talking about," Tom said as he stood abruptly and gathered the plates. He moved into the kitchen and Emily heard the plates and pans clattering in the sink.

Emily sat at the table, regretful that she had made the remark. Then, in a move that required all of her effort, she stood and hobbled on the crutches into the kitchen, blocking her father's retreat. "I just want you to know that it would be okay with me, Dad. It's would be a little strange for me, but I want you to be happy. And I know Mom would want you to be happy." Tom avoided her stare and continued to make himself busy cleaning. Emily continued, undaunted. "Do you really want to lead a solitary life for the rest of your life?"

Tom slammed his hand against the kitchen counter, rattling the plates and silverware in the sink. "Enough, Emily. I've heard enough." He put his hands up in the air as if to steady himself. "I am fully capable of deciding what I do and with whom. I don't need you or anyone else to tell me otherwise."

Neither Tom's tone of voice nor his visible anger deterred Emily, and she remained resolute. "I'm not telling you how to lead your life, Dad. I just want you to be happy."

Tom turned back to the sink. Here was the beginning of the inevitable: the child becoming the parent and the parent becoming the child. She wasn't being intrusive or overbearing and she meant well. He realized that he hadn't seen her in person since he began doing better. The last time they had been together he had been wallowing in self-pity, which he imagined fueled her instinct to mother him. He needed to allay her concern, for their mutual benefit.

"You don't have to worry about me, honey," Tom said as he moved toward her and put his arms around her. "I'm going to be just fine. I *am* fine."

Emily wiggled away and pushed back from him, almost losing her balance in the process. She managed to right herself on the crutches as he reached out to help steady her. "Is that just to appease me? Or are you really?" Emily looked at him intensely, trying to discern if he was being truthful. He seemed to be sincere, and he was certainly acting much more controlled than the last time she'd seen him. "I'll leave you alone, but when I want to tell you something I want you to listen to it with an open mind. And promise not to get angry with me."

"Okay, I promise. I'm willing to listen," Tom said as he sat on the arm of the couch. As Emily dropped back onto the chair she let out a yelp as her leg moved within the cast. Tom immediately jumped back up and was at her side.

"I think I'm going to need something a little more powerful than ibuprofen," Emily said a little too matter-of-factly, and they both broke up in laughter.

* * *

The time that Tom and Emily spent together after Emily's accident was therapeutic for them both. The personal interaction and being able to speak face-to-face was a pleasant respite from the hurried phone calls and even shorter texts which had taken over their communication. They filled their abundance of time together with conversations that meandered from topic to topic, from personal issues to politics, from present living to future plans. Tom learned more about Emily's job and friends, and in particular, about her relationship with Bobby. By her description he seemed to be caring and a gentleman, which was borne out from Tom's observations of him. She didn't know if he was the "one" and seemed unconcerned about the issue. For now she was content with spending time with him and "discovering" him, as she put it, and just seeing how things played out.

Tom and Emily never revisited their conversation in the kitchen or its implications. Nevertheless, Tom had heard what Emily said and it struck a nerve—one that he had never allowed himself to trigger in all of the years that he had known Jenny. At first he was amused by it and thought that it was sweet that Emily had conjured up a relationship for him. As he gave the idea of a relationship with Jenny beyond their friendship some thought, he acknowledged that it could seem like a logical step to take, if logic was what ruled relationships. He loved her, as one loves their best friend. He needed her, as one needs companionship and friendship. The question that Tom kept asking himself, the one that he couldn't answer, was why, when they were younger and had the opportunity to be together romantically, they hadn't chosen to do so. If they had been meant to be together, why hadn't it happened? He couldn't put his finger on it but something had kept them apart, and that something was many years in the making. If he had been too blind or too dimwitted to see it before, he now he had the time and the opportunity to contemplate their friendship and figure out what the future held for them. He just didn't know if he was even ready for something like that to happen in his life.

Tom stayed in Washington for several additional days, but at Emily's insistence he gradually reduced his role in her care. Actually, that role was almost immediately transitioned to Bobby. It was the young couple's first experience of having to care for one another in sickness, perhaps a foretelling of a future life together. Tom, considerate of their wishes, made himself scarce, and found himself looking for things to do. He filled his time walking around Georgetown and Adams Morgan, revisiting museums and historical sites. He was growing used to being alone, but every once and a while he found himself turning to make a comment about something he had seen, with no one next to him to hear what he had to say. He equated it to the amputee who still "felt" a missing limb, and it always shocked him back to what he deemed to be his reality—what his life now entailed.

The time came for Tom to head back to Sandy Cove and back to his real life. He did need to get back to the store and take care of his business, while Emily needed to get back to living her life as a single young woman and all of the social and intellectual joys and sorrows that entailed.

Tom had decided to rent a car rather than have Jenny drive back to pick him up, and as they waited in the lobby of her building for the rental car to be delivered, they talked about Emily and Bobby coming to Sandy Cove for a visit once she was well enough. Emily's time there had dwindled after Sarah died, and they both agreed that a long weekend trip would be therapeutic for her, both physically and mentally.

After the car showed up and all of the paperwork was signed and the keys handed over, Tom turned to Emily and gave her a lasting hug. "You know I can stay longer if you'd like."

"I know, Dad. I appreciate the offer, but I think it's time," she said even as she luxuriated in the security of his embrace.

Tom continued to hug her, then gave her one final squeeze with his arms wrapped around her. He picked up his bag and started for the door, then turned back to her. "If you need anything . . . ."

"I'll call you, immediately," Emily responded by rote.

They both laughed and he walked back over to her and kissed her on the forehead. "Bye, babydoll."

He opened the door and walked out to the car. The day was already heating up and the sun was beating down, mixing with the bustle of the street as people hustled past on their way to work. Heat shimmered off the roof of the car and Tom rolled the windows down to cool the interior. He threw his bag into the back, then settled into the driver's seat. Emily stood in the doorway watching as he shifted the car into gear, mouthed one more goodbye and waived to her. As the car began to move away from the curb they both felt a pang of sadness—the sadness that comes with changing lives and time's inevitable marching onward. But they also felt a warmth wash over them: the warmth of knowing that they were each other's guardian angel and constant; the warmth of knowing that no matter what highs and lows life determined would come their way, they had each other to lean on and to confide in; and the warmth of knowing that he was, and would always be, her dad, and she his little girl.

Chapter 20

When Tom finally arrived home from D.C. the sky was already darkening as the sun set over the mainland. He pulled into the carport and parked, then grabbed his bag from the back seat and walked up the stairs to the front porch of the house. Something in the light caught his attention, either a shadow or a glimmer of reflection, and it drew his eyes toward the ocean. The water was rough and the waves were crashing lustily into the shoreline. It was high tide and the water was rolling up close to the wooden walkway that led from the house to the beach. The movement of the ocean was as mesmerizing to him now as when he was a child sitting on the sand, looking outward and wondering who and what existed beyond his view. He walked around the porch toward the walkway and took a step onto it before stopping. This beach, this ocean were his ultimate joys, the things that inexorably tied him to Sandy Cove, the things that made him come back again and again. The things that as a child had so burned into his soul as to have made him one with that place, with that feeling of comfort and of home that he felt every time he returned.

He finally realized that his reluctance wasn't really about Sarah's absence; rather, it was about him—the lingering belief that he wasn't entitled to enjoy Sandy Cove, the thing that had brought him the most joy in his life. He had come to terms with everything else: the empty house, the loneliness, the way that everything he did by himself was accompanied with a hollow emptiness with which he was beginning to grow accustomed. But he wasn't able to allow himself that ultimate joy. Not yet, at least. He wasn't quite fully repaired. He gave a last furtive glance at the water over his shoulder as he turned to go inside. *"Someday,"* he thought. Someday.

* * *

The tourists were trickling in to the area with more and more frequency as the warm weather gained traction. The rental homes would stay mostly empty for a couple of weeks more, when the schools began to let out, but the luxury inns were full of couples looking for a romantic getaway. They got to see what Sandy Cove used to be like, what the locals still loved about the place, as much as they loathed the high season that brought with it the hoards of visitors.

Flowers and grasses were already growing tall, and the air had taken on a stable warmth that relegated the cold days of winter back into the recesses of memory. People walked, ran and biked by the sides of the main road through the village, shoppers meandered into and out of shops, and diners lingered over coffee and dessert at outdoor cafes.

Tom, like all of the merchants in the area, doubled up his time, taking care of the dribs and drabs of customers while also preparing for the summer onslaught. Not much had happened in his store for quite some time, not that the tourists were aware of his extended absences or the reason behind them. The store was almost squared away and ready, but miscellaneous chores kept creeping up to keep him busy and occupied.

He had spoken with Emily every day since he left her to fend for herself in D.C. She was still on the crutches but the cast was off and the doctors seemed encouraged by her progress at physical therapy. Bobby was taking good care of her and they seemed to be growing closer to each other since the accident. Emily didn't share much information with Tom about the relationship, and he didn't expect her to, but from what she did tell him it appeared that at least she had found a nice guy, and one who treated her well.

Tom was in the shop finishing up for the day and waiting for a couple to make up their minds so he could close and get on his way. He made himself busy while keeping an eye on them, chuckling to himself as he watched the man try to look interested while the woman hemmed and hawed over whether to make a purchase. She finally decided, both to Tom's relief as well as the husband's, who gladly pulled out his wallet and locked eyes with Tom as he handed over the money, as if to say "thank God she finally made up her mind," and Tom gave him a knowing look and a wink back.

He ushered the couple out of the store, turned the hanging sign to "Closed" and locked the door behind them. Tom knew that every early season sale was like found money, and he appreciated that he had business at this time of year, but he was tired and in need of a beer or two. He moved through the displays toward the back of the store, turning off lamps and light fixtures and shutting down the computer. He put the day's receipts into a bank bag and put it in the small safe he kept in the storeroom. He'd have to get in early to run the money over to the bank and make a deposit. He paused as he headed out through the back door to do a mental check, then clicked the light switch and the store went dark.

The sun was low in the sky but potent enough to provide some warmth to offset the evening chill pushing inland from the ocean. He walked along the main road, waving belatedly at the cars that honked their hello's to him as they drove past. Today was the first official SLOB session of the year, and Tom had been looking forward to it all day. The first opportunity to catch up with everyone, to find out the local scuttlebutt. It also made him realize that the summer was upon them. As he walked he could feel the warmth of the sun on his shoulders and seeping into his bones. He glanced to his left and saw that the sun was creeping lower in the sky and he picked up his pace.

A car pulled aside him and slowed, and he smiled as the passenger window opened.

"Want a ride?"

"Sure thing."

"We're going to the same place, aren't we?" Jenny said as Tom nodded and slid into the car. She waited for him to buckle up, ignoring the cars that had started to accumulate behind her. Once he got situated she accelerated the car and they began the short ride to her shop. They were less than a mile away but after the long day Tom appreciated the ride. He had taken to walking to work in the morning, which he enjoyed, but the walk home at night was a chore.

"Where are you coming from?

"Down in Kill Devil Hills, picking up a new mixer and one of those fancy Italian espresso/cappuccino machines. Sam said we need to have more frou frou stuff to offer people to keep them from driving over to Starbucks in the morning."

"You mean people don't flock to you just to catch a glimpse of Sam's good looks?"

Jenny chortled. Sam had peaked in high school and his days as a looker were long in the past—and about fifty pounds ago.

She pulled into the small parking lot that serviced their shop as well as the three others contained in the complex. "Help me carry this stuff inside?" Jenny asked as she grabbed one of the boxes. Tom went to the rear of the car and attempted to pick up the box holding the mixer and winced as he tried unsuccessfully to lift it. He gave it a second shot, this time bending his knees and getting leverage under the box before using his legs to help him lift it. He grunted with the effort and took staggering steps toward the door as he struggled with the box.

Jenny looked over her shoulder at him and laughed to herself. He had thought she was just being nice in stopping to give him a ride when her ulterior motive was to get him to help her carry the heavy load. She moved ahead quickly so that she could help him get inside. She balanced the box on her knee and against the door frame as she opened the door and put her box inside, then turned and helped Tom with the mixer. They both exhaled audibly after they put the box on the counter and regrouped.

"Beer," they said simultaneously to each other and headed onto the deck where Sam and several other of their friends had already begun drinking. Tom grabbed two from a bin and opened them, handing one to Jenny as they clinked bottles together. The beer was ice cold and went down smoothly and easily.

More people began to show up and the deck got crowded and loud, as people who hadn't seen each other for months caught up on each other's lives. Those who hadn't seen Tom since his return were surprised to see him there and with a smile on his face. More than one person thought inwardly whether they could ever imagine going through his ordeal. He had been a mess for a while and hadn't done a good job of hiding it. And when he told the story of Emily's accident, they had to believe that it had sent him over the edge again. But he had held himself together and looked to be back to his old self.

No one seemed to notice that Jenny stayed by Tom's side for most of the evening, or that when they all stopped to watch the sun slip beneath the horizon, she was standing next to him. Since Tom returned from Washington something had changed between them. Something that brought a new ease to their being together. This subtle change in their relationship was not altogether lost on Tom and Jenny, but it also did not register on the scale that it may have, previously. It was friendship, plus something a little bit extra. Nothing of a sexual nature had occurred—nothing other than a comforting touch or backrub here or there. But the fact was that they were spending more time together than before.

When the day's light was waning, the assembled group gradually quieted to focus on the sunset. They stood staring at the mainland shoreline and watched the water begin to glow and shimmer. The scene struck a unique chord inside each of them, and they watched in silence. When the sun finally disappeared behind the tree line someone cracked a joke, the spell was broken, and the conversations and drinking resumed anew.

Tom spent most of the evening talking with Donnie Peters, a giant of a man who ran a wide-range of tourist-centric businesses, including deep sea fishing, parasailing, kayaking, and Pirate ship scuba diving excursions. Donnie was a native, one of the few who had actually grown up in Sandy Cove, and was, for lack of a better definition, the local surfer dude. He had spent his entire life trying to stay on top of or diving underneath the surface of the ocean. Although still youthful looking, with the perpetual tan, ever-present cargo shorts and sandals, his time in the sun had taken its toll, and the wrinkles around his eyes began to betray his youthful countenance. Donnie was younger than Tom, but not by much, and they had known each other since they were kids. Back then Donnie was a precocious child who always seemed to be getting himself, and his friends, into trouble, and who always—always—was looking for an angle to make money. He had taught Tom how to surf and how to trap crabs, how to track the wild Arabian horses that roamed to the north and how to play beach volleyball. More than once they had found themselves explaining how they had gotten themselves into trouble carrying out one of Donnie's plans.

The most memorable of those events was when they took a two seat sailboat out on the ocean in hopes of attracting the attention of a couple of girls on the beach. They figured that the girls would try to save them if they started acting like they were in trouble.

They put out in the boat and sailed it directly in front of the girls, making enough chatter and showing off enough to get the girls' attention. When they got out a decent bit from the shore the boys started screaming toward the girls, feigning an emergency and crying for help. They expected the girls to run into the water and swim to their rescue. Instead, the girls jumped up and ran in the opposite direction, off of the beach and out of sight. The boys couldn't believe that their plan hadn't worked, and had a good laugh at their own expense, then sat and took in the sun as the boat lolled back and forth in the chop of the water.

Soon, they heard a constant *thwap, thwap, thwap* coming from the distance and they both turned to see a Coast Guard helicopter racing toward their position, and it suddenly occurred to both of them that the copter was coming for *them*. Horrified at the prospect and now aware that their plan had gone awry, they hunkered down in the boat and tried to make themselves invisible. The *thwap, thwap, thwap* came ever closer and gradually rose in pitch before becoming a deafening roar, and each of them prayed to any God that came to mind — *please, oh please, oh please don't be coming here for me* — as the copter finally reached them and then hovered over them, expectantly. As if they weren't horrified enough, the door on the side of helicopter slid open and they saw one of the Guardians stick his head out and look down at them. At this point the helicopter's rotors, which hovered only twenty or thirty feet above the water, were whipping up the chop to four or five feet, and the tiny boat began to take on water. Now they *were* in trouble, although in later years Donnie insisted that they weren't so far out that he couldn't have made the swim back to shore if the boat ended up sinking. Before they knew it a rescue basket was being lowered down to them and then was plucking them off of the boat and lifting them up to safety. It wasn't until Donnie's dad began grilling him later that night about the boat and what emergency they had encountered that the truth came out. Donnie spent the rest of the summer in indentured servitude paying for the boat, which somehow had disappeared, never to be seen again.

Donnie's personal life as an adult had been somewhat of a mystery to Tom and Sarah. They didn't socialize very often—Donnie always seemed to have a young twenty-something beauty on his arm—and Donnie was usually on the water somewhere, while Tom and Sarah were tending to the store on land. They jokingly, and jealously, referred to him as "Peter Pan," and he seemed to relish the role of the perpetual child.

Like with most of his friends, Tom hadn't spoken much with Donnie since Sarah died. Initially, Tom had avoided or ignored everyone who had reached out to him, until eventually the entreaties stopped. Donnie had kept a respectful distance, figuring that when Tom was ready, he'd let him know.

The two of them stood leaning against a deck post, sipping from their beer bottles and talking about the dilemmas facing the local economy, the never-ending traffic and the plans to build a new access bridge to the Outer Banks. The plans for such a bridge had gained and lost favor over the years, like the ebb and flow of the tide. Now, though, it seemed as though enough people with clout had taken up the project that it might actually get done. The effect could be a boon to all of them, or a terrible mistake, depending on which side of the fence you sat. For Tom and Donnie it would be horrible if the plan involved widening the roads to accommodate the increased traffic, as it would cut through both of their properties. Tom had always joked that he would give up his land for the better good, but as that possibility became more of a probability, he became more reticent to speak so flippantly about the project.

Not long after the sun had set people started saying their goodbyes and began to make their way home. This wouldn't be one of those nights where the group stayed until late into night. Those nights usually happened only during the season, when they all really needed a break.

Tom and Donnie stood silently as they finished their beers, then each of them tossed their bottle into the garbage a couple of feet away as they prepared to leave. Tom pushed off the railing and stretched, reaching his arms toward the sky and then bending over at the waist to stretch his back, which had been bothering him lately. He straightened up and held out his hand to Donnie. "Take 'er easy, Donnie, boy wonder."

Donnie grabbed Tom's hand exuberantly, crushing it in his large grip. He had sea-man's hands—rough and calloused. Tom's were dainty and smooth in comparison. Donnie pulled Tom toward him and gave him a man-hug, patting him on the back several times before releasing him.

"You know, Tom, you could always have called me," Donnie said. "I would have been there for you."

Tom was surprised by the comment at the same time as he was used to hearing it. "I know it, Donnie. Just understand, I needed some time to get my head together. To sort everything out."

Donnie stood in front of Tom, trying to conjure up a way to have a heart-to-heart. It wasn't easy for him and it didn't come naturally. You could talk to Donnie for hours about fishing or surfing or sports, but when it came time to have a serious conversation, Donnie was incompetent. So what he said next came as a complete shock to Tom.

"I had a daughter, you know," Donnie said as he turned

his gaze down to the ground. "Remember that girl, Taylor? The UVA grad student?" Donnie looked up at Tom, expectantly.

Tom nodded his head. "No, Donnie, I'm sorry, but I don't."

"Yeah, well she was here one summer and we hooked up." Donnie was swaying from side to side as he again stared toward the ground. "Must've happened toward the end of summer, because she didn't tell me until she was back in school in Virginia. Called me up and laid it on me, straight up. She's pregnant and she's havin' the baby and that's that."

Tom stood still, waiting for him to continue. Donnie just kept swaying from foot to foot, looking at the ground.

"Never saw that kid. Never got to hold her. Not once," Donnie said. "Paid child support, though. More than I was supposed to pay. Every month. Even after Taylor got married and sent me the adoption papers and I signed away my rights."

"I'm sorry, Donnie. I never knew," Tom said as he reached out and put his hand on Donnie's shoulder. "It must have been torture."

"Yeah, it was tough," Donnie said as he bit down on his tongue and wiped absently at his face. "But I'm telling you this because you have your daughter, Tom," he said as he looked directly at Tom. "And you can hold her and hug her and talk to her. That's a blessing, and I would give anything to be able to do that with my daughter."

Tom didn't know what to say. The deepest conversation he had ever had with Donnie had probably been back in middle school, over a certain girl's anatomy. And he had never known that Donnie was a father. He'd never once mentioned it.

"Donnie, I know you're right, and I do appreciate my

situation."

"It's a glass half full thing, Tom. It's easy to overlook what you've got and focus on what you don't have. But you've still got a lot in your life. And good friends around you."

Tom nodded in agreement. He'd heard it before, and he was sure he'd hear it again. Donnie meant well, as did everyone who gave him advice on how to get his life together. In his own way Donnie just wanted to help, and Tom appreciated it. Maybe he did take what he still had for granted. Ironic, he thought, having already lost Sarah.

"Thanks, Donnie, for sharing with me about your daughter." Tom said.

"Sure thing, Tom," he said as he again swiped his hand across his face. "Any time you need me . . . ."

"I'll give you a call," Tom replied.

They shook hands again and Donnie shuffled away, leaving Tom alone on the deck. He went inside and found Jenny, who was tying up garbage bags full of empty bottles.

"You wouldn't believe the conversation I just had with Donnie," he said as he reached into the pastry case and grabbed a wayward cupcake.

"Did he tell you about his daughter?"

Tom looked incredulously at Jenny. "You knew?"

Jenny gave him an all-knowing look and continued cleaning up from the party.

"I'm ready to blow this joint," Tom said as he put a dollop of icing in his mouth. "How about giving me a ride home? It's the least you can do after suckering me into carrying in all of your things."

"Yeah, I'm ready to go, too. It's been a long day, and I've got to get up early to start baking for the weekend onslaught."

Tom helped Jenny lock up and then carried the garbage bags to the recycling bin.

"I can drive if you'd like," Tom said as they approached Jenny's car.

"Not if your life depended on it."

"Why, you don't trust me?"

"Actually, no, I don't. You've had a few too many tonight."

Tom feigned that he was hurt and climbed into the passenger seat. The ride to his house took less than five minutes. Jenny pulled up to the front of the house and he opened the door. "Hey, come in for a minute. I've got something for you," Tom said as he climbed out.

The yard was dark save for a spotlight that shone from the side of the house. They climbed the front stairs and Tom tapped the fixture next to the door and the light came on. "Magic," Tom said to Jenny with a smirk and unlocked the door. He flipped on the switch, threw the keys into a dish by the door and walked in.

Jenny followed behind him and was surprised to see that one whole side of the living room was taken up by moving boxes. She looked quizzically at Tom. "What's all of this?"

"Some of Sarah's stuff," Tom said over his shoulder as he opened the fridge and fetched two beers. He opened a drawer, rifled through it until he found an opener and popped the tops off of the beers. He handed one to Jenny and sat down on a bar stool at the counter. Jenny was still looking at the boxes. "I was looking for something that Emily wanted, then decided it was time to go through everything."

Jenny nodded her understanding but shuddered inwardly. She couldn't imagine how difficult it had been for Tom to go through Sarah's drawers and closets.

Tom picked up an envelope from the counter and held it out to Jenny. "Here, this is for you."

Jenny took the envelope and saw that it had her name written on it. She stared at the writing. It was Sarah's, and it said, simply, "Jenny."

"Tom, what is this?"

"I don't know. It's sealed, and I didn't think I should open it. It's for you."

Jenny turned the envelope over and over in her hands. "I don't know if I want this."

Tom thought a moment before responding, understanding that it could be unnerving to Jenny. "Look, Sarah wrote all of the time. She wrote letters to me and to Emily. She wrote letters to her family and to college friends. When I was going through her desk I found this one with your name on it. I assume Sarah meant to give it to you but never got the chance."

"What should I do with it?"

"Well, if you want to know what it says, I suggest you open it," Tom said as he gulped down the last of his beer and walked back to the refrigerator for another.

"I'm not sure I want to know what it says. I feel kind of strange opening it now."

"So, don't open it. Your choice."

"Don't you want to know what it says?" Jenny asked, incredulous that Tom was acting so nonchalantly.

"The way I see it, whatever that letter says is none of my business. Sarah wrote it to you and it was meant for you, not me."

Jenny thumbed absently at the envelope. "Okay, fine. I'll read it, but not here. Not in front of you."

"Suit yourself."

She looked at Tom again in wonderment. "What's with you, Tom?"

"Nothing. Nothing at all," Tom said as he swiveled back and forth on the bar stool and picked at the paper label on the bottle. "It's just that . . . . You have to understand, Sarah wrote all of the time. She wrote notes and letters and post-its and all manner of things. She was a beautiful writer," he said and then looked away as he thought about Sarah. "The point is that I have no idea what's in that envelope, and it could be that she just was thinking about something she wanted to tell you and wanted get it down on paper before it slipped from her memory. She did that alot when she was sick. Sometimes I'd even wake up in the middle of the night and find her sitting at her desk, writing something. There was no rhyme or reason to it. I think it was just therapeutic for her to put her thoughts down on paper."

"I know about Sarah's writing. I've gotten notes from her in the past. It was one of the beautiful things about her. I just don't understand why I didn't get this while she was alive."

"Maybe she meant to give it to you but never got the chance," Tom said as the suddenness of Sarah's death hung in the air.

"That's a possibility, I guess."

"The reality is that you'll never know why it was sitting in that drawer, but I think you're making more of it than it is. Just read it."

Jenny, still thumbing the envelope, nodded her head. She knew he was right, but something about the envelope in her hands, delivered after Sarah's death, seemed ominous to her. It didn't seem right to her, and it was like a voice from the afterlife. And she was in no rush to read what was lurking inside.

Chapter 21

The bags were finally packed and loaded into the car. Tom and Sarah were set to leave for their vacation in the morning and would simply wake up, jump in the car and hit the road. After placing the last bag in the trunk and going through a mental checklist to determine if he had forgotten anything, Tom came back into the house to find Sarah in the bedroom, asleep on top of the covers. He looked down at her and watched her sleeping, peacefully. He reached out and ran his hand over her head. Finally, after her long ordeal, she was able to sleep through the night.

Tom went back out to the kitchen. He looked around to see if anything needed to be done before they left. The house was quiet, save for the sound of the furnace blowing air through the vents. It was getting colder and colder at night as the season turned toward winter. He grabbed a coat and walked out onto the deck to see the beach lit brilliantly by the full moon, beckoning to him. He walked out along the wooden walkway that led to the beach and at the end walked down the steps and stepped onto the sand. He stopped momentarily and looked up and down the beach, taking in its desolation. Tom had always been fascinated with the feeling he got being on the beach at night with no one else in sight. It was untamed and it was wilderness, and he was the only one there to witness it. It was a powerful feeling of being one with the world, to the exclusion of all others.

He looked back at the house and saw how tiny it looked in comparison to the landscape around it. No storm had ever come through that was powerful enough to wipe out the tiny speck that they claimed as their own against the world. And so it was with their battle against Sarah's cancer. The metaphor had become their reality.

Tom walked down to the shoreline and stood at the edge of the water, watching the grayness of the ocean and the foam of the waves as the water pushed relentlessly towards him. He stood looking out toward the blackness of the infinite view as he had many times over the years. When he was a child he hated leaving the beach at the end of the vacation. Over the years his angst at leaving grew larger, to the point where he felt a dread come over him when he knew he was going to be gone for an extended period of time. This was home, and comfort, and stability, and they were leaving it behind, even if for a relatively short time.

He did his best to push those thoughts from his head, knowing that this time, leaving was necessary. Both he and Sarah needed to put Sandy Cove aside for a time and go elsewhere. They needed to do so for healing, more of mind than body. Sandy Cove wasn't going anywhere. It would be there for them when they returned. And when that time came Tom would again walk out onto the sand at midnight, alone. He'd watch the waves rush towards him and he'd be engulfed by the warmth of the ocean's embrace. He'd be home.

* * *

Tom was fast asleep. Sarah had awakened early, one of those days when you jump up and are instantly wide awake. It was too early to wake Tom and anyway, the fog had rolled in and their departure time was going to have to be pushed back. She'd let him sleep in.

Sarah walked aimlessly around the house, went through her packing checklist more than once and attempted, unsuccessfully, to sit in a chair and read a book. She was antsy and the walls of the house seemed to be closing in on her. She knew that they would be leaving soon enough, but that time seemed like it would never arrive. She realized that despite her past trepidation, she was truly excited for their trip. Tom had been right all along, and she kicked herself for having doubted him. And now she was climbing out of her skin in anticipation of leaving.

Finally, she couldn't take it any more. She decided that she'd go for a walk and try to get out some of her nervous energy. She left a note for Tom on the kitchen counter and went into the bedroom. She leaned over the bed and gave Tom a light kiss on the cheek. He smiled and his eyes opened a slit. She whispered in his ear that she was taking a walk and that he should go back to sleep. He nodded his head and rolled over. She looked down at him with as great a feeling of love as she had ever felt. He had been her rock, through the roughest of times. How had she been so lucky to have found such a wonderful man, she thought to herself. She couldn't wait for the rest of their life together, as Tom put it, to start. Then she turned and walked out of the bedroom, went to the front door, and left for her walk.

* * *

Tom woke with a start. He couldn't remember if it was a dream, but he thought he remembered Sarah saying goodbye to him. He got out of bed and called out to her, hearing no response. He walked out into the house, but Sarah wasn't there. As he walked into the kitchen he saw her note on the counter. It read, simply, "Tom, woke up early and was antsy. Decided to take a walk. Be back soon. Love you, S." Tom read the note a second time and rubbed the sleep out of his eyes. He looked out the kitchen window toward the beach and couldn't see anything farther than five feet away. "Fog," Tom said silently to himself, and went to take a shower so that he'd be ready to leave when Sarah got home.

Tom was drying off when he heard a knock at the front door. He wondered who it could be so early in the morning.

"Be there in a minute," he called out to whomever it was at the door. He hurried to put on some clothes as the knocking continued, unabated.

When he finally opened the door he was surprised to see Gabriel Woodhall, Sandy Cove's chief of police, standing before him.

"Hey, Gabe." What brings you out here so early?" Tom asked as he continued to dry his hair with a towel. Gabe had a strange look on his face, and stood turning his hat over and over in his hands. Tom mistook his silence for a signal that Gabe was waiting to be invited in.

"You want to come inside?" Tom asked and stepped to the side to allow him to enter.

Gabe looked up from his hat and cleared his throat. "Tom, something's happened. You need to come with me."

Tom, confused by Gabe's demeanor, was growing concerned. "Go with you? What's wrong? Did someone break into the store?"

"It's Sarah, Tom," Gabe said, haltingly, his voice growing thick with emotion. "Sarah's dead."

Chapter 22

The Outer Banks is known for its abundant water-fowl, and either by virtue of its location or some innate ornithological migratory sense, Sandy Cove in particular teems with them. The area is replete with abandoned hunting grounds and their accompanying duck blinds, harkening back to a bygone era before the tourists and the development necessary to accommodate them overran the area. As it evolved into a tourist destination the hunters gradually disappeared from Sandy Cove, and age-old hunting grounds became strip plazas that extended into the sound, filled with t-shirt shops, kitschy novelty stores and ice cream stands. Yet many of the duck blinds remained, even though most of the people who happened upon them had no idea what they were or for what purpose they had been used.

Duck blinds are used to provide a camouflaged hunting spot, and are usually simple, rudimentary dugouts covered by branches and leaves. They are the waterfowl hunters' version of ice fishing huts, but provide the utility of allowing the prey to get near without the hunter being detected. Then it is figuratively like shooting ducks in a barrel.

Most of the leftover blinds that littered the area were overgrown and long forgotten. Except for the blind on the Avery Estate. Actually, the Avery Estate was a misnomer, as Old Man Avery considered any land he owned to be the Avery Estate, even if it wasn't contiguous with other Avery land, or even in the same State. And Woody Avery had accumulated a lot of land. Still, even though the "Estate" wasn't a unified piece of land, the locals had bought into the nomenclature, and had come to refer to all Avery land as such.

The Avery duck blind was not really a duck blind, in the purest sense or form. It was not small nor did it melt into the landscape as part of the scenery. It was actually the size of a small house, with amenities. Heat and air conditioning, running water, and of late, satellite television made a mockery of the concept upon which a hunter would utilize a blind: to become one with the scenery. Old Man Avery had been a hunter but had no yearning to rough it. He felt he had earned the right to hunt without the hassle and hardship of actually doing it while weathering the elements.

The structure began in the near-shore grasses and extended over the water, the entire sound-side of the house taken up by massive panes of sliding glass. When he felt like hunting, Old Man Avery would place his favorite easy chair in the middle of the room facing outward, push open the glass sliders and sit looking out to the sound through the open wall, at times shooting without leaving his seat.

LenDale Avery couldn't remember his father ever bagging a duck, or any other bird, for that matter. He just remembered playing on the floor with his toys while his father sat and watched the birds fly by, and heeding his father's warning to "Cover your ears, boy" whenever the time came to shoot.

When the wall of the hut was open it was like being one with nature, and that fact was not mutually exclusive to the human part of the equation. One day as Woody Avery dozed in his easy chair with LenDale playing nearby, a mother and four of her young ducklings flew in and landed at Woody's feet. LenDale froze as he looked up from his toys, mesmerized by the ducks as they waddled around the room and acclimated themselves. They were harmless, save for the droppings they left scattered around the room. LenDale couldn't remember how long the ducks were there or the exact details of what happened, but his best recollection was that his father, who was snoring loudly, let out a particularly loud honk and the ducks honked back. Woody, jarred awake from his sleep, let out a yelp as he instinctively jumped up on the chair, fumbling with his shotgun as his brain tried to make sense of the chaos of the noise and the flapping wings and the flying feathers. He was so startled by the noise and the sight of the ducks in front of him that he almost shot his own feet as he wildly shot the gun at the squawking birds. The birds managed to get away unharmed, leaving behind floating feathers, smoke and droppings, as well as a confused man and a bemused young boy. Woody Avery had managed to avoid his feet, and he missed the birds, but to this day there was still buckshot embedded in the wooden flooring.

Though their house was a mansion and offered every possible amenity, LenDale was more comfortable in the duck blind located a couple of miles to the north. After his father died, LenDale, who had never been fond of hunting, developed an affinity for sitting in the easy chair in the middle of the room with the glass wall open, as he recalled his father doing. He enjoyed watching the birds flying by and the insects darting about, listening to the sounds of the water and of the outdoors. He watched the glimmering sunsets and the twilight of sunrise with the mist hovering over the water. Although his father had cleared some of the land for a road and a carport, LenDale almost never drove to the hut. More often he would be seen walking along the side of the road on his way to or coming back from the blind, usually late at night or early in the morning. He knew that people found it odd, but if that's what defined him as being eccentric, then so be it. He liked what he liked and he did what he wanted to do.

Of late, though, he had been spending less time at the

blind. His ever-existent bad luck had struck him as a consequence of him being there, and since that time he couldn't shake the feeling that the place was jinxed, just as he was.

He was sitting in the easy chair in the blind, looking out at the whitecaps on the choppy water. The wind was blowing at a good clip, causing a maelstrom of swirling papers around him, to which he was oblivious. He was several layers deep in thought about his life and the events to which he had been an unfortunate participant. A Sad Sack, as his father used to say.

LenDale's bad luck seemed to always hit at the time that was least likely. Until the most recent incident he had never spent time analyzing the "when's" of his misfortune, only the "why's." He had never thought about the fact that he was ignoring half of the equation: being in the wrong place (why) at the wrong time (when). It never occurred to him that his proclivity to wander when he shouldn't, at times that others wouldn't, was when his luck tended to fail him.

Lately, though, he had given more thought to the proposition, and now it seemed so obvious as to be equally unlikely to be true. More often than not it was his fault that he was in the wrong place at the wrong time. And this latest, and worst, spate of misfortune had been the tipping point, the catalyst to change. Why was he walking by the side of the road that day, at that early hour? If he had been in bed in his home like the rest of the world that morning, he wouldn't have been stricken by another instance of bad luck.

He had gone over and over it in his head. He had woken up hung-over, and for the life of him he couldn't remember whole swaths of the night before. He knew he had ended up at his favorite bar, Crabby Al's, from the credit card receipt he found in his pocket later that morning. Apparently, he had quenched his drunk-munchies sometime before 2:00 a.m.—his deduction from another receipt, this one from the 24/7 gas station/minimart, at which he had no reason to stop other than for food, because he wasn't driving that night. He didn't remember hitching a ride with anyone, either. If he had walked all the way back from the 24/7 he figured that he would have gotten to the blind at around 2:45, given that he was probably not power walking and may have had to stop once or twice to either relieve himself or to throw up. A likely scenario, and one that brought to his mind an ironic twist on the investment mantra that past results do not predict future events. In his experience, yes, they do.

He figured that he arrived at 2:45, passed out at 3:00, and was up and walking back to his house at 6:45. Of all days, and given his condition, he would never be able to figure out how or why he awoke so early, or how that fateful, unknowing decision to get out of bed and walk back to his house would change his life, forever.

He remembered that the morning air had been cool and that a mist hung over the water. The water was still and seemed to melt into the air above it, resembling not so much a fog as a sheer curtain of water hanging above the water. It was the kind of morning that foretold of a dreary, rainy day to come, when in fact as the temperature came up the mist would eventually rise to reveal a perfect, cloudless day. He had made note of it as he looked out of the window wall before leaving, wondering if he was going to get caught in a downpour on the way home.

He had been walking for about twenty minutes and was almost home when he noticed a solitary bird flying about in a weird way, as if it was going crazy. The bird would fly ten feet one way and back the other way, and LenDale was mesmerized by the movement, which seemed to float inexplicably in coordination with his walking.

It was a pretty bird, a crow, with raven blue-black feathers. It was regal, elegant even. Suddenly it flew away and LenDale watched as the bird grew smaller and smaller before being swallowed by the mist, only to reappear and come screeching back towards him. The bird's actions were frightening LenDale and he began to instinctively cower backwards when the bird tilted its body, caught the wind and landed gracefully in a tree about twenty feet in front of him. It began squawking loudly, an awful shrieking that was as discomforting to LenDale as the spastic flying. It was only then that he noticed what appeared to be a pile of clothes on the berm of the road.

As he walked toward the bird and whatever was on the side of the road, the bird continued to squawk its kaw k-kaw, but now it was also flapping its wings as well. It reminded him of the herons he watched from the duck blind warding off potential threats. He walked on and drew closer to the bird, his eyes glued to its crazy, spasmic gyrations. He was almost upon it now, and the bird abruptly stopped its squawks, but continued to move its wings in a strange way. It was at that moment that a dread came over LenDale, and he knew, without even turning to look, that the pile of clothes by the side of the road, wasn't, in fact, a pile of clothes.

In hindsight, he wished it had just been someone's overcoat flung out of a car window or perhaps laundry from one of the ever-present linen trucks that trolled back and forth from the restaurants and the inns each day, laden with table cloths and napkins, sheets and pillowcases. Anything but a person, lying there by the side of the road. As if asleep. It didn't make sense to LenDale. His eyes were seeing the image but it wasn't registering in his brain. The bird and the squawking and the movement of the wings were now foreign to LenDale, blocked from his consciousness as he struggled to comprehend the horror of what his eyes were viewing.

She looked beautiful. Peaceful and beautiful, lying on her side with her back to the road. He remembered that he had kept wondering why she had decided to lie down there, in that particular spot, to take a nap.

Initially, the reality of the scene just could not break through his consciousness. Then something clicked within his brain and the horror hit him full bore: it was Sarah Ralston lying at his feet, and she wasn't taking a nap. He knelt down and tentatively touched her, almost poking her. No response. He shook her by the shoulder, moving her torso side to side three times, hard enough to wake someone. Again, no response. He was becoming frantic and was on the verge of hysteria. He leaned over and put his ear to her nose and mouth, something he had seen done on a crime scene television show once. He wasn't sure if he was supposed to hear something or if he would feel the wind of her breathing, but he neither heard nor felt anything. A small whimper escaped his lips as he scanned up and down the road for help, to no avail. He was alone, and Sarah wasn't moving, wasn't breathing. He thought the impossible: she might be dead.

LenDale didn't know what he should do. Should he go get help or should he stay and wait for a car to drive by? Should he leave her where he found her or should he move her? A million thoughts collided in his head in a silent cacophony that made him grab the sides of his face like a child. What should he do? WHAT SHOULD HE DO?! He felt as though he was losing control of himself—of reality—when something deep inside of him took over. He kneeled down and gathered Sarah in his arms, cradling her against his chest like a baby, and he began walking. Walking toward nothing. He didn't think about where he was taking her, only that he couldn't just stand over her and do nothing, couldn't leave her lying there while he sought out help. He couldn't believe how light she was in his arms. Light as a feather. He made the mistake of looking down at her once, and the sight of her head twisted away at an abnormal angle caused his stomach to seize and contract.

So caught up in the surrealism of the moment, he had

no recollection of how long he was walking, and he only vaguely recalled when the truck screeched to a stop shortly after passing him, and of the driver jumping out and racing around to come to LenDale's aid. He said nothing as the driver took Sarah from his arms and placed her in the back seat of the cab, only mumbling something incoherent and pointing back toward the direction where he had found her by the side of the road. The driver had to help him into the cab of the truck and close the door for him.

The ride to the hospital was a jumble of random memories. He was holding her from falling off the seat as they sped around the curves in the road that wound through Sandy Cove. He wouldn't—couldn't—look down at her. They drove in horrified silence the entire way, and when they finally reached the emergency room, the driver lifted Sarah's body out of the truck while LenDale sat impassively, staring blankly ahead. It wasn't until one of the ER nurses pulled him out of the truck that he snapped out of it and related what had happened. But of course what he had seen didn't matter. She was already gone and the doctors and nurses and technicians couldn't do anything for her.

He knew at once that no one would believe him. No one who knew him would believe that he walked innocently up to a body lying on the side of the road. A body that was there before he arrived. Sarah Ralston, of all people. The one person who had gone out of her way to be inclusive with him. Dead on arrival.

He had a reputation, mostly undeserved, for being a troublemaker. A more accurate characterization: he was the type of person whom trouble tended to find at every possible interlude. In this instance, he literally walked up to the trouble that awaited him as he walked home. Now people whispered as he approached and turned away from him. The worst of the gossips spread the word that he had killed Sarah and made up the whole by-the-side-of-the-road story. And worse.

Chapter 22

It took days for the doctors to finally determine what had killed her. Pulmonary embolism. A result of the chemo or the radiation or a combination of both. Something just broke loose, and like that, she was gone. Much to the surprise of almost everyone—the hospital staff, the police, the townspeople of Sandy Cove—the truth was that LenDale had had nothing to do with Sarah Ralston's death. He really had just stumbled upon her. Just a stroke of bad luck.

Chapter 23

J enny arrived at work early and dove into making the day's allotment of croissants, tarts and pastries. She knew that a month down the road she would yearn for a day like today, when she could sleep a little later and wouldn't have to double or triple her output, but she was exhausted, nonetheless.

When she went off to school and worked in New York, she had never considered that one day she'd be back in Sandy Cove elbow-deep in flour and confectioner's sugar. Like most people, she had awakened at mid-life wondering how she had ended up doing what she was doing, and lamenting all of the things that she had failed to do during her life.

Still, running the store with Sam had turned out to be a good fit for both of them. They worked hard but in return got to see the direct benefit of their hard work. They didn't have to punch a clock or answer to higher-ups, but they bore the weight of knowing that if they didn't do what needed to be done, down to the smallest menial task, no one else was there to do so. Every successful small business owner knew and lived this principle, and Jenny winced inwardly every time someone commented on how lucky they were to own their own business and make their own hours. Jenny often thought that those people would change their tune if just once they had to get up at three in the morning to start baking, or if they had to work late balancing the books.

Sam's summer trip was going to be hard. With him gone she would have to do both of their jobs, which meant getting up that much earlier, staying that much later, and not have anyone to fall back on if she was sick or just needed a break. She was happy to let him get away, and he promised her that she could do the same next year, but they both knew she couldn't take an extended trip, or any trip, for that matter. Without her, there were no pastries, no cakes, none of the things that brought the customers in, and in their business, once people stopped coming, it was hard to get them to come back again.

After finally finishing loading the displays with the fruits of her hard labor, she went onto the deck and sat down with a cup of coffee and a croissant. The sun was rising steadily into the blue sky and she turned her face up to it to gather in its warmth. She had put in the equivalent of a days' work and it wasn't yet noon.

Hard as she had tried to put aside Sarah's letter by diving into her work, now that she had a free moment, her thoughts went back it. She hadn't opened the envelope yet, and despite Tom's entreaty for her to just read it, she hadn't been able to do so. It still sat on her kitchen table, to her mind's thinking calling out to her much like Poe's Telltale-Heart, beating and beating a louder drumbeat as she fretted about it.

Jenny knew Sarah well, and nothing in Sarah's life occurred by happenstance or as a result of a lack of foresight. Sarah was methodical and organized. Jenny knew that if Sarah had wanted her to have the letter, she would have given it to her, rather than stick it in a drawer. And Tom seemed oblivious to what seemed obvious to Jenny—that Sarah hadn't meant to give her the letter. Not while she was alive. That is what unnerved Jenny and gave her pause when Tom handed it to her.

Jenny took a last bite of the croissant, washed it down

with a sip of her coffee and stood to go back inside to finish cleaning up for the day. Enough was enough, she thought. She would just open the letter, and whatever Sarah had written to her, she'd deal with it.

* * *

Tom was in the back of the shop rearranging his inventory when he heard the door chime jingle. "Be out in a second," he called out as he lifted a box into place and stood back to view the result of his efforts. This was the first year that he had to handle all of the chores in the store and he spent more time than he'd anticipated getting the displays ready, leaving the storeroom a mess. He was far from being done but had made some progress. He figured that another afternoon or so would get the job done.

He came out from the back room and pushed through a curtain hanging from the doorframe. He looked around the shop and initially thought he must have imagined the chime ringing because he didn't see anyone. Then, in the easy chair that was set into the far corner of the shop he saw some movement, and felt an immediate pang of regret as he realized that the person sitting in the chair was LenDale Avery. LenDale rose to greet Tom and noticed the change in Tom's expression from happy and expectant to . . . something different. Tom's reaction to seeing him was not abnormal in LenDale's experience, and he shrugged it off and walked over to Tom.

"Hey, Tom," LenDale said as he held out his hand.

"Hi, LenDale," Tom responded and shook hands. He realized that his expression betrayed his emotions and quickly attempted to deflect LenDale's attention. "I've meant to call you for a while now."

"Yeah, I've meant to stop by to see you for a while, too."

No matter how hard he tried to be someone else, and despite having all of the resources at his disposal due to his wealth, LenDale just had the type of body language that made him come off as a sad sort. It hung over him like a black cloud.

"How've you been lately?" Tom asked.

LenDale did his normal half-hunched over, sad sack routine. "I've been doing okay, I guess," LenDale said with a shrug of his shoulders.

Tom looked LenDale over and thought that he didn't look like he was doing well. He noticed upon examination that LenDale was dirty. His clothes looked like they hadn't been washed for some time, and from the stubble on his chin it appeared that he hadn't shaved in a couple of days. Tom felt sorry for him, even more than he had in the past. Word had filtered back to Tom that LenDale had been asking about him. He knew why LenDale wanted to talk to him, but LenDale had a way of being inappropriate, of saying the wrong thing to the wrong person at the wrong time. Tom knew he had been selfish to avoid him, but what LenDale knew and wanted to discuss was not something that Tom wanted to hear. They stood at arms length, neither of them speaking, in an uncomfortable silence, when LenDale's chin began to quiver.

"It wasn't my fault, Tom," LenDale blurted out, his voice cracking.

Tom was shocked. Of all of the possible things that he thought LenDale might have wanted to say to him, an apology was the last that he had considered, and he realized that LenDale had been torturing himself, thinking that Tom was blaming him for Sarah's death.

"Of course it wasn't your fault," Tom said, as he reached out and put a steadying hand on LenDale's shoulder. "It was no one's fault, LenDale. It was . . . ." Tom paused as he attempted to come up with an apropos designation of what had happened to Sarah. What had caused her to be here one minute and gone the next, for no reason other than a microscopic speck letting loose inside her body. "It was fate, " Tom finally said. "I've never believed in fate, but it's the only thing by my way of thinking that reconciles what happened."

LenDale looked forlornly at Tom. "She looked like an angel, lying there on the side of the road," LenDale said, catching Tom off-guard. This was the conversation that Tom had done his best to avoid. He didn't want to know the details of that morning. He would not be any better off knowing those details. But LenDale was there and seemed bent on telling him all of them.

"Stop. Please stop," Tom said. "I don't want to hear about this."

"I'm sorry, Tom. I didn't come here meaning to upset you." LenDale seemed to shrink in size before Tom as he turned toward the door to leave.

LenDale was feeling sorry for himself in the self-deprecating way that had always rubbed people the wrong way. Tom knew that if he let him leave, LenDale would wallow in self-pity. Tom reached out, grabbed his arm and stopped him. "You don't have to rush out of here. I knew you had something you wanted to tell me. I'm just not ready to hear it yet."

"I understand," LenDale nodded. "I just, well, I think I need to talk to somebody about it, and there's no one else besides you that can truly understand. Sarah links us."

"Aren't I the lucky one," Tom thought to himself. LenDale was harmless, but annoying. Now, every time they ran into each other he could expect to have LenDale talk about the worst day of Tom's life.

"I didn't believe in fate, either," LenDale said as he played absentmindedly with a miniature wind chime on the checkout counter. "But I believe in it now. I mean, how else can you explain that it would be me walking on that road on that morning and at that specific time? A couple of minutes earlier I'd have missed her, a couple of minutes later someone else probably would have found her."

Tom looked at LenDale in astonishment. His trepidation seemed to have been lost on LenDale.

"I see that as a good thing, though, in a strange way," LenDale continued matter-of-factly.

"A good thing? How was it a good thing?" Tom asked.

"Well here's the thing. I think if I hadn't been there to find her, I wouldn't have her watching over me now."

Tom gave him a double take, but LenDale was dead serious. "Oh, come on, LenDale. Enough of this nonsense."

"I don't mean as in literally, Tom. I mean as in she's changed my karma. I've given this a lot of thought, and I've noticed that since I found Sarah lying there, everything has gotten better in my life. Call it fate, karma, whatever. Tom, you know me well enough to know that bad things tend to happen to me."

Tom's lack of a response was confirmation of LenDale's statement.

"Well, since that day, things seem to have turned around for me," LenDale continued. At first I thought I must be imagining it. But I wasn't. I started to notice that whenever I figured something was going to go wrong for me, it didn't. When I've had to rely on someone, they actually came through for me. I can't put my finger on it, exactly, but things in my life have really changed for the better. How do you explain that?" For once LenDale seemed to actually straighten up and stand tall as he spoke to Tom.

"I can't," Tom said, wanting the conversation to be over more than ever. "Look, I hear what you're saying, but let's be realistic. Maybe your luck has just changed. It doesn't have to be tied to Sarah."

"So, you don't want to believe it's Sarah looking over me?"

This conversation is nonsensical, Tom thought. But he felt a certain obligation to appease LenDale, given everything he had been through. "I didn't say that. I'm just not a believer in the paranormal."

"Well, neither am I, Tom. I mean, I never have been in the past. It's not like I'm talking about signs from above. It's more subtle than that." LenDale thought for a minute before continuing. "For example, I was over at the Sunset Lodge for happy hour the other night and they did a drawing. You know, one of those you-have-to-be-present things that they do every so often. And I won. Do you know how many times I've ever won something like that?"

Tom shook his head.

"Never," LenDale said, answering his own question. "Never that drawing, never any drawing. Or contest. Or anything. Ever."

Tom noticed that LenDale had developed a tick, a double movement of his eyelids which seemed to get more pronounced as he got more excited. This lent to an even stranger affect than was normal for him. Tom again felt sorry for LenDale. Only he could turn having better luck into a negative thing.

"Let me ask you this," LenDale said, his eyelids slapping down forcefully. It was like a stammer, and made Tom wonder if LenDale had been a stutterer as a child. "Do you know how they say that people carry a certain electrical charge—an energy—that science can't explain? Well here's what I think, and you can tell me if you think I'm crazy. That's okay with me." Again, the eyelids slapped down.

"Go ahead. I'm listening," Tom said, trying to not focus on LenDale's eye movements.

"I think that Sarah was one of the nicest, sweetest women I've ever met. She was always kind to me, when most people weren't. And up until the very end, she was lucky. The two of you had a nice life together."

Where this was leading, Tom had no idea, but he was starting to get concerned that maybe LenDale had suffered a break from reality.

LenDale continued, unabated. "Well, I think it was like in the movies, when two people switch bodies. It happened when I found her lying there by the side of the road. I came along right at the time that this energy was leaving Sarah, and somehow, now I've got it. And ever since that moment my life's been changed."

LenDale finished abruptly and the room was silent. Tom didn't know if LenDale was serious or if he was just looking for sympathy, but while he had previously carried an aura of only sadness with him, now he brought a certain psychotic element along with it.

Rather than dismissing him, Tom played along. He was willing to give LenDale a respectful audience given what he had been through. "Have you ever considered that maybe things are better in your life because you've made them better? Or because your attitude changed as a result of having gone through the trauma of finding Sarah?" Tom asked, providing a rational alternative to LenDale's conclusions.

As LenDale contemplated Tom's suggestions his countenance seemed to change and he appeared less sure of himself, his shoulders slumping little by little as Tom's reasoning worked its way through his brain. Tom thought that he resembled a balloon, slowly deflating from a pinprick hole. He could understand if LenDale was looking for an explanation, for some reconciliation of what he saw as a change in his life. LenDale's personality had always been filled with negativity. He was a walking example of Murphy's Law. But the person who suffers from a trauma is usually the last to realize it or to notice the changes caused by it. The fallout from trauma is a stealthy thing.

Tom was now well aware of the trauma he suffered in losing Sarah, and looking back on the past months he realized how much it had altered his life. It was like climbing out of a deep hole to get back to where he had been. Yet he was also aware of how profoundly he was changed as a result of that experience. He was not the same person he had been before Sarah died. That person had, in some real ways, died along with Sarah. And so it was for LenDale, as he was apparently deeply affected by the circumstances of Sarah's death.

He was certain that he had put an end to LenDale's nonsensical thoughts and was about to suggest that they leave, when LenDale asked a question that rocked Tom to the core. Something completely out of left field. Something that LenDale had no way of knowing. Something of which only one person—Sarah—could possibly know the significance.

"Hey, Tom—why haven't you been able to go on the beach?" LenDale asked robotically and without emotion, his eyelids snapping forcibly open and shut. And a wave of nausea flooded over Tom.

Chapter 24

Jenny's house was dark save for the flickering light of candles glowing in the bathroom. She wasn't much for baths, maybe filling up the tub once or twice a year when she was really stressed or really relaxed. Tonight she felt oddly a little of both. For the other three hundred and sixty-odd days a year the tub sat unused except for the clothes that she shedded while half asleep, morning or night, which ended up piling up inside the tub or draped over its side.

It was a standalone tub with claw feet of brushed silver. She'd found it at an estate auction a couple of years earlier. It had been in dire need of a scrubbing and some tender loving care, but beneath the dust and stains was a thing of beauty. She had always had an eye for such things. The tub was solid cast iron and weighed a ton. Sam had taken one look at it and walked out, so she hired a local crew to do the heavy lifting. It had taken three men and a lot of sweat to get it up the stairs and into the bathroom. Once it was in place they joked that the house would fall down around it before the tub would be moved out of its spot.

The only bad thing about the tub, as she found out, to her embarrassment, was her difficulty getting out of it. Getting in was a breeze, one foot in, then the other, then sit down and lean back. The parabolic shape fit her perfectly and reminded her of the gilded baths in European castles or at the Biltmore Estate. Getting out was another thing, altogether. Either her body wasn't meant for its shape or vice versa, but one night she just couldn't lift herself out. In hindsight it was an issue of leverage, and her lack of it. She tried every which way to climb or lift herself out, from her back, from her stomach, hands along the sides, feet over the sides. Nothing worked. Eventually she turned over onto her stomach and crawled her way high enough at the foot end of the tub to be able to throw one of her legs over the side and roll onto the floor. She had lain wet and naked on the tile floor laughing hysterically at herself, but the next day she awakened to a sore back and a welt that ran the entire length of her inner thigh. She was so mortified at herself that she wore pants for the entire three weeks it took for the black and blue mark to fade.

When she bought the tub she'd imagined herself using it all of the time, images playing in her mind of peaceful nights with a glass of wine and a bunch of candles giving the room a golden glow. Although she hadn't used the tub as much as she'd envisioned, that fact didn't take away from her enjoyment when she found herself lying back with the water lapping over her. Tonight she was half way through a bottle of Cabernet and was sitting in warm bliss watching the shadows of the candles play like a movie upon the bathroom walls.

She was a little drunk and was reminiscing, thinking about when she was a little girl and her mother would come in every night as she bathed, running a comb through her long hair, working through the tangles until it was perfectly straight and silky smooth. It was still hard for Jenny to believe that her mom was gone. Every once in a while the reality of her absence struck her again, and she felt the raw ache of loss in her belly anew.

Jenny remembered her mother as a kind and caring woman who was supportive and accepting of the choices Jenny made in her life, but who also wasn't afraid to tell her things as they were and to give constructive advice. Unlike her father, her mother was thrilled when Jenny decided to leave to go to school in New York. She lived the adventure and the excitement vicariously through Jenny, and would listen intently to Jenny's stories whenever she'd call or travel home on a break. When she was young Jenny had never realized that her mother was interested in anything outside of Sandy Cove, having spent her whole life there. But her mother grew up in a different time, when expectations for young Southern women had more to do with getting married and having children than going off to far flung places for an education and in search of an exciting life. Jenny's experiences—the ones that she chose to share—were her mother's, as well, even if her mother never set foot in Manhattan, never sat through a college lecture, never walked on the paths of Central Park and never shopped on Fifth Avenue.

As she got older Jenny came to realize that she understood her mother more and herself less. Her mother had been satisfied with her station in life and seemed to have come to terms with it at a young age, although she never really had a choice in the matter. Her parents married almost as soon as they graduated from high school and Jenny was on the way not long thereafter. Out of necessity her father worked any job he could land, two and three at a time, in order to support his fledgling family. It was a different world than today. They didn't get any help from their families and didn't ever ask for it. They understood that they were responsible to make their lives work, whether that meant that they rarely saw each other or that they would be required to fill the then-traditional roles of provider and caretaker.

Eventually her father scraped up enough money to buy the local general store and he put both her and Sam to work stocking shelves and sweeping floors. This was their norm, the only life they knew, and when their father told them to do something they did it, no questions asked and no complaints accepted. The shelves and aisles became their playground, working at the cash register versus in the stockroom their battleground. Their existence was typical of small business owners' of that era, descendent of the country's agrarian origin, with the whole family pitching in and doing their part.

Jenny's memories of her childhood were so intermingled with her memories of working in the store that she could barely recall any youthful experience outside of it. And now she was running her own business out of the same building. Not that she had any regrets. She was happy—had been happy since she returned to the security and safety of the only real home she had ever known.

Her parents had both died young, her father of a heart attack at fifty-two and her mother of complications from smoking a few years later, both victims of the excesses of their era. Jenny and Sam considered closing the shop and moving away, but Jenny's experience in New York tempered any thoughts she may have had about leaving, and Sam had never felt the pull of greener pastures. Still, Jenny felt an emptiness settle in when her mother died, and all of the self-assuredness and confidence of her youth had given way to worry and doubt—and loneliness.

She took a sip of wine and put the glass back on the table by the side of the tub, then reached for a washcloth to wipe the perspiration off of her face. She knew the wine/bath combination wasn't a good one for her and that she would feel it in the morning, but right now she felt good and loose and relaxed. She leaned back and sank down in the tub, letting the water lap over the undulations of her body. It was warm and womb-like. Her cell phone rang out from the bedroom but she wasn't ready to get out of the tub. Whoever it is will leave a message, she thought, then went back to thinking about Sarah's letter and what she needed to do as a result of it. Or did she need to do anything, she wondered.

After she finally decided that she should open the envelope, she'd rushed home and tore it open, taking in the flowing handwriting like a starved animal. When she'd finished the letter she read it again, and again still. Sarah had been a very perceptive woman—and apparently had some type of premonition that her luck at beating back the cancer was soon to be undone. Was it a preternatural feeling or a dark foreboding borne from her recent brush, Jenny wondered. Sarah had always been so optimistic and upbeat. That she had become so fatalistic was a fact that she had hidden well, even from Tom, apparently. He had certainly never mentioned anything about it to Jenny.

Ultimate, Sarah's letter didn't reveal any deep, dark secret, didn't provide any revelations and, in fact, didn't reveal anything to Jenny other than the fact that Sarah was observant and perceptive and knew her husband and Jenny well. It was simple and it was direct:

Jenny,

I feel that I should write this letter to you, despite my recent good news. I leave this knowing that in my absence, Tom will give it to you.

You have been such a special friend to me, and to Tom, of course, and for this I thank you with all of my heart. At this point I can't imagine our lives apart, but nature will eventually take its course. I wouldn't be so presumptuous as to ask you to do anything for me once I am gone, but I do want to tell you something that you may not have allowed yourself to acknowledge for a long time, for obvious reasons.

As you know Tom is a wonderful person, father and

spouse. He was my dream come true from the day I met him. My marriage has been a fairytale, yet, the only bad thing, the one negative, is that I am not and could never be Tom's true love. That would be you, and despite both of you burying your feelings for each other for all of these years, at times I could plainly see it. Always respectful and at a distance, but those feelings are alive, if only under the surface.

So, what I want to ask of you is not something you can do for me but something you can do for yourself and for Tom: follow your heart. Let go of whatever long ago-expired pact the two of you made as children to just be friends and follow your heart. Hopefully it will lead you to each other, and then you will find the happiness together that was meant to be since you were children. Follow your heart, Jenny, to the man whom I promise will treat you with respect and give you the life you have always deserved. Follow your heart to my beloved Tom, so that he can be happy and at peace in a life shared with you.

With all of my love

Sarah

Jenny reached over the edge of the tub for the wineglass and sipped some more of the Cabernet. It was strong and full-bodied and it hit her like a sledgehammer with every sip. As far as people went, Sarah was as close to perfect as anyone Jenny had ever known. And now she had set the bar even higher. She had perceived something that Jenny didn't even realize was there. Jenny had thought that whatever teenage crush she may have had for Tom was water under the bridge, and long forgotten. But Sarah had sensed something there, and not just with her, but with Tom as well. *"So now what do I do?"* Jenny thought as her cell phone chimed again. Jenny turned and looked quizzically into the bedroom toward the sound of the ringtone. Once late in the evening could be ignored. Twice in short succession meant something was up. Jenny jumped at the repeated sound of the ringtone and did her maneuvering to exit the tub, slopping water over the side of the tub and onto the tile as she ran naked into the bedroom to retrieve the phone. She grabbed it and instinctively glanced around the room to make sure the blinds were down and no one could see her from the outside. She looked at the screen on the phone but didn't recognize the number.

"Hello?" she said as she began to walk back to the bathroom, shivering slightly as the air hit her.

"Jenny?" A young voice she couldn't place.

"Yes?"

"This is Bobby. Emily's . . . friend."

Jenny stopped walking and caught her breath. "Oh, hello. Hi there. Sorry I didn't recognize your voice. Is everything okay? Is Emily alright?"

"Yes, of course. Everything is fine. Just fine." Jenny heard a muffled voice and a laugh in the background. Water was pooling at Jenny's feet and she was confused by the call.

"So, not to sound rude, but what's going on? Why are you calling?"

"Because Emily won't," he said, as he semi-giggled into the phone. It sounded like he'd been drinking.

"Look, I was in the middle of something . . . "

"Wait. Hold on. Let me get Emily." Again the laughter and giggling in the background.

"I'm losing my patience," Jenny said to no one as she

waited for him to hand the phone over.

Finally, she heard Emily on the phone, and before she could say anything further Emily blurted out, "Jenny, we're engaged!" and Jenny could hear the unadulterated excitement in her voice.

Jenny was caught so off-guard that she couldn't say anything at first as she attempted to process the good news, then tears welled up in her eyes. Emily was the closest thing she had to a daughter, and the wine, the letter and the bath were conspiring against her. "Oh, my," was all she could manage to say through the tears which were now running down her cheeks, and she thought about how ridiculous she looked standing naked in a pool of water on the floor, crying hysterically.

"She's crying," she heard Emily say to Bobby under her breath.

Jenny rushed toward the bathroom for a towel and a tissue. "Emily! My God—what wonderful news!" Jenny gushed into the phone as she dabbed at her eyes with the tissue. "I'm so happy for you. Your father must be thrilled."

"Well, that's one of the reasons why I called," Emily said, hesitatingly. "I haven't told him yet."

Jenny instantly became still. "You haven't told him? Why not, honey? Is something wrong?"

"Don't sound so worried. Nothing's wrong. I just want to tell him in person, and I want it to be at the proper moment, which is why I called you. I want you to help me surprise him. Unless you don't think it's a good idea."

"Not at all! I think it's a wonderful idea and I'd be happy to help you. What did you have in mind?"

"Bobby and I are going to drive down next weekend and surprise him. I just need you to make sure that he's with you and not away on some antique goose chase."

"A whole week? You want me to keep my mouth shut for a whole week? Your father will kill me once you tell him."

"He'll do nothing of the sort. Bobby and I agreed that we want to do this the right way, in person. Dad will understand. We just need you to make sure that he's in the shop next Friday at around 6:00. Is that possible?"

Jenny was already running the excuses she would make to Tom around in her head. "Even if it's not, I'll make it work."

"Great. Now for the other thing I needed to ask you— I'm going to need some help with the wedding, since Mom's not around. Will you help me plan it?"

Jenny's eyes welled up again and for a minute she couldn't manage to speak. The tears came out of happiness for the honor of being asked to help and of sadness for Emily and Sarah. A daughter deprived of her mother at the most special time of her life, a mother deprived of sharing that moment with her daughter. "Of course, I will, honey." she managed to say through the tears. "I'd be honored."

* * *

The summer after their sophomore year in high school was a turning point for Jenny and Tom. They were no longer the children who played in the surf and built sandcastles together. Age and maturity and hormones had conspired to change them, and as well, their relationship. That summer the boys were hanging out with the boys and the girls with the girls, and Jenny and Tom found themselves making excuses to their friends whenever they were caught spending time together. Yet, even as they toiled with the intricacies of becoming young adults, they still retained a certain childishness, and still liked to spend time together doing the things that they had done together, summer after summer.

Jenny's summer life was typical of a local kid in a re-sort town. She didn't come from means and didn't have the luxury of lazing around during the summer on vacation. Her summers were for working and earning money for the coming year.

That summer Jenny was working in the store more days than in the past, getting in as many hours as she could to save up for a trip to New York that she had been dreaming of taking. She had always been enamored of New York City and fantasized about the excitement that the sights and sounds and crowds offered. Her parents didn't understand where her fascination with city life had originated or why, but figured that it was an outlet she needed from Sandy Cove's slow pace. They hadn't agreed to allow her to go on the trip, but they had challenged her to earn the money to pay for it, thinking that she would fall short or give up the idea. To their chagrin, she took them up on the challenge and was well on her way to earning enough money to make the trip.

She didn't take many days off that summer, but one day in August she and Tom made plans to spend a day fishing on the Kitty Hawk Pier. As it stands today the Kitty Hawk Pier is only a fragment of the great pier that existed when Jenny and Tom were children. The pier was iconic in the area, jutting out far over the water, hundreds of feet from the shoreline, seemingly a testament of man's triumph over nature. Yet over the years, storms and age and neglect had decimated it, so much so that one had to wonder whether or not it was entirely safe, although that didn't seem to deter the fishermen who regularly cast their lines over its edges. It was known to be a prime fishing spot, the place to regularly catch large striped bass, king mackerel and bluefish. The pier was mostly destroyed after Hurricane Isabel blew through the area in 2003, and only the portion nearest the shore that remained standing was restored. The only remnants of the great pier that had extended much farther over the ocean were two wooden pilings still sticking out of the water far from the end of the current pier, like two pick-up sticks stuck haphazardly into the water.

Tom was not a fisherman, but once or twice a summer he would borrow a pole and grab a bucket and he and Jenny would spend the day in Kitty Hawk fishing from the rickety pier. In contrast, Jenny had grown up on the water and had been fishing since she was able to hold a pole. When they were younger she would help Tom, and she taught him how to bait the hook, how to cast the line and how to lure the fish to take the bait. Over the years she became more subtle in offering help as Tom became more stubborn and less willing to accept advice, even though his skills never seemed to improve.

They didn't know it at the time but their outing on this particular day in August would be their last day spent together fishing from the pier. The next summer Tom's parents decided to tour Northeastern schools and spend time on the New England coast, and college loomed on the horizon. They would never again trudge together down the beach road to the pier, would never again sit on overturned paint cans having a conversation or saying nothing at all, eating sandwiches, drinking orange crushes and sucking on frozen popsicles bought from the vending machine next to the pier office. On this day, however, they weren't thinking about the future. They were just happy being kids, away from the judgmental and questioning glances of their friends, taking in the blue sky and the sun, the ocean and the surf.

They had settled in, gotten organized and spent some time fishing—without success, as usual. Jenny was used to Tom's futility and found it to be comical, while Tom began to get frustrated and grew angrier as the day progressed. They took a break to eat lunch, after which Tom re-cast his line and continued his elusive quest. He looked down over the side of the pier at his slack line which had started to wend its way under the pier. He cranked the handle on the rod to reel in some of the line so that it wouldn't go all the way under the pier. He didn't know much about fishing, but he knew that the best place to find fish was under the pier, and that you didn't want to hook something on the other side of the pier and fight the pilings in trying to reel it in.

Jenny got up and stood next to him, stifling the urge to offer him assistance even as she watched his ineffective attempts to fish. She knew it took a certain skill, and Tom just didn't have it. They stood side by side with elbows on the rail looking out from the pier. They always took up position halfway out on the pier, not because it offered better fishing, but because when they were younger it was as far out as they felt safe. They had both been scared to death being at the very end of the pier, feeling as if it would give way at any second, dropping them into the water far from the shore.

Along the beach was a speckling of people lying on towels or sitting in chairs, with fewer still in the water enjoying the surf. Most of the oceanfront houses sat tucked behind the dunes, single story low-riders that were built to use the dunes as protection from storms. The mansion-like homes of the future were still a quarter-century away and not something that anyone of that era could even contemplate being built.

When Tom's line suddenly grew taut, he was startled and he fumbled with the rod, almost losing it to the ocean. He braced against the pull of the line and struggled to crank the reel. Jenny, excited by the first take on the bait of the day, leaned far over the rail to see where the line ended. It was a far way down and the mix of the movement of the waves, of hanging almost upside down and of the excitement of the moment caused Jenny to suffer a bout of vertigo. Her body started to swivel over the rail and her arms flailed out at the air, and an overwhelming sense of panic started to take over.

"Gotcha!" Tom said as he grabbed the back of her shirt and pulled her off the rail. She really hadn't moved much more than a couple of inches, but to her it felt like she had fallen half the distance to the water and like the hand of God had reached out and pulled her back from the abyss. The panic left her but the adrenaline continued to course through her body, and she stood next to Tom for a second, wide-eyed and speechless. Suddenly, she threw her arms around him and hugged him tight. It was natural and instinctive and although he was surprised, Tom didn't pull away. He put his arms around Jenny and patted her back, comfortingly. But then something happened that neither of them anticipated: they held their embrace. And there they stood, on the Kitty Hawk Pier, hugging each other.

In the scheme of such events a moment in time, a flashpoint, changes lives. A touch, lingering just a moment longer than expected, speaks a thousand words. It means nothing and it means everything. Jenny's head was on Tom's chest, feeling it move with each breath he took. She could feel the strength of his arms around her. Tom breathed in the sweet smell of shampoo from her hair, felt his arms touch the skin on her back, felt the press of her chest against his. They lingered, holding the embrace for just a moment longer than expected, a little bit tighter than required, and a spark ignited in each of them, an electrical shock pulsing through their veins, through the connections and the synapses of their brains, embedding the moment forever in their shared memory. And then the moment ended, the embrace subsided, and they parted. They looked at each other and laughed and got back to fishing. But in that brief moment they had discarded their platonic friendship and a seed had been planted. A fleeting second and everything was different, but nothing had changed. Each of them allowed the thought to momentarily cross into their mind, then pushed it back. And the moment was gone.

Chapter 25

J enny kept an eye on Tom as unobtrusively as possible the next week, subtly maneuvering to get him to agree to go to dinner with her after work on Friday. Usually that would not present a problem, but as if on cue he had such a busy week that it was not as automatic a proposition as would normally be the case. Jenny called him every day and made small talk until she could manage to sneak in a question to make sure that their plans were still on, and twice he told her that he might not be able to make it on Friday. She was a nervous wreck thinking that at the last minute he would back out.

The week turned out to be an emotional roller coaster for Jenny. She was thrilled that Emily wanted her help, but felt guilty that she was filling a role that was rightfully Sarah's. Between Sarah's letter and the wedding planning, Jenny couldn't help but feel that she was suddenly living someone else's life, not to mention that in the back of her mind she was pondering what it would really be like to be romantically involved with Tom. She had become accustomed to her relationship with Tom and his marriage, and now it felt to her like her whole world was being turned upside down. This was not some novel or fantasy—it was her life playing out in a way that in the past she had never allowed.

She and Tom had known each other for so long and knew each other so well that the only element missing from their relationship was that last step: romance. But Jenny wasn't even sure if she wanted that from Tom. To add to her emotional conflict, Tom was just . . . himself. He didn't seem to look at her or treat her any differently than he had since they were children. She *was* aware that he seemed to be keeping a closer presence to her lately, but she attributed that to her being his security blanket. She was happy to play that role and to fulfill that need for him, and she wasn't entirely sure if she wanted or needed anything more from him.

By the time Friday arrived Jenny was on pins and needles, so much so that she had a glass of wine with lunch just to calm her nerves. Because Tom seemed to be so distracted with work, Jenny had convinced Emily to change the plans during the week. Instead of meeting at the shop they decided to meet at the bar of their favorite local restaurant. Jenny told Emily that it would be better to get Tom away from the distractions of the store and work and into a more relaxed atmosphere. Jenny didn't mention that she had arranged to have a small party on the lawn outside of the restaurant later in the evening to celebrate the engagement with some of their local friends.

When Tom came sauntering in at the appointed time Jenny practically leapt from her barstool to give him a hug. He laughed her off and noting her empty wine glass chidingly said, "Couldn't wait for happy hour?" Jenny laughed nervously and glanced at her watch. Emily and Bobby were set to arrive any minute but Jenny was so out of sorts that she couldn't even make small talk. Tom took her silence as being due to the wine and ordered a drink for himself. He looked through the restaurant to see if any friends were eating, seeing no one familiar. He turned back around and nodded to the bartender as a fresh martini was placed in front of him. He picked up the glass, raised it toward Jenny and clinked glasses with her. "Rough week," Tom grimaced as he swallowed a gulp of gin, then picked an olive off the toothpick and popped it in his mouth. Looking at Jenny staring straight ahead he gave her a quizzical look. "What's up with you today?"

"Why? Nothing. I'm fine. Just . . . it's been a long week for me, too."

"Well, relax. It's Friday. Let's have some good wine and eat some crabcakes and be blissfully ignorant for a couple of hours."

"Sounds good to me," Jenny said as her eyes caught a glimpse of Emily at the hostess station over Tom's shoulder. "By the way, have you spoken with Emily lately?"

"Not for about a week. I called her last weekend and left a message."

Jenny saw Emily wave and hold up a finger as if to say *"give me a minute."* Tom was focusing on the crawler on the television behind the bar. "I talked to her last week," Jenny said, trying to keep Tom's attention. She didn't want him glancing around.

"Really? What did she have to say?"

Bobby had joined Emily and they started walking toward the bar. "She said that she really missed you and wanted to see you," Jenny said as she motioned over Tom's shoulder. Tom turned in response to her motioning just as Emily reached him.

"Hiya, Daddy," she said and gave a half wave, then wrapped her arms around him.

"Emily, what are . . .why are you here?" Tom said incredulously as he stood and reached out to shake Bobby's hand while Emily still clung to him. Bobby shook his hand and as Emily pulled away from him he looked at her, then at Jenny, then back to Emily. "What's going on here?"

"Well, I called Jenny last week and asked her if she'd help me out," Emily said.

"And I told her, of course I would help her," Jenny chimed in.

"Help? Help with what?" Tom said to both of them, then noticed Bobby standing behind Emily with a grin on his face.

"Really, Tom? Can't you put two and two together?" Jenny chided.

Still, Tom had a puzzled look on his face, then blurted out, "Oh my!" as he began to understand what was happening.

As if on cue Bobby stepped forward and said, "Mr. Ralston, we came here because I told Emily that I had to do this in person."

Tom held up his hand in front of Bobby to stop, then stood next to Emily, put his arm around her shoulder and faced Bobby. "Now, proceed."

Bobby, now less confident in himself, stammered as he continued. "So, the um, the reason that we're here is so I could ask you for your permission to marry your daughter."

Tom said nothing at first, alternating his look between Emily and Bobby, then Jenny, then back to Emily and Bobby. Finally he said with an impish grin, "You're asking for my blessing?"

"Umhmm, yes," Bobby said as he shifted his weight back and forth, clearly uncomfortable with Tom's wit. It was all Bobby could do to get the words out, now that Tom was on to him.

Tom let it play out some more, acting as if he was pondering how to answer as Bobby continued to squirm in front of him. Emily elbowed him in the chest for having fun at Bobby's expense. Finally, he said "Yes, Bobby. My answer is yes. You have my blessing, and yes you may marry my daughter." Then Tom, grinning widely, reached out and grabbed Bobby to give him a bear hug, and Emily reached out for Jenny and they all stood at the bar hugging each other.

They spent an hour at the bar talking about the engagement and the wedding plans before their friends started showing up, then everyone went out on the lawn overlooking the sound for hors d'oeuvres and to watch the sun set on the sound. Gas torches lent a warm glow to the area to go along with the soft sound of the water lapping at the grasses near the shore. Jenny found herself standing next to Tom as he greeted people and introduced them to Bobby, and next to Emily as she told people that the wedding was going to be held at their house in Sandy Cove and that Jenny was helping her with it. Jenny knew that everyone was thinking the same thought: that Sarah should be standing by Tom and Emily's side and that Sarah should be helping to plan the wedding. Ironically, everyone but Tom and Emily, it seemed to Jenny, paused at the thought. She could see the curiosity in their eyes, the unspoken questions on their lips. Even though they all knew that Tom and Jenny had known each other forever and had remained best friends over the years, the news piqued their friends' interest. Did this mean that Tom and Jenny were now a couple? Was there something going on that the local gossips could run with? Jenny cared but didn't care. They all could think what they wanted to think and the joke was on them, because Jenny herself didn't know the answers to those questions.

* * *

The weekend was a whirlwind of meetings and planning and then Emily and Bobby were on their way back to Washington. Behind them they left Tom and Jenny, who were simultaneously exhausted and frazzled and excited. Thankfully, Emily wanted to have the wedding in Sandy Cove, but for some reason she seemed to be in a rush to tie the knot and wanted the wedding to be this summer, which raised a litany of problems. It would be high season, which meant that housing would be in short supply, and even if they managed to keep the number of people on the invitation list relatively small, they would have a hard time finding places for them to stay. In addition, Tom and Jenny would be swamped with work and neither had an extra set of helping hands for the first time. The one thing going for them was that they were locals, and despite the late date they were able to arrange for vendors to supply the wedding, and for catering and flowers. Jenny was going to bake the wedding cake and a band made up of Tom's buddies agreed to supply the music. Miraculously, they had made all of the plans in less than forty-eight hours.

After the kids left Tom convinced Jenny to stay for dinner. He threw some steaks on the grill and told her to put her feet up and relax while he cooked. Jenny obliged him and napped on the couch while Tom prepped in the kitchen. He woke her when the steaks were done and they ate the meal robotically. Both of them were mentally spent from the weekend's excitement. Jenny had been so wrapped up in the commotion of the weekend that she didn't have time to think about her and Tom and all of the issues that she had been going over in her mind before Emily arrived.

When they were finished Tom gathered up the plates and retreated to the kitchen, re-emerging a minute later with two cups of coffee. He handed one of the cups to Jenny and then sat heavily in his chair. The coffee was strong and welcome.

"You know I really appreciate you helping Emily," Tom said finally, breaking the monotony of the meal. "I couldn't have done what you did for her this weekend."

"No need to thank me. I had fun."

"No, it went above and beyond, and I know how much it meant to Emily. And to me," he said and smiled at her while reaching over the table. He grabbed her hand in his and squeezed.

Jenny looked down at his hand holding hers and wasn't

sure what to do. Was this the time to show him affection? Was this the right moment to start down that path? And then, as if it was the most natural thing in the world, Tom's fingers moved on top of her hand, rubbing lightly against the top of her fingers.

A surge of energy flew through Jenny's body and nearly took her breath away. She sat silently as Tom continued to caress her hand. "Jen?"

Jenny's heart was pumping so hard she could barely catch her breath. "Yeah, Tom?" she managed to say back. He was still holding her hand.

"Do you remember that last summer, back when we were kids, and we were both getting ready for college?"

"I remember."

"And that we said we'd come back here every summer together?"

"'No matter where we go, no matter what we're doing, no matter who we're dating, we come back here for each other,'" Jenny said as she recited the mantra they had come up with in anticipation of where their lives were headed.

"You remember! I wasn't sure you would."

"How could I ever forget? You said it over and over again that whole summer."

"I wanted to make sure I got my point across," Tom laughed.

"Your point was well-taken. Unfortunately, we didn't follow through very well. You met Sarah and I, regrettably, met Trip. The rest is history."

Tom paused before continuing, then his eyes met hers. "I came back, Jen," he said, and again gave her hand a light squeeze.

"Yes, you did, but not exactly in the same way we had discussed."

"I don't mean back then, Jen. I mean now. After Sarah died. I came back." He moved around the table, closer to her, and now both of his hands were holding hers. "I came back here when I could have run away and never looked back."

An unexpected tidal wave of emotion washed over Jenny, but she wasn't sure how she should respond.

"That was months ago Tom, and you had obligations here," she managed to say. "You had to come back."

Tom sat back in his chair and looked at her for a moment before continuing. "But then I stayed, Jen."

She could hear the emotion in his voice, and she knew this was their moment of truth. Still, she was scared to take that step. "Tom, that's sweet, but I think you're saying that just because of the excitement caused by Emily's engagement. I mean, you've never said a word to me, never given any indication."

"No, listen to me. I'm laying it all out here. I know I didn't say anything before, but now I am. It just took me time to get my head together, and I'm saying it now. Now is what matters."

"It's not as easy as that, Tom. We've been friends for all of these years and I don't want to lose that. It's too important to me."

"No one is saying we'd lose that."

"But we'd be taking that next step, and there's no returning from it. We're playing with fire." She heard the words coming out of her mouth and almost wondered who it was who was speaking. Why was she being so defensive? Hadn't she really been waiting to hear these words since they were kids? Jenny pulled back as if to stand up and Tom grabbed first one, then the other hand again and held them softly in his. Jenny looked down at their hands together and this time responded to him by reciprocating the warm touch. "What do you want from me, Tom? I don't know what to say," she said, the resignation and weight of the emotional strain with which she had been struggling draining her voice.

"Say anything you want. Tell me I'm an idiot for taking so long."

"You *are* an idiot," she said, laughing at how farcical it all was. She felt like a teenager again, with all of the angst and anxiety of being asked out by a boy for the first time. As they held hands she felt all of the stress and doubt fall away. It was just her and Tom sitting and talking and holding hands. For the first time since that day on the Kitty Hawk Pier, she allowed herself to feel that tingle run through her body at his simple touch, and she knew that after all of those years her wait was finally over.

They sat looking at each other as if for the first time, each feeling a rising tide building up inside, something that neither had ever felt, or allowed to happen, in all of the years they had known each other. Tom reached over and touched her cheek and Jenny tilted her head into his hand. She moved closer to him and put her head on his shoulder. She felt exhausted and relieved at the same time and was spent from all of the worrying and wondering that had been tormenting her for the last week. "I hope you know what you're doing," she said as she snuggled into him.

"So do I," he responded as he turned her toward him.

They kissed, at first tentatively, then more assertively. Whether it should have happened years earlier or whether it was meant to happen only now was irrelevant and forgotten. The fury of their bodies' response was testament to the fact that it was right and was what each of them wanted to happen. They rose from the kitchen table and moved to the couch in conjunction with each other, locked in their embrace, as if they were both afraid to break the spell that had come over them, for fear that it wouldn't return. They sat, then lay on the couch, kissing and touching and exploring with curiosity, as if they were still the inexperienced teenagers of their youth. It felt natural to both of them, and neither showed any hesitation or trepidation as they forged further and further down the path of intimacy.

They shed their clothes gradually and methodically, savoring each step of their journey together. The touch of Tom's fingers on Jenny's skin was soft and tantalizing, and Jenny's lips prodded and poked at Tom's neck until she found his most sensitive spots. They teased and taunted each other, building up to that moment they now both wanted more than anything in the world. They both luxuriated in the moment, Jenny in feeling the security of Tom's weight on top of her, and Tom in feeling Jenny's softness under him. They were hurried by the urgency of their excitement yet did not rush their lovemaking, taking their time to indulge in their intimacy. When they were finished they lay together on the couch, exhausted as much from the emotional as the physiological release, and they fell asleep in each other's arms and slept on the couch entwisted together.

Tom woke with a start from the morning sun blazing through the windows and took a moment to gather his thoughts, but upon doing so he immediately realized that he was alone. He rose and walked over to the kitchen, feeling self-conscious that he wasn't wearing anything despite the fact that he was in his own home. He found a note on the counter that said "Thanks for last night. It was wonderful. Call me in the a.m." Beneath the writing she had drawn a heart and signed her name. Tom smiled as he read the note again and thought about the previous night. He felt neither doubt nor embarrassment, but was worried that maybe the same could not be said for Jenny. He wondered why she left so early and why she didn't wake him. Had they gotten caught up in the moment as a result of a mix of exhaustion and wine?

As he went through the various scenarios in his head

he realized that he had to see her, had to make sure that she felt as he did and wasn't regretting what had happened. He rushed through the house, hurriedly washing his face and brushing his teeth, then threw on some shorts and a t-shirt and ran out the door and down the front steps to his car. He jumped in and gunned the engine, spitting gravel behind him as he took off in search of her. He had only one thought: he had to look her in the eyes. Only then would he know if the night before had been a mistake.

Chapter 26

The wedding weekend was approaching fast and they had a major problem: the number of people who were coming exceeded the amount the house could accommodate. Even with the limits Emily had put on the number of people invited, they couldn't all fit. Worse, all of the local halls were booked, and Tom hadn't yet told Emily, hoping that somehow he'd figure out a solution.

Tom and Jenny were sitting at her shop sharing a day-old scone and trying to solve their dilemma. Sam looked over the counter and smiled as he saw Jenny's hand sitting idly on Tom's forearm. They hadn't said anything to him, or to anyone else for that matter, but he knew almost immediately that something between the two of them had changed. An extra long look, a hand on the arm. Sam's initial thought was that it was about time. He, like most of their friends, knew that the two of them were meant for each other, but coming as it did out of Tom's tragedy, no one felt it proper to suggest anything to either of them.

Tom had found Jenny that morning after in her shop, elbows deep in flour and immersed in baking the day's output. When he came through the door he was anxious, but any angst he had conjured up was dispelled by Jenny's broad smile upon seeing him. She came around the counter acting coy and they stood apart for a moment before embracing, both of them thus being relieved of any questions they might have had about the other's feelings.

They decided to keep things quiet until after the wedding, not wanting to take away from Emily's moment. They also didn't know how she would react to them being together. Jenny was always treated as Emily's Aunt and almost as an older sister. Even though she gave Tom the impression that she would be accepting of them being together, he knew that it was going to be complicated. The abstract was easier to accept than the reality. Not that there was much to tell her at this point. They truly hadn't had time to delve into their new relationship, being consumed with the wedding and work and what seemed like a million loose ends that needed to be tied up.

Their backs were turned to the shop door and neither of them noticed the door opening, or the door chime ringing, or that LenDale Avery had entered the store and now stood at the display case trying to decide what to buy. They continued to talk quietly as Sam took LenDale's order and as LenDale turned around to see them sitting there. As was normal in things involving LenDale, they were surprised and somewhat put off when he tapped Tom on the shoulder to make his presence known to them, and more so when he started talking to them about Emily's wedding.

"So, your little girl is getting married, huh?" LenDale said, matter-of-factly.

"Seems that way," Tom replied, barely concealing his aggravation, which was how people always seemed to react to LenDale. Ever since that day in his store Tom had tried to be friendlier to LenDale but he always seemed to show up at the worst times and places.

"How have you been, LenDale?" Jenny said as she slowly pulled her hand away from Tom's arm, hoping that LenDale didn't notice. Women always seemed more accepting and less put off by him, and his demeanor brightened upon hearing her voice.

"Doing fine these days. Just fine." He stood smiling and

glancing back and forth between Tom and Jenny, as if he had just gotten the punch line of a joke. They sat looking at him with anticipation, waiting for him to fill them in on what was funny.

"You know that I live right down the way from you."

"That's right, LenDale, we're not that far apart." Tom replied. "What about it?"

"So you need more room for the wedding, huh?"

Tom stole a glance at Jenny. He wondered where in the world this was leading, because with LenDale, one never knew. He had a reputation for scattering divergent thoughts throughout a conversation.

"I'm just saying, well, I overheard the two of you talking and it sounded like you don't have enough room for the wedding."

Tom instantly realized where the conversation was leading and moved to dispel any thought that LenDale might have that he would have anything to do with Emily's wedding. "That's nice of you but . . . ."

"We do need more room," Jenny interrupted. "Do you know of a place?" Tom shot a look at her as if to say "are you crazy?"

"That's what I was sayin'. I have a place."

"Where? Where is it?" Jenny asked, ignoring Tom's glare.

"Like I said. It's just down the way from you." He continued when neither of them displayed any comprehension of what he meant. "It's quite a large place, the ballroom. My dad had it built for my mom to be able to throw grand Southern galas, but she left and we never used it. But it's quite big." He looked expectantly at them, while both Tom and Jenny sat dumbstruck. Tom again started to notice Len-Dale's eyes snapping shut, and coupled with the bizarre conversation, he felt like he was slipping into a dream sequence. Or more like a nightmare.

Finally, Jenny managed to speak. "You have a ballroom?" she asked as she cleared her throat. Tom couldn't believe she was encouraging him.

"With a stage and everything. My mother's family was known to host the best parties in Newport when she was a little girl. She insisted on a ballroom here."

"LenDale, I've lived here almost my entire life and I don't ever remember any parties at your house," Jenny said, her skepticism starting to take over her initial interest.

"No, I never had any parties there, or anywhere for that matter. You know I'm not the most sociable of people. Well, actually I am, it's just that I'm off-putting to people."

LenDale put up his hand as Jenny and Tom began to protest. "It's ok, I know what people think: 'What's LenDale doing here? LenDale's here, the party's over. I hope LenDale doesn't come over here.' You both know that's how it is with me. But like I said, I'm alright with my life right now. Things are different now," he said as he looked at Tom, in search of some acknowledgement of their last conversation.

"And I do have a ballroom," he continued, impervious to Tom's consternation at the entire conversation. "I think it would be a nice place to have a wedding, and it would be nice if it finally got used."

"Honestly, LenDale . . . ," Tom said, trying to put a stop to the conversation. He was not about to give LenDale a role in Emily's wedding. But LenDale stood expectantly looking down at them, his eyes snapping open and shut as if governed by a metronome.

"Look, if you don't want to use it that's fine. But don't dismiss it out of hand. Why don't you at least come over and check it out?" Across the store Sam called out that his order was ready and without another word LenDale left them and scurried over to the counter to pay. He looked like a troll, Tom thought, then caught himself. Sarah had always given LenDale the benefit of the doubt, had always been kind and accepting of him. For her, at least, he should fight back whatever it was inside of him that was irritated by the man.

"Well?" Jenny asked, breaking through his thoughts. "Should we go take a look?"

"Do you honestly think there's any chance . . . ?"

"Not really, but we don't have much choice at this point in time, do we?"

Tom's body language betrayed his thoughts. He slumped in his chair as he realized that they were stuck with no place to hold the wedding and with LenDale, of all people, who offered them a solution. "I guess it couldn't hurt to give it a look." He turned to call LenDale over but he was gone. He had left the shop without another word. Tom looked back at Jenny and they both chuckled. Same old LenDale.

* * *

When LenDale said "ballroom," he meant *"ballroom."* As in enormous. On the scale of Tara. Tom and Jenny were speechless as they turned round and round and took in the room. LenDale was a lot of things, not many of which comprised redeeming qualities, and he never hid the fact that he came from money. But he never let on to how rich he was. Jenny had spent nearly her entire life in Sandy Cove but, based on what her eyes were taking in, she had never realized how much money the Avery family had.

LenDale stood off to the side as Tom and Jenny took in the room. They were awe-struck by the size of it. It had a twenty-five foot ceiling and was lit by three immense crystal chandeliers. The long walls on the sides of the room were lined with floor to ceiling palladian windows which were covered by gold brocade curtains that were pulled back and held in place by red rope ties. Hand-woven tapestries covered the walls in between the windows. The floor was hardwood with a parquet insert for dancing. The room would easily accommodate their wedding party. It could easily accommodate three times their wedding party.

"Pretty cool, huh?" LenDale said as he walked over to them. "Supposedly, my mom brought in some famous interior designer from New York to decorate it."

"It's stunning," Jenny said as Tom nodded in agreement.

"You know, I never knew my mother. Well, I knew her when I was a little kid, maybe when I was three or four, but I never saw her after she left and went back home." LenDale looked around the room as if to catch a glimpse of her within. "I don't blame her, really. My dad was fooling around and she never wanted to be here in the first place, never wanted to be a mother, either, I suppose." He walked over to one of the red ropes and pulled it off it's hook and allowed the drape to unfold over the window, as if to see if it would cover it or not. The floor creaked with his footsteps as he walked back over to them, groaning from years of sitting idle.

He stopped in front of them and stood silently, staring at them. Just as they both were becoming uncomfortable he said, "You two are good together, you know." His eyes started the strange staccato snapping again. "You make a good couple."

It was strange for them to hear someone refer to them as a couple and both of them instinctively began to correct him when they were interrupted by Tom's cell phone. He excused himself to take the call and left Jenny and LenDale waiting in the middle of the ballroom.

"I never had a serious girlfriend," LenDale said more as a comment to himself than to Jenny. "There *was* this one girl who I thought was going to be the one but then someone told me that she was bragging in the bathroom at the Harbor Grille that she had hooked a whale and was reeling him in, meaning me," LenDale explained to Jenny, although Jenny understood exactly what he was saying.

"You deserve better than that," Jenny responded and put a comforting hand on his arm.

"It's ok with me . . . how my life has turned out, I mean. I know I'm lucky in some ways and not in others. I know people get annoyed with me. The funny thing is, I try really hard to *not* bother anyone, but somehow it doesn't play out that way."

He walked over to the window again and stared outside. "My dad used to send me off to boarding school. A place up in the middle of Pennsylvania." He looked back over his shoulder at Jenny to see if she was listening, then continued. "I used to hang out with this one guy. Carl. We were a lot alike. He was one of the few people I ever met who didn't make me feel like I was a nuisance. But then his family moved out West and they sent him to a school near where they lived and I never saw him again."

"That's so sad, LenDale."

LenDale shrugged his shoulders. "That was a long time ago. Water under the bridge." He moved the curtain back and forth across the window and then tied it again with the rope and adjusted the folds until they were uniform. Satisfied with his efforts he turned again toward Jenny. "I hope Tom realizes how lucky he is."

"How so?"

"Well, first he had Sarah, and now he has you."

Embarrassed, Jenny felt her neck and cheeks warm as she blushed. "That's sweet of you to say, but . . . ."

"No, really. He's lucky. You two have been friends forever, and everyone around here always wondered why you never got together."

Jenny remained silent, not knowing how to respond. Should she be embarrassed that everyone wondered about why things turned out as they had? It wasn't like she hadn't had feelings for Tom before he and Sarah met, but once they did, Tom chose his course and it didn't include her. The look on her face revealed her consternation and for once, LenDale realized that his comment had made her uncomfortable. He changed the subject.

"So, do you think the room will do?"

"If anything, it's too big," Jenny responded, glad for the reprieve. "Are you sure you want to do this, though? It will be a lot of people to have here."

"Actually, it will be nice to use this place for once. What a waste it's been for all of these years."

"Sorry about that," Tom said as he walked briskly back into the room. "Minor problem at the store. My new assistant couldn't figure out the register." He looked both of them over and got the feeling that something had happened while he was gone. "Is everything ok?" he asked as he looked directly at Jenny.

"Everything's fine," she said, brushing aside his inquiry. "We just need to decide if we are going to go ahead with this and inconvenience LenDale."

They both turned and looked at LenDale, giving him a chance to rescind his offer.

He thought a moment before providing them with his response. "You know, Sarah always went out of her way for me. She was always kind to me when she didn't need to be. I always thought of it as a one way street. I mean, what did I have to offer to her in return for her kindness?" He paused, then continued. "The way I see it is if I can do something to help out with her daughter's wedding, to make it as special as it can be, then it will be a chance for me to pay something back."

"So, you're sure?" Tom asked, while still thinking to himself that they might be making a mistake.

"I'm sure." LenDale replied with a wide smile, and they shook on it.

As they drove away Tom turned to Jenny and gave her a look.

"What?" she asked with a laugh.

"You didn't have to be so encouraging."

"Tom, we're pretty much out of options."

"We could still do it at my place."

"You can't fit everyone inside. What if it rains?"

"Then we could use LenDale's place as a rain location."

Jenny rolled down the window and the warm, humid air filled the car. She was a beach bum at heart, and preferred the heat over the air conditioning. "Look, I think you need to put your reservations aside," she said. "It's a beautiful room, and it will make the wedding that much more memorable for Emily."

"That's what I'm worried about, quite honestly. That the memory will be something involving LenDale. He always seems to have problems."

"He's just quirky, that's all."

"Exactly, and do we want the wedding to be affected by it." He turned the car into the parking lot in front of her store, pulled into a stall and put the car in park. They sat there, pondering what they should do.

"So we're a couple, then, I guess?" Tom said as he reached out to hold Jenny's hand. She laughed and put her hand in his.

"I know why it's strange for me to hear someone say that," she said. "Is it strange for you?"

"A bit. I mean, for me, along with those kinds of comments obviously there's an unspoken element . . . about Sarah."

Jenny sat nodding her understanding as she stared at their hands together. "Does that make you uncomfortable?" Tom asked. "For me to mention Sarah?"

"Truth?"

"Sure."

"Yes, it is a little offsetting to me. But not for the reason you might think." She pulled her hand away and leaned back against the door, facing him. She was searching her mind for the right way to say what she was thinking.

"Are you sure you want to do this? I mean, do you know what you really want?"

"Of course I am," he said as he attempted to hold her hand again, only to have her pull away. "Do you doubt that?"

"I just don't want to be your rebound. I let myself go once in my life and it ended in disaster. I don't want to ever feel that way again."

"You're comparing me to Trip?"

"Not at all. I just don't want to get hurt," she said, but realized that she was sending a mixed message. This time she reached over for his hand. "I know it's a bit unfair, but what I'm saying is that I want to know what we're doing. Is this for real or am I going to wake up alone one day, and this time without my best friend."

"Jenny, Sarah is gone. If there's one thing I've learned from her death it's that there are no guarantees. So, we are who we are and who we've always been to each other. I'm here right now, and I don't have any desire to be anywhere else or with anyone else. That's the best I can do."

Jenny knew that she was being unfair to ask for a commitment, and in fact, she didn't want a commitment from him. She didn't know what she wanted these days, and felt like her life was getting out of control. She was afraid that her relationship with Tom was on a slippery slope that would end in disaster.

"Hey, look at me," he said, reaching out and shifting her chin toward him. "Let's just take this thing slow, day by day, and do it together. We'll figure it out."

She nodded in agreement. He was right, and he was being reasonable, while she was . . . losing her mind. "Alright, Tom. Just promise me that you'll be honest with me."

He leaned forward, pulling her toward him, and kissed her. "I promise."

Chapter 27

Tom pulled off of the road and found a spot to park between two overloaded SUVs sporting the requisite white oval OBX stickers on their rear windows. If you'd been in business in the Outer Banks long enough you knew that the sign of someone's success wasn't whether they were busy around the weekends, when the hordes of tourists arrived and departed. That was easy pickin's, when a slew of catchy signs could attract tourists like flies to tarpaper. The locals knew that the true sign of success was when people left their vacation retreats behind during the week and drove away from the beaches to shop.

Tom was respectfully envious when he saw several cars in the lot on a Tuesday afternoon. He had hoped he'd get some time to sit and talk with her, even though he was dropping in unannounced. The days had been passing by and the wedding was approaching with such speed that he found himself scrambling to complete the items on his to-do list. This was one of the things he needed to do before the wedding, but just hadn't been organized enough to set up in advance.

He walked through the front door and heard the familiar creaking of the floorboards as he stepped within. It dawned on him how inviting and comfortable the place felt, an atmosphere which in and of itself was something that most merchants tried and failed to create. Miss Ray had her back to him, answering a customer's question while keeping an eye on others who lingered throughout the store. She half-turned to welcome her newest customer, and when she caught sight of Tom, she smiled broadly and held up a finger and mouthed "one second." Tom nodded and sauntered around the store, watching the customers and listening in on their comments. Miss Ray was one good businesswoman to have honed in on the ever-more fickle sensibilities of today's shoppers.

When she finished with her customer she walked over to Tom, who was turning an item over in his hands, trying to determine its use. She approached him with her arms outstretched and wrapped him in a hug. It was as comforting as he remembered feeling when he was a child hugging his grandmother.

"It is so, so good to see you, Tom," she said as she squeezed him tight. She released him and took a step back, solemnly surveying his face. "You're in a better place now than you were the last time I saw you." It was a statement rather than a question.

"Yes, I am, partly in thanks to you," he said, remembering that he had his breakthrough on his way back from meeting Miss Ray that particular day. She looked at him in confusion, and he said, "Never mind that. It's a long story."

Tom looked around the store, admiringly. "It looks like your business is thriving."

"Yes, thank the good Lord above," she said with a glance upward. "I've been blessed with good fortune here. But as you know, it's never good enough," she said, then quickly added, "Although I'm not complaining." They both chuckled at what every small business owner has thought a thousand times.

"So are things going well with you then, Tom? she asked as she appraised him anew. "How are you coping these days?"

"I'm in a good place, living my life, day to day," he said. "I realized that I have a lot to live for and that I shouldn't squander a moment of it. But it took a while to get my head straight."

Miss Ray looked at him closely, saying nothing at first, then asked him, "You've found somebody, haven't you? I can see it in your face."

Tom was starting to get used to hearing the comments about him and Jenny, but he felt a tinge of self-consciousness at Miss Ray's observation. She had always been close with Sarah, not him. He wondered if her comment revealed any antipathy.

As if she could read his mind, she said, "I think it is wonderful if you have. You have a long life ahead of you, Tom. You deserve to live it like the rest of us."

He didn't know why it mattered to him what Miss Ray felt about him, or why he accepted being judged by her. Maybe it was her motherly aura or just that her approval provided the confirmation he needed that he wasn't a bad person if he stopped mourning and re-started his life. Whatever the case, her words soothed him.

"I appreciate that, more than you can know," he responded. "And yes, I've found someone. Actually, I've known her almost all of my life."

"Jenny Powers?" Miss Ray said, matter-of-factly.

"Yeah . . . yes," Tom said, surprised. "How did you know?"

Miss Ray laughed. It was a deep, tumultuous laugh that filled the room with its energy. "Honey, don't ever be surprised by what Miss Ray knows," she said, as the thunderous laughter continued. The customers turned to look as the sound of her laughter took over the room.

Finally, after the laughter stopped and she composed herself, she re-appraised him, then said, "So, you're ready to dance again, Tom?"

Tom chuckled, recalling their last conversation. "Yes, yes. I think I am," he said. "It's funny you would mention that, because that's part of the reason I'm here. Emily's getting married."

"I heard that," Miss Ray said, raising her eyebrows to ward off another "how did you know" comment.

Tom took the cue. "So I think it's time for me to retrieve the dancers. I thought that Emily should have them." He looked at Miss Ray expectantly. "You still have them, don't you?"

"Of course I do. I promised to safekeep them for you." She stood up and started for the stairs, then turned around to him and said, "I think you're doing great, Tom. So much better than the last time. And Emily is going to love the dancers. They will mean so much to her."

She continued up the stairs and disappeared around the landing. Tom listened in on the customers' conversations and comments, and as he waited for her to return he walked over to a window and looked out to the garden in the back. As he had expected, it was in full bloom, roses of every color and variety surrounding and wrapping around the wooden pergola in the center. It was a beautiful and restive place, and was obviously the result of many hours of hard work. Gardens are a labor of love, and he could imagine Miss Ray sitting on the bench under the pergola in the evenings, taking in the bounty of her efforts in the serenity of the garden.

He heard the stairs creaking and turned around as Miss Ray descended with the box in her hands. She walked over to Tom and handed the box to him.

"Miss Ray, I don't . . . ," Tom said as he struggled to find the right words to say to her.

"Hush now, Tom," she said, cutting him off. "You don't need to say anything to me. You just go on and be happy."

She looked over her shoulder and held up her index finger as a customer asked for her help, then turned back to him. "I'm so glad you came to see me, Tom. And I saw you looking at my garden. Promise me you'll come out some night and we can sit together and visit."

This time it was Tom who gave her a hug, then he drew back and said, "I'm looking forward to it, already. But there's one more thing and I wanted to ask you in person. Will you please come to the wedding?"

Miss Ray broke into broad smile and patted her chest to ward off tears. "Of course I will, Tom. I wouldn't miss it for the world." She grabbed him and hugged him again, and he disappeared in her arms.

Chapter 28

High season in Sandy Cove brings cloudless skies, long, sunny days and little respite from the heat. Native grasses and brush are hearty and resilient, genetically predisposed to withstand the ever-present winds and the salt-enriched air. The locals, like the flora, having adapted to the climate, seem oblivious to the scorching sun, while the tourists scurry from air conditioned homes into backyard pools or the ocean in order to keep the heat at bay.

In the mornings the tourists trudge like ants in formation toward the beachfront, overloaded with towels and umbrellas, coolers and toys, on a quest to stake out a patch of sand for their daily interlude. They spend the day in a repetitive cycle that involves lathering on sunscreen, overheating and cooling off in the water. The sounds of the shore, of children's laughter and dogs barking, of blaring music and crashing waves, mix together and then are seemingly whisked away by the ocean winds.

The masses of humanity assembled on the beach were blissfully oblivious to the vagaries occurring with some particular locals on the weekend of the wedding. Tom and Jenny were busy dealing with the last minute problems that always arise with weddings, while Emily and Bobbie tried to keep each other calm. They had only had one or two tiffs leading up to the wedding, and nothing significant enough that a hug from Jenny or some of Tom's gentle nurturing couldn't resolve.

Friends and relatives were staying at an inn a comfortable distance away.Tom had been lucky to get a block of rooms at a steep discount over normal summer rates, the result of his friendship with the owner, for which he would long owe a debt of gratitude. The rehearsal dinner the night before had been a success, and the playful roast of the couple given by the wedding party and their close friends provided a snapshot of Emily that was previously unknown to Tom. While he had memories of her as a little girl and with Sarah, she had established a life of her own, separate from his, and of which he was glad to be given a glimpse, even if that glimpse was of her foibles or idiosyncrasies.

Tom was comforted in watching the couple interact with each other and their friends, to see how calm and comfortable the two of them were together, how they sought reassurance from each other with a touch of the hand to the forearm, or with a gentle stroke on the back of the neck. They seemed a good match and a good compliment to each other, and it eased his concern—the concern of every father—that his daughter would be taken care of and be treated well.

The suggestion of having the wedding at LenDale's had been a hard sell to Emily, that was, until she saw the room for herself. They all were still a bit uncomfortable using it, and of having LenDale be such an indispensible part of the weekend, but he had done what he said he would do, staying out of the way and not interfering. He had even resisted coming to the wedding, but they had insisted, and he only relented when Emily put her arms around him and hugged him, refusing to let go until he agreed. It was funny and awkward and sweet, and they all laughed together as LenDale squirmed away from her embrace.

Emily had come in early, on the Monday preceding the wedding, to help with the final preparations, such as decisions regarding the placement of decorations and seating and the hundreds of other little things that needed to be accomplished in the impossibly short period of time leading up to the wedding. Every day had its task, and on Thursday Emily and Tom decided to tackle putting together gift bags for their guests. They were sitting at his dining room table methodically piecing together the bags when out of the blue, Emily asked, "So, what's happening with you and Jenny?"

Tom was caught by surprise by the comment and by the fact that Emily had any idea of what was going on between them. He hadn't mentioned anything to her, and he and Jenny had decided to downplay it during the wedding.

"Me and Jenny? Nothing. We're the same," he said, trying to sound matter-of-fact.

"Oh come on, Daddy. You think I'm blind to what's going on with you two?"

"What's going on with us?" Tom wasn't sure from Emily's tone whether she was upset or being playful with him.

She stopped stuffing the wrapping paper into the gift bag and gave him a deadpan look. "Dad. Really?"

Tom had thought it would be better to keep the burgeoning relationship under his hat for a while with Emily, especially around the wedding, but like everyone else, Emily seemed to know and wanted answers. "Honey, it's a little complicated."

Emily sat silent for a moment, as if trying to decide whether she should push for more information, then resumed stuffing the gift bags. For several minutes they both concentrated on their task, working in silence, before Emily brought it up again.

"You know I'm okay with it, don't you?" Emily asked, without looking up. "I mean, I want you to be happy."

Tom looked over at his daughter, who was now a beautiful young woman, and felt his heart well up with joy. Life awaited her, with all of its ups and downs, its trials and tribulations. She had so much of Sarah in her, from her com-

Sandy Cove

passion to her facial expressions to her mannerisms. And even though she had lost her mother she had put on such a brave face, had tackled that demon head on, and had come out the victor.

"I am happy, honey," Tom said as he reached over and cupped Emily's chin in his hand, just as he had always done since she was a little girl.

Emily smiled and squeezed his hand in return. "I'm glad for both of you. I think it's nice for you two."

"We've known each other our whole lives."

He saw her brow furrow and she again looked down at her handiwork. "So, why didn't you end up together way back when?"

"Honey, we . . . because I met your mother," he stammered. "Life isn't linear. It's all about timing. When we were younger we each had our own lives and went our own ways, and I fell in love with your mother."

Emily nodded but didn't respond. "Does it bother you that we're together now?" Tom asked. "Is it too soon?" He, too, now sought solace in his work and he grabbed a bunch of snacks to stuff into the bags.

"I don't know. It's strange in some ways, but seems right in others. I just . . . I always heard the stories about how you knew each other since you were kids and how you were best friends. I just wondered how that didn't ever translate into a relationship."

"I don't know how to explain it. It just never did."

"Well, if it makes you two happy, then it's good."

They continued to assemble the bags in silence, then Tom added, "You know, she'll never replace your mother, if that worries you."

Emily looked at him with a pained expression on her face. "Is that what you think?"

"I still miss your mother. I always will."

"Daddy, of course you do. So do I."

"Well, we never really talked about it." Tom said as he stopped working and looked directly at Emily.

Emily contemplated the comment, which was also an invitation to discuss her mother's death. She had waited so long for her father to open up to her, but now was not the time that she wanted to have that discussion. "You have to put her in your heart and keep her there with you while you move on," she said, hoping to circumvent that conversation.

Tom nodded and took the clue. She was right. He wondered how someone so young seemingly had figured out life.

Emily stood and walked into the kitchen to get something to drink and Tom sat alone, deconstructing their conversation. When she returned she stood by the table for a moment and took in the room. Somehow she hadn't noticed before that her father had changed things. He'd removed some of the pictures from side tables and mantel, and looking around now, the room felt empty and devoid of its former character. She had put on a brave face for her father, but the subtle differences in the room bothered her. Suddenly, the room didn't feel the same to her.

She sat down and attempted to resume her task. "By the way, Dad, did you ever look for mom's necklace? I wanted to wear it at the wedding," Emily said as she tried to shake off the odd feeling in her stomach.

"I did. In fact, I tore this place apart, but I couldn't find it. Somehow it must have gotten lost when . . . ." Tom stopped in mid-sentence, not wanting to complete the thought. "But hold on a minute, I have something I want to give you," he said as he stood suddenly and hurried toward the bedroom. When he returned he was carrying a giftwrapped box, which he handed to Emily.

"This isn't the way I had envisioned giving this to you, but now's as good a time as any."

Emily looked at the box as if she were a child on Christmas morning. She carefully unwrapped the paper and opened the outer box to reveal what lay within. She studied the box for a moment, then pulled it out of the package and placed it on the table in front of her. She rubbed her hand over the smooth black lacquer lid, then opened it to reveal the dancers, and the music began to play. They sat in silence watching the dancers twirl to the music before she slowly closed the lid, watching as the dancers disappeared inside.

"Daddy, I don't know what to say. They're beautiful."

"They were supposed to be your mother's," Tom said, then explained that Miss Ray had gotten them for Sarah but never had a chance to give them to her.

Emily simply nodded her head, still looking down at the box and rubbing her thumb over the inlaid designs on the lid.

"Are you ok?" Tom asked as he reached over and put his hand on her shoulder.

She nodded and turned to him with a brave smile. "It's just that I know how much this would have meant to mom. She loved these things."

"She certainly did. I can't tell you how many times we were traveling and she'd manage to find a store that carried music boxes. She didn't buy a lot of them, though. She just liked hearing them and watching the dancers. I think they were comforting to her."

Like a curious child, Emily opened the lid again and as the dancers began to pop up she closed it, then opened it a bit more, allowing the dancers to come out more. She repeated this several times until the lid was wide open, then she closed it and sat looking down at it. Suddenly, she pushed the box toward Tom. "I think you should keep this,

Dad," she said, as she moved it closer to him.

"Emily, no. I want you to have it."

"I know, and I appreciate it, but here's the thing. One of my fondest memories of the two of you is when I watched you dance together. You both always looked so happy in each other's arms like that. And I think that's why Mom loved the dancer boxes so much. I don't know if you ever noticed, but the ones she liked weren't ballerinas. They were always the ones with couples dancing together."

Tom thought a moment, then realized she was right. How had he never noticed? Still, he knew that Emily was just being protective of him. She knew how special certain things were between her parents, slow dancing being one of them.

"Emily, this is yours. You need to have it and it will make me happy knowing you have it."

"Daddy," she implored him.

He shook his head and reached over for his daughter and gave her a hug. "Just promise me one thing," he said.

"Of course. Anything."

"Promise me that you'll save a dance for me at the wedding."

She looked at him in feigned horror, then laughed. "I promise."

Chapter 29

Jenny was struggling to get her dress on, silently swearing at her lack of self-control over the past weeks. *"Great,"* she thought. *"Now I have to worry about falling out of my dress in addition to all of the other things I have to deal with at this wedding."* She reached down to the bodice with both hands and did a half jump while pulling up with her hands to get the dress into place, but having not quite succeeded, she twisted and turned to straighten the dress, then let out a silent cheer as the dress finally conformed to her body.

The preceding twenty-four hours had been filled with minor catastrophes of the sort that plague every wedding: from mis-counts and mistakes to no-shows and add-ons, to flaccid orchids and mismatched linens, just to name a few. Jenny had done her best to run interference during the weekend so that Tom and Emily wouldn't have to deal with any of the problems. Tom had done as good a job as could be expected of him leading up to the wedding, but he was not Sarah, and could not do the things that normally would be Sarah's province. In addition, Jenny had tried to keep as busy as possible so as to avoid spending too much time with the two of them. She had become more and more uncomfortable during the weekend. Emily was Sarah's daughter, and although Jenny could offer her help and fill in when needed, she was not Emily's mother, nor Sarah's surrogate.

Jenny hadn't mentioned anything to Tom, and Tom had seemed blissfully ignorant, but Jenny wasn't so sure how well Tom was going to handle the actual wedding. There are only a few life events a parent gets to experience: The birth of a child. A graduation. A wedding. Absent a divorce, or in this case, a death, the wedding of one's child is meant to be shared. When Tom turned toward Jenny during the wedding for solace, wouldn't he really be looking for Sarah? Jenny knew him well, and knew that he had put on a brave face many times when he was reminded of Sarah, but his wound was deep and still relatively fresh. It would take more than a couple of months for him to see Jenny when he was actually looking for Sarah. That was partly why Jenny had resisted being in the wedding, despite Emily's persistent entreaties.

Still, Jenny had a lot on her plate for the wedding and was rushing to get dressed, get her makeup on and get out of the house. She was running behind schedule, so when the phone rang her impulse was to ignore it, but then she thought that someone might be calling about the wedding, so she picked it up. To say that the call caught her off-guard was an understatement.

"Jenny, hi . . .um . . . it's LenDale. I think we might have a little problem."

* * *

When she pulled up to the house she was met by a convoy of service trucks and workers bustling to and fro. Flowers and tables and chairs were being moved into place with such order and purpose that it seemed like she was watching a perfectly choreographed dance. Jenny exited her car and stumbled as her high heels sought purchase on the gravel drive. She caught herself, straightened her dress and half-ran toward the house. She had to find LenDale and deal with him before Tom and Emily arrived.

He was in the ballroom, sitting at one of the windows,

watching the workers set up the chairs for the ceremony. They had arranged for a tent in case it rained, but the sky was crystal blue and devoid of clouds, so the tent was being disassembled and would be gone before any of the guests appeared. LenDale was wearing shorts, a t-shirt and a base-ball hat. The shirt said "Get Shucked at Badass Bill's" and had a caricatured image of a redneck holding a shell in one hand and a shucking knife in the other. Jenny noticed that LenDale had a glass in his hand containing what she assumed to be scotch.

"LenDale, what is going on?" Jenny huffed as she came scampering into the room. Her hair was already starting to wilt from the humidity and was clumping to her cheeks.

LenDale stared out the window, saying nothing. He looked like he was on the verge of tears. Finally, he turned toward her and mumbled something. When Jenny looked at him with puzzlement, he repeated himself, this time a little louder but still just above a whisper. "I think I made a mistake."

"A mistake? Jenny looked at him with such exasperation that he shrank before her. "LenDale, the wedding is in a couple of hours. What do you mean, you made a mistake?"

"I shouldn't be here. I mean, the wedding shouldn't be here. It's all wrong."

Jenny couldn't believe her ears, and as she struggled to maintain her calm as her brain exploded with a myriad of potential responses, she realized that she had to get control of the situation and deal with the problem. She pulled a chair over, placed it facing LenDale and sat down in front of him. "LenDale, tell me what you're thinking. What's bothering you?"

He looked at Jenny with such a sad expression that her heart melted. He looked defeated. "I shouldn't be here because I'm a reminder to everyone of what happened to Sarah," he said. "I'm bad karma and everyone knows it.

They're going to think I'm jinxing the marriage."

"Well, first of all, drinking is not going to help the situation," Jenny said, taking the glass out of his hand. The one thing no one wanted at this wedding was a drunk LenDale Avery, and thankfully he seemed to be relatively sober. He offered no resistance but still sat slouched in the chair watching all of the activity going on outside. Jenny needed to get him turned around, quickly.

"LenDale, listen to me," she said as she placed her hands on his shoulders and squared him to her. "No one, and I mean no one, thinks that." She searched his face for a response, but got none.

"You had nothing to do with Sarah dying, other than happening to find her," she continued. "That's all that happened, and everyone knows it."

"They all have their theories. I've overheard people talking."

"They're just ignorant, stupid people," Jenny blurted with such ferocity that she finally got LenDale to look at her. "Those people don't know what they're talking about. They don't really know you. Whatever they say is irrelevant."

LenDale looked at her with a desperate, lost expression. "But people do talk. And especially today, when people see me, the thing they'll say is that there's the guy who found Sarah."

"So what."

"Well, it's hurtful. And it makes it sound like I'm responsible."

"No it doesn't. It is a fact that you found Sarah. She was lying on the road and you came upon her. And she was already dead. And nothing you did or didn't do affected her situation."

LenDale's chin began to quiver and sink down to his

chest and Jenny reached out to stop it, literally lifting his gaze to her.

"You. Did not. Kill. Sarah."

He began to nod in agreement, but he still looked sad. She wasn't getting through to him. Through the window Jenny saw Tom and Emily pull up in the driveway, which meant she was out of time.

"LenDale, we've got a wedding that's about to start. You made the offer to have it here. Now is not the time to re-think that offer. If you don't want to be here, fine. But I've got one task to take care of today, and that's to make this wedding the best it can be for Emily. Personally, I think you've got it all wrong. You're paying homage to Sarah by hosting this wedding. I knew Sarah very well, and I know how much it would have meant to her to have her kindness to you repaid this way. She would have been so pleased."

"Really? You think so?" LenDale said as if that prospect never crossed his mind.

"Of course she would. But you know what's more important than that?"

LenDale looked at her with childlike anticipation, which made Jenny pause before proceeding, but her time was gone so she forged ahead.

"You know that you and I have known each other probably longer than anyone else around here." LenDale did not acknowledge the fact, but she had garnered his attention. "When I was a toddler and my father was trying to get his business going, my mother worked odd jobs to bring in some extra money. One of the things she did was clean houses, and right now we're sitting in one of them."

"Your mother cleaned this house?"

"Um hmm, she did. Since she didn't have a sitter for me, she brought me with her, and you and I used to play together while she cleaned. In fact, it wasn't until after we came here to look at this room for the wedding that my memory was jarred."

"I don't remember that at all."

"Well, you are younger than I am, and I barely recall it."

LenDale sat silently as he caressed the revelation around in his head, but he still seemed out of sorts, so Jenny forged ahead again.

"Yeah, I was kind of surprised when I saw this room and the stage and the chandeliers and later that day it all came flooding back to me. Like how sweet and kind you were back then. Just a sweet little boy who was happy for a playmate and some attention."

LenDale's demeanor brightened noticeably even though his brain was devoid of any memory of that time.

"And you know," Jenny continued, "I think we're all just bigger, older versions of who we were when we were kids. That's what's deep inside of us." She took his hands in hers. "You're a good person, LenDale. You have not had it easy in this life. But deep down you're good and you mean well. And that's why we're here today. Because deep down you knew the right thing to do was to offer your home for this wedding."

LenDale nodded his head and finally smiled. His insecurity was appeased—for the time being. Then he was overtaken by a panic. "Look at me," he said, pulling at his t-shirt. "I've got to get changed." He jumped up and took a couple of steps, then stopped abruptly and turned back to Jenny. He grabbed her and hugged her tightly—too tightly, like a child. Then he released her and hurried away.

Jenny looked around the room and down at her rumpled dress. *"Good lord,"* she thought, *"I only have so much energy. Please let me get through this day."*

She stood to go find Tom and Emily and realized she was holding the glass of scotch she had taken from LenDale. She looked at the glass in her hand, contemplating what to do with it, then raised the glass to her lips and gulped it down. She felt the burn in her throat and the heat rising through her head, and with it she felt her tension and anxiety begin to recede. Rejuvenated, she put the glass down on a table and set off to find Emily. She had a wedding to attend to.

Chapter 30

For all of the preparations, for all of the time put into planning and executing, for all of the worrying and anxiety, the weekend was really about the wedding ceremony. Afterward there would be food and drink and dancing and carousing. But first would come the ceremony of vows and supplications and the joining of the two young adults in the time-honored tradition of binding matrimony.

Tom and Emily had arrived to the tumult of workers scrambling to finish setting up. Inside, centerpieces and place settings were being moved into position in the ballroom, while outside the final touches were being added for the ceremony. Pedestal stands holding chalice vases lined the aisle, with alternating white orchids and flat white candles suspended in water. Workers were straightening the rows of chairs, laying down the white cloth runway and placing the programs that Emily and Bobby had made on each chair.

Tom and Emily stood watching in awe of all of the activity when Jenny suddenly swooped in and grabbed Emily and rushed her inside the house. Tom found himself standing alone without any purpose. Someone from the florist handed him a flower to attach to his lapel, and as he struggled to attach it Jenny again appeared, this time for Tom's benefit. "Give it here. I'll put it on for you," she said with a smile and a half-wink.

"I don't know what I'm supposed to be doing," Tom said in an exasperated voice.

"Just excess baggage, I guess," Jenny joked and gave him a nudge.

"You joke, but that's what it feels like."

"You're not excess baggage, Tom. You're the father of the bride." She finished attaching the boutonnière and patted him on the chest. "There. All done. You look great." She looked at him and saw him a wavering look in his eyes, as if he was about to get swallowed up by the event. She kissed him on the cheek, gave him a comforting squeeze, then said, "It's going to be fine, Tom. Don't worry."

Tom nodded at her and straightened his back. "Is everything okay with Emily? Where did you take her?"

"She's inside having her hair done." Jenny considered telling Tom about her earlier discussion with LenDale, then thought better of it. He was a nervous wreck and didn't need to start worrying if LenDale was going to be a problem. "Did you finish writing your speech?"

Tom's attempts to write his toast over the preceding days had not gone well. He had struggled to come up with the words that would convey what he wanted to say to Emily and Bobby. More than once he had thrown away what he had written, thinking that he should simply give a short congratulatory note to the newlyweds, only to go sifting through the garbage later to retrieve the draft.

"For what it's worth, it's done," he said with a shrug. He sighed, then reached out and held Jenny's hand. "Do you think she's doing the right thing?" Tom asked. "She's still so young."

"I think she's in love and she's doing what feels right to her," Jenny said as she rolled her eyes at him in mock exaggeration of what she and Tom were in the midst of doing.

"Yeah, that's a recipe for disaster," Tom joked. "It's just

hard for me to believe that she's all grown up," he said, more seriously.

Jenny pulled on Tom's hand. "Come on. Stop being morose. This is supposed to be a happy day."

Tom smiled at her. "You're right. Enough of that nonsense," he said as he leaned toward Jenny and kissed her gently. "Thanks for being here for me."

Jenny leaned back and gave him a "are you kidding me" look, as if she wanted to be anywhere else. Then she reached out her closed hand and held it in front of Tom, motioning for him to hold out his hand. At first he was confused, then he appeased her and held out his hand under hers.

"I thought you might need this today," she said as she opened her fist and dropped what she had been holding into his awaiting hand. Tom stared at it, then chuckled. It was an atomic hotball. In all the years they had known each other, Tom had always been the one to calm Jenny by giving her atomic hot balls. She had never given him one.

He unwrapped the cellophane covering and popped it into his mouth. "It's good," he slurped, which came out sounding like *"hips shood,"* as he attempted to speak despite the orb in his mouth. They both laughed—a laugh reflective of years of friendship, of childhood pranks, of adult jocularity and now, of a burgeoning romance.

* * *

The guests finally arrived and were seated on the lawn facing the sound. A light wind had whisked away the afternoon's humidity, providing a comforting counterbalance to the late day heat. As the ceremony began the sun had just reached that certain point on the horizon where the sky took on various hues of orange and pink and lavender. It was as if the heavens were providing accent lighting for the wedding.

Emily was beautiful in her simple gown and Bobby was the picture of the nervous groom whose eyes lit up upon seeing his bride in her wedding dress for the first time. Tom walked Emily down the aisle, kissed her and gave her a lingering hug before passing her hand to Bobby. A father never easily yields the province of his daughter's protection to another, and Tom struggled at that moment to remain stoic. The young couple looked at each other expectantly, then took their positions and nervously held hands. The vows were taken, the rings were exchanged, and then, finally, they kissed to seal their commitment to each other. And it was over, not without tears shed, both of happiness and of sorrow.

Once inside for the reception, the new couple was introduced for the first time as husband and wife, toasts were made and the celebration got underway. Tom felt relieved and oddly devoid of sadness. He lamented that Sarah did not live to experience this life event, but he did not allow himself to slip back into the despair. This was Emily's day and she deserved for it to be full of cheer and happiness.

For Tom the wedding was a whirlwind, a kaleidoscope of images and a cacophony of sounds. He was pulled from one person to the next, from family to longtime friends, all of whom wanted to say hello or congratulations or to whisper in his ear that they were happy that he and Emily seemed to be happy.

When he finally was able to break away from one of the well-wishers, he began to make his way to the bar when he felt a hand on his shoulder. He turned around to find it was Miss Ray. She was wearing a colorful dress and an elaborate church hat with a large bow festooned on the side and feathers sprouting high above her head. She looked elegant and was smiling broadly at Tom.

"What a lovely wedding, Tom. And what a beautiful

bride that daughter of yours makes," she beamed.

"I'm so glad you were able to be here and share this with us, Miss Ray. To be honest I wasn't sure how I would be today, with all of this," he said as he motioned with his hand at the festivities.

"You did fine, Tom. Just fine. And I wouldn't have missed it for the world. Not for the world."

Despite his best efforts Tom's face must have betrayed his emotions, and Miss Ray reached for him. "You listen to me, Tom Ralston, and *hear* what I'm telling you. You're the father of the bride, and you're allowed to be emotional at your daughter's wedding. There's no need to hide from it. You're a human being, not some kind of robot."

Tom laughed. For some reason this woman's wisdom cut through all of the chaff and honed in on his psyche as if she had known him forever. She was right. He had just spent so much effort holding back his emotions lately that he had needed to be reminded.

"Sarah would have loved this," he managed to say as the words caught on his tongue. "It's just that it's . . . it's so unfair that she isn't here."

Miss Ray let out a long sigh and looked him up and down. "Tom, she *is* here." She turned him and pointed across the room to Emily, who was dancing slowly with Bobby. "See, there she is, right there. And she's here, too," she said as she fanned her hand around her head. "And she's here, as well," as she pressed her index finger into his chest. "She's inside of you, and Emily, and me, and everyone she loved. She's never going anywhere, Tom. She's always going to be with us." It was so cliché but Tom knew that she was right.

Suddenly, a bright light shone in Tom's eyes and he heard a hush come over the room. At first, he was blinded by the light and confused by what was happening, then his eyes adjusted and he saw Emily walking toward him.

When she reached him she held out her hand to him and said, "Daddy, will you dance with me?"

Tom wiped at his eyes and stole a glance at Miss Ray. She nodded her encouragement and put her hands to her face as well. Tom grasped Emily's hand, and they walked to the dance floor together.

Save for the music the room remained silent as father and daughter took their places and began to dance. Everyone knew what they had been through, knew that the two of them were missing a part of their lives on this most special of occasions. They watched in silence as Tom and Emily made slow circles on the dance floor, proud father and his bride daughter, with him whispering in her ear, and few of those present escaped the moment without shedding a tear.

As the song neared its end, Emily turned her head and scanned the room. When she spotted Jenny she waived to her, indicating that she wanted Jenny to come to her. Jenny initially shook her head no, but Emily only waived more vigorously. Finally, Jenny relented and walked toward them. As she neared, Emily pushed back from her father and held out his hand for Jenny to take. Tom and Jenny both hesitated, then appeased Emily and began to dance. The band took its cue and began another song. Bobby joined with Emily, and the four of them danced together, alone in the middle of the room.

"Thought you'd be able to escape without having to dance with me?" Tom teased Jenny.

"I didn't want to upstage the bride," Jenny joked back.

They both laughed and continued to move to the music.

"Well, I guess our secret is officially out," Tom said. "Now what?"

Jenny thought for a moment before replying, then said, "A wise person once told me to follow my heart. So, how about we both just follow our hearts, wherever that takes us."

Tom nodded and Jenny laid her head on his shoulder, and they continued their slow glide over the dance floor.

Chapter 31

LenDale stood watching from a nook in the corner of the room as Tom and Jenny danced together. He smiled as he saw Jenny lay her head on Tom's shoulder and whisper something in his ear. Tom's head tilted back and he laughed—an easy, relaxed laugh, and they continued to dance in a tight circle, oblivious to the rest of the guests. They certainly seemed to LenDale to be a good couple, and he was happy for them.

LenDale had spent most of the evening alone in his house. He had purposely stayed at the periphery of the ceremony and away from the reception, not wanting to insert himself into Emily's moment. He had not seen such joy in his life, but while others might have felt uncomfortable being at a wedding to which they had no true connection, LenDale was not even slightly put off. He was used to being an outsider, and tonight was no different than many he had spent over the years watching others enjoy their lives.

As he watched the party he absentmindedly turned over a chain he had retrieved from his pocket. It was a necklace with a pendant attached. He had thought about giving it back to Tom on several occasions. At the funeral. At the store. He even went out to Tom's house once to hand it over and provide an explanation, but he turned away when he saw that Tom had company. When he offered his house for the wedding he thought it would give him an opportunity to bring up the topic, and perhaps he could give it to Emily when she came out, but he never could figure out how to explain to them why he had it in the first place. At this point it seemed like he would never be able to explain it and he tucked it back into his pocket.

He took one last glance around the room, turned and walked outside. The night air was still being warmed by the heat emanating from the ground after the hot summer day. An ocean breeze offset the heat and felt comfortable and re-freshing. Once the door closed behind him the party felt far away, the sounds from within muffled and diffused.

LenDale walked away from the house and began trudg-ing down the gravel driveway toward the road. His foot-steps were light on the ground as he felt buoyed by doing a good deed in providing the ballroom for the wedding. He didn't often get the opportunity to be the good guy and for once he hadn't screwed it up. He thought of his mother, who had abandoned him and left him to his father's upbringing. She would have been proud of him, this time.

He found it odd that the memory of his mother came to him now, of all times. He knew she was still alive, living in a home somewhere in Rhode Island. He also knew about the family she had after she left him and his father behind to fend for themselves. He shouldn't have cared whether he would please her or not, but he did. And he thought it ironic that his mother was more dead to him than Sarah was to Emily. Emily had fond memories of Sarah which she would be able to recall for the rest of her life. LenDale had none of his mother.

LenDale turned onto the main road and continued walking. Even though it was high season for tourists there were few cars on the road at this time of night. Sandy Cove was different from most beach towns in that way. Things pretty much shut down early, even in summer. The hot sun does a good job of wearing out children, and in most of the houses that lined the roads to the beach children were comfily tucked beneath the sheets by now.

As he rounded the corner in the road where the shops began the road was illuminated by fluorescent security lamps that lined the parking lots of the businesses. Swarms of moths and other assorted summer insects swirled around the lights, and for some reason it made LenDale think of a bee hive, and how the worker bees swarmed around the hive to deliver their pollen. Theirs was a well-orchestrated dance, but seemingly random, and LenDale wondered if the same thought could be had of the human race as observed by some larger and more intelligent species. Events might appear to happen by chance, but they really happen for a reason.

After passing through the village the road darkened again and LenDale wondered why he hadn't thought to bring along a flashlight. He could see where he was going but there was no sidewalk on this stretch of the road and he realized he wasn't wearing anything that would make him stand out. As he picked up his pace he heard a car approach from behind him and he consciously moved farther off of the road and waited for it to pass. It sped by without incident, the laughter of the occupants and the fading sound of Creedence's Midnight Special trailing behind as the car drove away. LenDale smiled at hearing the song's lyrics.

He finally reached the turnoff to his cabin at the duck blind and was relieved when he heard the tumbler click in the lock. As he stepped inside he was confronted with odors familiar to him since his childhood. He hadn't come to the cabin for some time and it was musty and dank and needed airing out, but at the same time it gave him a sense of comfort in being home.

The curtain was pulled across the broad window wall overlooking the sound and the room itself was pitch black, but LenDale moved with ease around the furniture. He pulled the curtain aside and the room instantly filled with moonlight, an eerie, dull glow casting long shadows along the floor and walls. He unlatched the lock and slid the window wall completely open, and the air and sounds wafted inward. Frogs and crickets and other creatures of the night called out to each other in a loud, dissonant symphony.

LenDale moved with purpose through the room, ignoring the onslaught of mosquitoes that were already buzzing at his face. He pushed the easy chair across the floor to the edge of the open window and plopped down, sending the air from the cushion whooshing out around his legs in an audible sigh.

The mosquitoes dive bombed at him and the frogs and crickets called for him, and he didn't know how long he had sat in the chair or if he had dozed off and he didn't care. He watched the lights move on the far end of the sound and felt the breeze waft in and around him, and he sat still in the chair taking it all in. This was a good day, he thought with satisfaction. Then a thought occurred to him and he reached into his pocket to retrieve the necklace and pendant. He held them in front of his face and rubbed his fingers over the pendant—what appeared to be a single form but was really two people embracing, as if dancing together.

He still didn't know why he had unclasped the necklace from around Sarah's neck while they were racing to the hospital. He just did it. And if he couldn't explain why he had done what he had done to himself, he couldn't explain it to Tom or Emily. Ever.

He had kept the necklace as some sort of memento, but now it was spoiling his feeling of having done a good deed, and he felt an overwhelming urge to rid himself of it. He crumpled it up in his hand, stood up and heaved it as far into the water as he could manage. He heard a faint plop as it hit the water, then saw the ripples of the water emanating outward from the point of entry. He sat back down in his chair and watched the ripples dissipate. He felt relieved.

Now, no one would ever know what he had done. Except him.

Chapter 32

The fog was so thick Tom couldn't see his hand directly in front of his face. He had a strange, otherworldly feeling that something just wasn't right. He was walking, but he didn't know where he was going.

As he walked along the fog would ebb and recede just enough so that he could make out the form of something ahead of him, but even when he picked up his pace he couldn't get any closer to it. He tried to call out but the sound of his voice was muffled by the volume of the fog, and his words came out garbled and jumbled.

He tried to push himself ahead and through the fog bank to get at whatever was ahead of him. Finally, he came around a bend and the fog was suddenly gone. He saw what he had been chasing and he stopped in his tracks. It can't be, he thought to himself.

"Sarah?" Tom called out. She was right there, right in front of him.

She looked at him and smiled. Then she turned and started to walk away.

"Hey, wait," Tom said as he tried to catch up to her. But he couldn't seem to move his legs. She kept getting farther and farther away from him. "Sarah! Come back!" he cried out. He started to run after her, his legs suddenly free, but she was too far ahead of him, and finally he gave up the chase. He watched as her profile got smaller and smaller, and then, just before she disappeared from his view, a bright light shone in his eyes, causing him to cringe and turn away.

He stirred from the dream as the sunrise filtered through the curtains. As he shook off his sleep, he looked beside him and took in the form on the bed next to him. She was sleeping with her back to him, a white sheet partially covering her.

He replayed what he remembered of the dream over in his head, and thought about how real it had felt. But it wasn't real. *This* is what's real now, he thought as he watched Jenny sleep.

He moved over and wrapped his arm around her, pulling her back close to him and placing his nose on the side of her neck, taking in her scent. She opened her eyes and let out a low contented murmur in response to the touch of his cheek against her neck. She rolled over and they stared into each others faces, the reality of the moment flowing over each of them.

She heard the sound of the waves as it filtered through the partially opened window and she turned to look at the beach. The sun had just risen above the horizon and she could see the pelicans flying in formation over the water. The beauty of the scene and of the moment buoyed her, and instantly she wanted to be a part of it.

"Can we go for a walk on the beach?"

The words flowed out of her mouth before she considered the implications of the question. Her realization of the mistake instantly spread over her face, betraying her. She wanted to take it back. She started to speak, but before she could say another word, he put his finger over her mouth, then pulled her to him and kissed her. A long and loving kiss. As they broke from their embrace he said, "Yes, I would love to go for a walk with you on the beach."

He was happy. As happy as he had been in a long time.

ACKNOWLEDGMENTS

This book could not have been completed without the help of friends and family who lent me their ears and gave me their constant encouragement. I thank all of you for your support during this project. Thank you also to Brad Meltzer and Jean Chatzky for your recommendations, and to Spencer Baum, who gave me his insight into the nuances of the publishing world and whose advice pushed me to move forward in publishing this book. To Howard Cohen, for your advice on writing and about the book industry, as well as your suggestions on what to "read next," I thank you. I owe a debt of gratitude to Jeff Caplan, whose creativity and courage to build something from nothing inspired me. *Wasaaabi*, my brother. To my soundingboards and readers, Ken and Lauren Rice and Carole Mantel, thank you, thank you, thank you—for your time, insight, suggestions and encouragement—but most importantly, for your friendship. To my wonderful children, Jacob, Sydney and Rayna, thank you for being you, for sharing all of your enthusiasm and excitement about this book, and for helping to push me to finish whenever I thought I couldn't. And to my wife, Geri, without whom this book would never have been written— would never have even been pursued—I am humbled by your faith in me and in my writing. You knew what I didn't know. I love you.

ABOUT THE AUTHOR

Steven Recht lives in Pittsburgh, PA, with his wife, three children and Airedale Terrier. He would love to read your reviews and hear your thoughts. Like him on Facebook at www.facebook.com/smrecht or visit him at www.stevenrecht.com for updates on future projects and additional information, or to just see what's on his mind.